AGATHA, ANTHONY AND MACAVITY AWARD-WINNING AUTHOR

HART

D0036392

A DEATH ON DEMAND MYSTERY

LAUGHED 'TIL HE DIED

"I'm a sucker for Carolyn Hart's Annie and Max series." ROBERT CRAIS

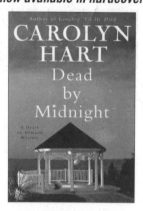

"Carolyn Hart is superb."
Green Bay Press-Gazette

Praise for CAROLYN HART and
LAUGHED 'TIL HE DIED

"The queen of the traditional mystery in
America. . . . [Hart's] plotting skills rival
those of Britain's Agatha Christie."
Cleveland Plain Dealer

"Hart . . . has developed an interesting and amusing
cast of characters and a surefire formula for the success
of her mysteries. Mystery fans will enjoy this book."
The Oklahoman (Oklahoma City)

"Well-developed characters and a complex, fast-
moving plot make for a satisfying read."
Publishers Weekly

"Hart excels at showing her sleuths at
work . . . and she keeps readers involved
in the ongoing search for justice."
Booklist

"A shining star in the mystery galaxy."
Jackson Clarion-Ledger

"If I were teaching a course on how to write a
mystery, I'd make Carolyn Hart required reading."
Los Angeles Times

By Carolyn Hart

Death on Demand

DEATH ON DEMAND • DESIGN FOR MURDER
SOMETHING WICKED • HONEYMOON WITH MURDER
A LITTLE CLASS ON MURDER • DEADLY VALENTINE
THE CHRISTIE CAPER • SOUTHERN GHOST
MINT JULEP MURDER • YANKEE DOODLE DEAD
WHITE ELEPHANT DEAD • SUGARPLUM DEAD
APRIL FOOL DEAD • ENGAGED TO DIE
MURDER WALKS THE PLANK • DEATH OF THE PARTY
DEAD DAYS OF SUMMER • DEATH WALKED IN
DARE TO DIE • LAUGHED 'TIL HE DIED
DEAD BY MIDNIGHT

Henrie O

DEAD MAN'S ISLAND • SCANDAL IN FAIR HAVEN
DEATH IN LOVER'S LANE • DEATH IN PARADISE
DEATH ON THE RIVER WALK • RESORT TO MURDER
SET SAIL FOR MURDER

Bailey Ruth

GHOST AT WORK • MERRY, MERRY GHOST
GHOST IN TROUBLE

LAUGHED 'TIL HE DIED

CAROLYN HART

A V O N

An Imprint of HarperCollinsPublishers

This book is a work of fiction. The characters, incidents, and dialogue are drawn from the author's imagination and are not to be construed as real. Any resemblance to actual events or persons, living or dead, is entirely coincidental.

AVON BOOKS
An Imprint of HarperCollins*Publishers*
10 East 53rd Street
New York, New York 10022-5299

Copyright © 2010 by Carolyn Hart
Excerpt from *Dead by Midnight* copyright © 2011 by Carolyn Hart
ISBN 978-0-06-145308-3
www.avonmystery.com

First Avon Books mass market printing: April 2011
First William Morrow hardcover printing: April 2010

Avon Trademark Reg. U.S. Pat. Off. and in Other Countries, Marca Registrada, Hecho en U.S.A.
HarperCollins® is a registered trademark of HarperCollins Publishers.

Printed in the U.S.A.

10 9 8 7 6 5 4 3 2 1

To Dorothy Sayre,
whose goodness shines like a beacon

LAUGHED 'TIL HE DIED

∴ *One* ∾

TIM TALBOT DROPPED his backpack. Oblivious to the chirping of birds and the chitter of squirrels, he hurried directly to a five-foot-tall saw palmetto. He carefully eased back a spiky frond to reveal a bale of hay. He pulled the bale out. His nose itched from hay dust as he worked the heavy bale across a dusty path to a toppled oak near a lagoon. He tipped the bale up and leveraged it onto a fallen tree trunk, then rubbed at his nose with the back of his hand.

He was sweating when he finished, the fifty-pound weight hard for him to heft. He worked the bale backward on the trunk, leaving a three-inch ledge exposed. The slender teenager nodded in satisfaction.

From his backpack, he retrieved a stack of five white Styrofoam cups and a packet of colored chalks. He sat on the dusty ground, his expression intent. Straight brown hair framed a thin, sensitive face. A jagged red scar marred one cheek. On each cup, he drew a large, heavy, masculine head topped by tight yellow curls. He used orange for the U-shaped mouth and brushed the cheeks with red. He placed the finished cups a few inches apart on the ledge in front of the bale. He dropped two quarter-ounce drop-shot sinkers into each cup.

He whistled tonelessly as he returned to the shrub. He brushed away a covering of leaves and picked up an oblong package, well-wrapped in a black plastic bag. His gait uneven, he walked about twenty paces to a big live oak. He favored his shorter leg as he climbed a rope ladder. As he worked his way up, he propped the package across sturdy branches, moving it in stages.

He stopped when he reached a fork and a broad limb about twenty feet above ground. He unwrapped the package, revealing a twenty-two rifle. He handled the gun with the ease of long practice.

Tim worked his way out onto the thick branch, holding the rifle carefully. When he was satisfied with his perch, he looked toward the cups, bright in the sunlight against the barrier of hay. He lifted the rifle, aimed, and pressed the trigger, once, twice, three times, four, five.

As the bullets reached their targets, pieces of Styrofoam flew into the air and lead sinkers clanked against each other. He was too absorbed in his task to feel watching eyes.

Booth Wagner tilted back in his oversized black leather desk chair, blue eyes merry in his reddish face. Short-cropped, wiry blond curls covered his massive head. His features were blunt: broad forehead, bold nose, square chin. He was a big man with big appetites and big laughter that erupted in whoops of amusement. His lips spread in a huge smile as he listened to the strained voice made hollow by the speakerphone.

". . . Now I need to raise money—if I don't I'm finished—and I've been checking. The value's not there."

"Hey, good buddy," the throaty rumble of laughter shook the words, "I didn't take you to raise."

"You said you'd looked everything over because there was some question about the origin, but for the money it was a real steal." The voice was harsh.

Booth lifted his shoulders, let them fall. "You got it in one, Larry. Definitely a steal." His laughter boomed. "Kind of like the deal you cut with me over the manufacturing plant in Honduras and it turned out the machinery was rusted and the goods were shoddy. Sure, I had the site vetted, but obviously the fix was on. I lost a bundle on that one. I don't like to lose." The voice was still warm and good-humored, but Booth's eyes were cold. "Better luck next time. Maybe this will give you more time to write about island history. I'll bet you can sell one of those pieces for, oh, how about twenty bucks." He whooped with mirth.

Jean Hughes stared into the mirror. She gripped the eyeliner brush with a hand that shook so badly she dared not apply the bluish color that emphasized her wide-set green eyes.

The mirror was not her friend this morning. Maybe the haggard image served her right. Ever since she was a little girl with golden blond curls, she'd loved looking in the mirror. She'd seen a saucy teenager, a seductive twentysomething, a flamboyant midthirties.

She stared at this morning's reflection: strained eyes full of fear, splotches on the cheeks that even a thick base would not hide, deep wrinkles bracketing downturned lips.

"Jeanmarie?"

The clear sweet voice hurt as much as a physical blow. Only Giselle called her Jeanmarie. Only Giselle looked at her with misty eyes of love and saw the Jeanmarie who might have been, not the Jean who was.

Using all the will at her command, Jean called out, "In a minute, sis. Running late. Got a bunch of meetings." For how long? Could she persuade him to change his mind? She'd try again to get him on the phone. If that didn't work . . . She reached in her pocket, touched a crumpled ad she'd cut out of yesterday's *Gazette*.

Quickly, mechanically, she worked on her face, bold strokes of mascara, layers of base and powder, color where there was none, garishness as a shield. When she was done, she dashed into the breakfast nook, grabbed a cinnamon bun.

Giselle's thin face turned toward her, though her sight was almost gone. She was thin as a wisp of corn silk, wasted by the illness that was draining her life away. However weak she was, however much pain she felt, her smile for Jean was a constant. "I'll try to tidy things—"

"No, you don't." Jean's voice was mock-stern, though tears burned her eyes. "Big sister means business. You have one job today. Sit on the deck and soak up sun and when I get home, I'll fix raspberry brownies. We'll have a feast." Jean rushed toward the door, her high heels staccato on the hardwood floor. "Mind me now." It wasn't until she was in the car that a sob shook her shoulders and the painstakingly applied makeup smeared as she swiped at her face and drove to work.

Meredith Wagner breathed hard, sweat beading her face and streaming down her back. She'd ridden as fast as she could on the hot bike path through the woods all the way from the Haven. It wasn't that far. Only about a mile. She had to hurry before somebody missed her. She'd skipped lunch, but she was signed up for the Chinese checkers tournament at one.

Ready to duck behind a thicket of bayberry if anyone stepped outside, Meredith stared at her house, quiet in the hot July sunlight. Accomplishing her goal ought to be easy but she stood frozen, listening over the whistle of her shallow breathing and the rush of blood as her heart pounded. If only she hadn't spent the money Aunt Rose had sent. She'd run through that two hundred dollars in one blazing shopping spree. When she was in stores, bright with beautiful clothes and jewelry, she didn't have to think about home and his loud laughter and the empty place in her heart. The moments of looking and choosing and saying, "I'll take that one," and carrying the boxes to her car made her feel safe and warm, the way she'd felt as a little girl when Ellen smiled at her.

Ellen.

Most kids didn't call their moms by their first names, but Ellen was different. Even when Meredith was little, she felt protective toward her mother, always aware of the shadow in Ellen's brown eyes and her air of fragility. She had to help Ellen.

Now was her chance. Beth would be in the kitchen eating lunch. Neva played golf most days. Tim wouldn't be here. He was supposed to go to the Haven with her, but who knew where Tim was. In the mornings, when she turned onto the winding blacktop that led to the Haven, Tim pedaled straight ahead, without a word to her.

Sometimes Meredith wondered where her stepbrother spent the summer days, but he treated her the same way he treated her dad, as if they were strangers he had to be polite to. Meredith would have been resentful, but she couldn't resent Tim.

Her dad's car was gone.

She was hot, but she felt cold. He was probably at the Men's Grill, regaling other golfers with one story or another. No one could ever tell a funnier story better. The skin would crinkle around his blue eyes, he'd slap a huge hand onto his thigh, he'd start to laugh midway through a sentence and pretty soon everyone in the room would be aching with laughter. Sometimes people laughed until they cried. Everything was funny to him.

Even when the story wasn't funny to someone else.

If he caught her, she could imagine the joke he'd tell— maybe the next time she had friends to dinner—". . . So how do you know if your kid's cut out to be a felon? A sure tip-off is . . ."

Tears burned Meredith's eyes. What was she waiting for? She'd count to ten and then she'd go fast, really fast. She could use the French window into his study. They were never locked in the daytime. She had to get the money.

". . . Three . . . four . . ."

She knew where everything was in the study, the bookshelves, the fireplace, the leather sofa, her dad's desk. In the right-hand drawer of the desk, he kept an envelope full of cash, a thick stack of hundred-dollar bills. He liked to have cash on hand. There was more, lots more, in the safe behind the painting of Neva over the fireplace mantel. The painting wasn't a very good likeness. He always had a good laugh when he pointed at the painting and dramatically proclaimed, "There's where my heart lies. A beautiful woman and plenty of money. Now if I had to say which mattered the most . . ." Again that rumbling laughter.

". . . Five . . . six . . ."

With a sob, she turned away, ran to her bike, swung on the seat, and pedaled, eyes blurred by tears. She was too scared. Tomorrow. Neva was at the spa on Fridays. Her dad played golf. Beth shopped for groceries. She'd try again tomorrow.

Hubert Silvester, better known as Click, patted his pocket as he climbed the tall tower toward the platform. Two hundred bucks. That was more money than he'd ever had at one time. The minute the deal was made, he'd priced a used Ninja 49cc Super Bike for a hundred and fifty dollars. A bright silver one. He'd have almost fifty bucks left over for gas. When he had the scooter, he'd have everything he'd ever wanted. Life had been great ever since Ms. Hughes helped him land the part-time job at José's Computer Repair. He had a computer he'd put together himself with old parts. José had given him a used laptop for a Christmas bonus. Pretty soon the silver scooter would be his. He'd give his bike to his little brother.

The job itself couldn't have been easier. At first, he'd been a little worried. Still, once he had the handwritten note in his hand, which explained who hired him and why, he'd agreed to give it a shot. He wished he could go along in the morning and watch, but he'd find out everything at the program tomorrow night. What was really neat, he was going to be announced as the brains of the outfit. That would be cool. He figured Mr. Wagner couldn't fuss too much. He played more jokes than anybody.

His face furrowed in thought as he climbed the steep steps to the platform twenty-eight feet above the lake. He'd have to come up with a story about the scooter for Uncle Arlen. He'd tell him he was using money he picked up from computer repair jobs to rent the scooter from another guy at the Haven.

Uncle Arlen settled into a beer-sodden stupor after dinner every night anyway. He never paid much attention to his dead sister's sons. He gave them a place to sleep and food to eat and was glad they spent their free time at the Haven.

Click swatted at a dragonfly. Sweat beaded his face. He'd never been to the nature preserve before. He'd lived on the island all his life and he took egrets and herons and alligators and dank still waters for granted. He spent most of his time inside, either working at José's Computer Repair or using the wi-fi at the Haven for his laptop.

He climbed, panting a little. So he carried a little extra weight. The jocks made fun of him, but he sneered at the jocks. Why run when you could walk, or stand if you could sit? Most of them weren't good enough to play in college, but, if everything went well, he'd have a scholarship to the technical college. Mr. Darling had promised to write him a good rec. Someday he'd have his own repair store and show those stupid jocks.

On the platform, he looked out at the lake, shimmering in the heat. Three alligators sunned on the far bank. There was nobody else around on a muggy July afternoon. People had better sense. They were inside, where it was cool, or on the beach, where the breeze dropped the temperature about ten degrees. Although he understood the plan to keep everything secret until the last minute, he wished they could have met somewhere cooler.

He pulled at his sweat-dampened Braves T-shirt. The weather would be hot tomorrow night at the program, but the sun would be going down and there would be shadows everywhere. The program was going to be lots of fun. Everybody would have a big laugh. He'd bet Mr. Wagner laughed loudest of all.

Scuffing sounds signaled someone climbing the ladder.

Click turned, excited and eager. His eyes widened when the climber reached the platform. Click wondered if he'd have a costume for the program, too.

"Agatha, you really shouldn't." Annie Darling moved toward the coffee bar.

The plump black cat lifted a paw to swipe at Annie.

"If the health department finds you on top of the coffee bar, I'll get a citation."

Agatha's ears folded back.

Annie realized her somewhat chiding tone was not being well received.

She approached cautiously, a veteran of many losing skirmishes with her gorgeous but iron-willed cat. The choice of Agatha to honor Agatha Christie had perhaps been a mistake, since the celebrated Queen of Crime had been known as a kindly person. Maybe she should have named Agatha, gender aside, for Mickey Spillane.

"I know." Annie softened her tone, added a coo of adulation. "I let you sleep on the coffee bar in the winter and you don't see why summer makes any difference. It's the people." Not that her beloved mystery bookstore was currently teeming with readers, much less buyers. This summer's slow traffic reflected the tourist downturn since the financial bust.

Agatha flattened like a snake. A guttural growl rumbled in her throat.

Annie swerved away from the coffee bar. Her mama hadn't raised no fool, as they liked to say in Amarillo where Annie grew up. Living on a South Carolina sea island with alligators and snakes had reinforced her cautious nature. It wouldn't do any harm to let Agatha remain on the counter-top as long as they were alone in the store.

Annie paused in front of the fireplace and looked up. If she had been a ballerina, she would have danced to a memory of Strauss's lovely "You and You."

She hummed the melody and waltzed across the floor of the coffee bar and back. Sometimes, when she was happy, she had to dance. She was happy today, happy to be in her wonderful bookstore, happy to adore her demanding cat, happy that she and Max had planned a very special evening tonight, and happy with the watercolors hanging above the mantel.

Every month a local artist provided Death on Demand with five watercolors depicting memorable scenes from wonderful mysteries. This month's paintings represented the first books in series that Annie considered among the best in the mystery world. The first customer to correctly identify author and title received a free book (noncollectible) and free coffee for a month. Annie refused to add up how many months of free coffee had been enjoyed by Henny Brawley, the store's best customer and Annie's good friend. Maybe this month would be different . . .

In the first painting, a tall, slim young woman with strik-ing reddish-blond hair stared in horror at the overflowing bathtub. She clutched a maid's cap in one hand and wore a black maid's uniform. A fully clothed man, even to a black overcoat, lay submerged in the water, staring upward with dead, glassy eyes. His dead face was unprepossessing.

In the second painting, a petite young woman leaned against the side of a lakefront cottage, looking up at the porch and two burly men, one with blond hair held by a bandana do-rag, the other with a massive wiry brown beard.

In the yard, a dozen motorcycles were bunched. Their riders looked big, rough, and dangerous.

In the third painting, a small African woman, her back twisted, one leg shorter than the other, struggled to mount the steps of a wooden scaffold where a noose hung waiting. A crowd of thousands, black faces and white, watched in frozen silence. Not far from the wooden structure stood a young white woman, her face strained but determined.

In the fourth painting, a young woman with short dark hair, dressed all in black, from her polo sweater to her black leggings, crouched behind the balustrade of the minstrel gallery to peer down into a candlelit village hall at seven figures in black hooded cloaks drinking beer. A black cloth covered a table near the back wall.

In the fifth painting, protective face visor lifted, a woman stared in horror at putrefying human remains scattered on the ground. She was a startling figure in the desert moonlight, her head bristling with electronic wires and probes, her body encased in a lightweight metal contraption of arm and leg braces, a web vest fastening her to a computerized spine.

Each book was utterly original. Annie loved recommending these authors and she was thankful for mysteries, old and new, that made her bookstore a magnet for mystery lovers. Annie was convinced her customers also came for the ambience, a molting raven perched above the children's section near a photograph of Edgar Allen Poe's tomb, comfortably cushioned wicker chairs and potted ferns à la the days of Mary Roberts Rinehart, and posters from famous mystery movies, including *The Cat and the Canary, Charlie Chan Carries On, The Thin Man, Ellery Queen and the Murder Ring,* and *Murder by Death.* Pride of place went to the vintage poster for *The Maltese Falcon,* worth a cool $3,500. Humphrey Bogart was the quintessential Sam Spade: wary, suspicious, battered but never broken.

As she made another graceful swoop, the storeroom door banged open.

"Some people get to dance." Max Darling stood in the doorway, holding a sturdy cardboard box.

As always, Annie's heart danced, too. Was there a man anywhere as handsome, sexy, and fun as her tall, blond husband?

At the moment, he was trying hard not to smile, attempting, in fact, to appear apprehensive. "Other people steal sand from the beach. I wonder if I broke any laws. At least I didn't take a sand dollar."

"Max, you're here!" Her exclamation indicated sheer delight. "Bring the sand up to the front. I've got the books ready."

Annie walked swiftly down the central corridor, her flats slapping on the heart pine floor. She hurried to the front window, humming "Summertime." Quickly she removed the books that had celebrated the Fourth of July: *Roanoke* by Margaret Lawrence, *Blood and Thunder* by Max Allan Collins, *Red, White, and Blue Murder* by Jeanne M. Dams, *Murder on Lenox Hill* by Victoria Thompson, and *The Drop Edge of Yonder* by Donis Casey. No books were more American than these.

Annie never tired of showcasing mysteries sure to please. Well, they might not please everyone, but they pleased Annie.

A thud sounded behind her. "Damn." Max's exclamation was anguished. Perhaps a trifle too anguished?

She turned. "Are you all right?"

Her husband bent to massage a sandaled foot. "Dropped on my big toe." He gave the sand-filled box a kick, grimaced. "I may never walk again." He reached out to drape himself against her. "I need solace. Lots of solace."

Mmm. Trust Max.

But she smiled. It never mattered when she saw him, movie-star handsome in a tux, sleepy-eyed with bristly cheeks in a T-shirt and boxers, muscular and tanned in swim trunks, sweaty in a polo and shorts on a tennis court, every glimpse evoked the same swift, passionate delight. Her husband, her wonderful husband.

His blue eyes gleamed, and his arm slid more firmly around her shoulders.

She wriggled free. "Your toe will be fine. Get some ice from the coffee bar. I need to arrange the sand." She spread a drop cloth and troweled beach sand from the box.

Agatha suddenly appeared and, with an effortless leap, landed in the display. One swift paw whipped out to bat at the trickle of sand.

"Uh-oh." Annie put down the trowel and reached for the cat, who eluded her grasp. "Agatha, don't even think about it."

Behind her, Max laughed.

It took some effort and a tempting dish of cat salmon to entice Agatha out of the window and down the aisle to the kitchen area. Annie returned, somewhat breathless. "In a little while, maybe you could put up a lattice so she can't jump into the window."

"A lattice, the woman says. Presto." He snapped his fingers. "One lattice coming up. Where's the lattice store?"

"Try the lumberyard." There was a plea in her voice. "Maybe you could go get it while I arrange the sand."

He leaned against the wall. "I buy lattices and you arrange sand. You can't say we aren't original." His tone was musing. "Now, what would anybody say if they heard you announce that you were arranging sand? Doesn't that have a Laurelesque quality?"

Annie laughed. "I'm not in Laurel's league." Was that ever true. Max's mother, a gorgeous blonde who enchanted men from eight to eighty, was, to put it kindly, a free spirit who was ever and always unpredictable.

"Even Laurel never asked me to carry sand. Do you have any idea how heavy that box was? Why not just put up a beach chair? People who read books can imagine anything. Show them a beach chair and a stack of books and they'll make the connection: beach books! That would only take a few minutes and then we could go home and make some beach music of our own. As for a lattice, that comes later."

This time his hand started at the back of her neck and began slipping . . .

Annie ducked away. "Look how much I've taken out. Now you can pick up the box and pour."

He moved with alacrity. "Then we can go home?" His dark blue eyes told her that she was desirable, that they could be home in their splendidly restored antebellum house in a matter of minutes, that the sun would spill into the master bedroom . . .

She should finish setting up the new display. There were orders to fill and e-mails to answer. But Max was so near and she ached to tangle her fingers in his thick blond hair and lift her lips—

The front bell jangled as the door opened.

"Max." Jean Hughes's strident voice broke a golden spell. She burst into the central corridor, attractive yet with a frowsy look, a bit too much makeup, clothes a little too tight.

Jean rushed toward Max without a glance or murmur to Annie.

Annie folded her arms, determinedly maintaining a pleasant expression.

Max took a deep breath, then managed a quick wry grin and a promissory glance before he turned.

Before he could speak, Jean blurted, "I saw you through the window. I'd been to your office. I don't want to bother you, but please, can I talk to you?"

Annie considered clearing her throat since she was apparently invisible to Jean.

Jean reached out and gripped Max's arm, tugging him toward the door. "Please. Oh, please. I need help. You're a nice man. Everyone says so. Please help me."

Annie's resentment was abruptly swept away. The quaver in Jean's voice was real, and the desperate appeal in her eyes revealed a depth of misery.

Jean held out a trembling hand. "I've seen your ad in the paper. Confidential Commissions. Problems solved in a heartbeat."

That was a new ad, in which Max took great pride. He did not hold himself out to be a private detective, nor was he offering legal counsel. He was a member of the New York bar, but had never taken the South Carolina bar. Max was firm in insisting no special qualification was needed to provide advice to those in travail.

"I've got an awful problem." There was nothing artful in Jean's language, but her stricken face told a tale of despair. "Please help me. I don't know what to do."

Max recognized heartbreak. His resistant look faded. He nodded toward the door. "Sure. Let's go over to my office. Maybe it will help to talk—"

The door closed behind them.

Annie watched until they were out of sight. What had reduced the woman to such a pathetic state? Although Annie was well aware that their South Carolina sea island of Broward's Rock wasn't a paradise, even if it often seemed so, the island certainly wasn't the proper backdrop for an Ibsen drama. Still, she didn't like the possessive way Jean had clung to Max's arm as they walked on the boardwalk.

Annie shrugged. She'd know soon enough. She worked briskly on the new display, artfully placing the titles face up on the sand. The books, all superb mysteries, had the added cachet of offering stories set in South Carolina: *The Mercy Oak* by Kathryn R. Wall, *Hush My Mouth* by Cathy Pickens, *Mama Pursues Murderous Shadows* by Nora DeLoach, *Too Late for Angels* by Mignon F. Ballard, *Monet Talks* by Tamar Myers, and *Murder in the Charleston Manner* by Patricia Houck Sprinkle.

Of course, Jean had been a disaster from the first. Hiring her to be the new director at the Haven had been on a par with choosing a chorus girl to head up a nunnery. Max wasn't on the board at the Haven, though he'd been invited. As a volunteer, he wanted to avoid any conflict of interest, but he'd regretted that decision when Jean Hughes was appointed.

What were the board members thinking?

Annie didn't need to be a mystery expert to know the answer. Not for the first time in human annals, when money sizzled, good sense fizzled.

Max still volunteered, teaching sailing and tennis, coaching basketball, but he avoided gatherings attended by board members. That wasn't accurate. When possible, he avoided one particular board member: Booth Wagner. Island bigwigs, including the mayor and heads of charities, had been ecstatic when Wagner retired to the island and turned his considerable energies to island affairs—his energies and his apparently limitless wallet.

Jean as Haven director was a fait accompli when Max came home to tell Annie that the board, responding to Wagner's offer to fund a new gym, selected her on his recommendation. Max had been wry. "She's about as qualified to run anything as a panda."

Annie brushed sand from her fingers. Maybe Max would finish soon and they would close up their respective shops and go home for more fun than even the best mystery provided. After all, Jean Hughes wasn't their problem.

∿ *Two* ∿

JEAN'S HARSH SOBS brought Max's secretary, whose heart was as big as her beehive hairdo, to his office door. Summer-bright in a yellow tunic and white capris, Barb looked at him questioningly.

As awkward as most men in the face of feminine meltdown, Max cleared his throat. "How about some iced tea, Jean? Hey, Barb, bring us some of your special fruit tea and good lemon pie."

Since Max's business was sporadic, Barb took advantage of her spare time to create tantalizing desserts in the back room that also served as an amazing tiny kitchen.

Jean, using a handkerchief provided by Max, wiped her face, leaving purplish smudges atop puffy redness. She looked shyly at Barb when she returned. Barb placed a tray with two big tumblers and two plates on the desk. "Goji berries and guava, my own private blend. Guaranteed to refresh. And lemon pie made this morning."

Jean managed a smile. "Thank you." She took a bite of pie. "Hey, that's good. I haven't eaten much, I've been so upset. Booth texted me yesterday, told me the board was going to fire me. I kept calling and he never answered. I finally talked to him this morning. He laughed and said it's a done deal. I saw your ad in the paper yesterday afternoon. I cut it out." She looked at Max with red-rimmed eyes. "I know you think I'm stupid." There was resignation in her voice instead of indignation. "I don't know the kind of stuff people are supposed to know to run things. But the kids like me."

Max felt a rush of embarrassment. He'd been disdainful. He'd chalked Jean up as a bimbo forced on the Haven by Booth Wagner and hoped the board would come to its senses and not renew her contract this summer.

"Yes, the kids like you." He looked at her with new eyes. She spoke the truth. Most of the kids thought Jean was great. The Haven offered games and classes and afterschool snacks to latchkey kids in winter and a full recreational program in the summer that drew kids from both modest and affluent backgrounds. Kids had to feel welcome or they wouldn't come. Since Jean had become director, attendance had swelled. Was that success enough to counterbalance her lack of understanding of accounting procedures and slapdash record-keeping and the sometimes voluptuous appearance that worried the mostly single moms whose hormonally charged teenage sons clustered in craft classes around Jean, instead of strenuous games designed to siphon off some of their excessive energy?

She leaned forward. "I know what everybody thinks. Some of it's true." She looked forlorn. "I met Booth last summer at a jazz bar in Atlanta. I'm a singer. Maybe not a very good one. Good enough. And I didn't sleep with the customers. Plenty of them tried. I could have picked up a lot of money. I needed money, but I didn't do it. Then Booth came and he treated me really nice and he acted like he cared for me, really cared. Do you know what he did?" She talked as fast as angry wasps milling from a spilled nest. "When he realized I cared for him, he started talking about my coming to the island. He said he and his wife were separated. I didn't know that was a lie. He asked me if I liked kids and I told him I did. I loved babysitting when I was growing up." There was an innocence in her voice that made Max wince. "He said he'd help me get a job at a rec center for the kids. How could I have known that he wanted me hired because it would make this old lady on the board mad? Booth thought it was a scream. He laughed and laughed about the way Miss Prentice acted around me, like I was something dirty a crow had dropped. I talked to Booth this morning. He doesn't think the joke's funny anymore, me and the board." Once again the tears brimmed. "He's mad and getting back at me because I told him I wasn't anybody's other woman and I wasn't going to sneak around behind his wife's back. He took my life and used it and now he's stopped laughing. He told the board members my résumé's phony. He's the one who put the résumé together. I didn't even know what was in it until after I was hired and then I couldn't say anything, could I? When I asked him why he did it, he laughed and laughed and said he'd really pulled the wool over the board's eyes and it served them right because they were so stuffy. Can you help me?" She used the back of one hand to wipe away the tears. "Will you help me?" Her voice broke.

Annie's eyes flashed. "He's despicable." She paced in front of Max's desk.

Barb stood with her hands on her hips. "What can we

do?" She looked as affronted as a mother cat defending her kittens against a barking dog.

Max held up a cautioning hand. "As they say in the newspaper business—"

Annie knew the nearest Max had been to a newsroom was a role in *The Front Page* for the local little theater.

"—'Your mother says she loves you. Check it out.'" He flicked on the speakerphone and dialed a number.

"Yo, Darling." Booth Wagner's voice was ebullient. "How's the world treating you?"

"No complaints, Booth." Max's tone was easy. "I understand you fabricated Jean Hughes's résumé without her consent."

There was a pause. Then a whoop of laughter. "Prove it, good buddy. Her word against mine. Anybody can take one look at Jean and know she's a dame on the make. Anyway, she's a little late complaining, isn't she? Don't worry yourself about all of this, boy."

Max's jaw ridged.

"The board agrees with me," Wagner boomed. "We vote at the annual meeting next week. I got my votes lined up. She's out as of July fifteenth. Tomorrow night's shindig will be her going-out party. Be sure and come. I'll do a little roast of Jean, give everybody a laugh, Jean confronting her first spreadsheet, Jean encountering Robert's Rules of Order and asking who Robert was." Another whoop.

So much for afternoon delight, Annie thought ruefully. Or evening, for that matter. Instead of dancing cheek-to-cheek at the country club to celebrate the evening they first met, Max hunched at the computer in their upstairs his-and-her study, a half-eaten salad pushed aside. Dorothy L., delighted to have her favorite human at hand, draped herself comfortably in his lap and purred.

Not one to ignore meals, Annie took her last bite of a scrumptious cheeseburger from Parotti's Bar and Grill, wiped her fingers on a red-checked napkin, and punched a telephone number with pleasure.

Henny Brawley, tipped off by Caller ID, answered cheerfully. "I've already heard Booth Wagner's version. Between me and thee, Jean has some challenges running anything, but she has a good heart so tell Max he's got my vote. Max may be able to swing it. I'm sure he's already talked to Frank Saulter. Larry Gilbert's a possibility. Larry and Booth used to be big buds, but at the last board meeting it didn't take a swami to figure out the boys were crossways. Nothing overt, but there was no clap-on-the-back bonhomie between them. Whatever Booth suggested, Larry was against it. In fact, this was actually funny though it didn't get a laugh from Larry. Booth proposed cutting five hundred dollars from the summer rec programs. Larry immediately proposed increasing the budget by a thousand. Frank Saulter and Pauline Prentice were all over an increase as was I. After votes placing the motion on the agenda, et cetera, the increase was approved. Booth guffawed and managed between bouts of hilarity to explain the increase had been his plan all along. Anyway, the vote may have to be delayed unless Booth has a proxy for Pauline. She spends July in Italy. Now for a matter of greater interest to me, has someone beaten me to it with the paintings?"

Annie felt a quiver of delight. Maybe this time, Henny would be stumped. Annie was careful not to let her voice reflect her hope. "Gee, Henny, I don't think so. I had a customer from the mainland this morning," fiction was not reserved exclusively for authors, "who had all but two."

Henny was gruff. "Which two?"

"She wasn't sure about the fourth painting. She said she was sure she knew the book and pretty soon she'd remember the title. And she wasn't positive about the fifth."

"The fifth is a piece of cake. But that second one! No wonder she didn't get the fourth one. I haven't either." Henny sounded relieved. "You know, fair's fair."

Annie prepared to do battle. "Everyone has equal opportunity—"

"If a reader of my sophistication is baffled, that strongly suggests the painting doesn't accurately reflect the book. There is a fair solution. Exclude the fourth painting."

"You have the other four." It wasn't a question.

"On the money."

Annie was firm. "Takes five."

"Fair's fair." Henny was emphatic. "Think about it. See you and Max tomorrow night at the program." The line clicked off.

Annie glared at the phone. "We'll see what's fair."

The phone rang. Annie glanced at Caller ID. "Hi, Laurel."

"Annie, my sweet." Her mother-in-law's husky voice brimmed with concern. "Your message sounded strained."

Laurel had empathy to the tips of her toes. Annie wasn't surprised that her mother-in-law had detected stress. Jean Hughes was dominating their evening. Moreover, it looked increasingly likely that tomorrow night she and Max were going to be in the thick of the Haven's annual summer talent show, but enjoying the fun would not be their priority.

Annie looked at Max, intent and intense as he sent e-mails. Short of slapping a gag on Booth Wagner, Annie didn't see anything but trouble ahead at the Haven. But she wouldn't have it any other way. Jean had come to Death on Demand seeking a kind man. That was what she found.

"Maybe a little stressed. Max and I are trying to round up people to come to the talent show at the Haven tomorrow night to lobby the board members for the director's reappointment."

"Really? From what I've heard, there's some question about Ms. Hughes's suitability."

Annie knew how to approach her mother-in-law. "Some people oppose anyone who is fresh and different." Annie pushed away a memory of Jean's too-tight clothes and abundant makeup. Tastes differed. "More kids are coming to the Haven than ever before. She's been a little disorganized, but she's going to take some classes over the Internet, some basic accounting. Frank Saulter's promised to help with the books." The retired police chief, Frank was highly regarded on the island. "A bunch of the boys are making posters for tomorrow night."

Laurel's laughter was throaty but delighted. "I have a soft spot for the unconventional. That may surprise you—"

Annie squashed her immediate inward hoot. Conventionality and Laurel were mutually exclusive concepts.

"—but I'll be glad to come on board. Tell me what I need to do."

Annie knew that Emma Clyde, the island's gruff mystery writer, was enjoying the euphoria attendant upon completing a manuscript and sending the e-files to her editor. During this happy time Emma could likely be persuaded to do almost anything short of dancing on top of the piano. However, protocol—and Emma's ego—required a thorough discussion of the just-completed manuscript, the huge difficulties Emma had faced, and her brilliant solution to an intractable plot problem. Only then had Annie segued into the reason for her call. She almost had her spiel memorized. ". . . Please call these five names and urge them to come to—" A little whiffy beep signaled another call on the line. Annie glanced at Caller ID. "Oh, hey, Emma, I've got a call I should take. Anyway, please persuade them to come to the Haven talent show tomorrow night and seek out board members in support of the director Jean Hughes." A second beep. "Lay it on thick about the island coming together behind her because of her rapport with the teenagers." Not to mention, and Annie wouldn't, Jean's undeniable sexual appeal for horny teenage boys. "I'll let you go. Billy Cameron's on the other line." She clicked. "Hey, Billy." Her voice was warm. Police Chief Billy Cameron was not only a good steward of his island, he was Annie and Max's dear friend.

"Hi, Annie. Is Max there?"

Billy's voice told her this call was official. "Yes." Her reply was swift and breathless and she was on her feet and holding out the phone to Max. "It's for you. Billy Cameron."

Shadows grew as the summer sun slipped behind huge loblolly pines that bordered the lake. Though spears of rosy light still touched the center of the lake, dusk cloaked the woods. Birds chittered as they settled for the night. An owl hooted. A light breeze rustled magnolia leaves. A faint scent of fragrant magnolia blossoms overlay the danker smell of the lake. Nearby pines threw dark shadows across the wooden viewing platform.

Billy Cameron held a flashlight trained on a body at the base of the ladder. The young black teenager's face was slack in death. He'd had a chubby face. "Held him until you got here. Doc Burford's been and gone." Billy pointed at the braided green-and-black friendship band around the right wrist. "Most of the guys at the Haven wear those. Kevin's got one."

Max nodded. Billy's teenage stepson was a regular at the Haven. Kevin was the driving force behind the Haven's first rock band. A memory bobbed in the back of Max's mind: Jean Hughes patiently teaching chords to an aspiring guitarist.

Billy looked expectant. "I figured you might be able to ID him."

Max felt a wash of melancholy. This lovely summer day, a day when living should have been easy, had ended in the much-too-soon death of a kid who'd had great promise. Max's voice was heavy. "Click Silvester. Hubert, actually. A really good guy. Worked part-time at José's Computer Repair. Click was a whiz with anything electronic. He could do a paintball gun faster than anybody. That's why they called him Click. No parents. He and his little brother live with an uncle, Arlen Garvey. The little guy, he's maybe seven or eight, hangs out at the Haven, too. I don't think they had much of a home life. What happened?"

"Accident, maybe." Billy nodded at the ladder. "He could have been up there, looking at birds, and when he started down the ladder, he could have lost his grip, fallen backward. Doc said massive hematoma on the back of his head. Or maybe somebody whacked him with something firm, but not sharp-edged since there's no cut or scrape, lugged him to the edge, and pushed him over. Whatever happened, somebody was here when he fell or found him later." The police chief's quiet voice was taut with anger. Billy Cameron was a gentle giant, but he had zero tolerance for lawbreakers. He was imposing in his crisp khaki uniform, a big man with short-cut blond hair, a broad face, and bright blue eyes.

"How do you know that?" Max looked around. The only figures he saw were Billy's officers, Lou Pirelli and Hyla Harrison. Obviously summoned from off-duty, Lou wore a Braves T-shirt, baggy sweat shorts, and running shoes. He moved step by careful step around the perimeter of the crime scene, set off by yellow crime-scene tape. Lou's flashlight beamed at the gray dusty ground. Hyla held a notebook, her reserved face preoccupied as she made quick notations. As always, Hyla's uniform was fresh and crisp.

"Look." Billy pointed at the pockets of the dead boy's blue jean cutoffs. Both pockets were pulled out, the white interior lining distinct despite the gathering gloom. "Empty pockets. Same thing in back when we turned him over. Did somebody accost him, make him hand over everything in his pockets? I don't think so. If he took everything out himself, why would he pull out the lining? That looks more like he was robbed after he died. Somebody pulled out the pockets, took everything he had."

Max frowned. "He wouldn't have had much. Anybody going to the trouble to kill someone to take their stuff would pick a victim with a better payoff. I'd be surprised if Click had ten bucks on him."

Billy's eyes narrowed. "Whatever he had, it was taken. The guy who found him, a tourist on a bike, said the pockets were pulled out. He buzzed 911. I called you when I saw the friendship band from the Haven. No ID on him. No cell phone. So maybe he had something that linked him to somebody. You say he wouldn't have had much money. How about drugs?"

"Not Click." Even as he spoke, Max knew drugs were always a possibility. He didn't believe that Click, who had been cheerful and eager to please and good-natured, had used drugs. He would have been shocked if Click sold drugs. But he had been shocked before.

"Maybe. Maybe not." Billy's voice reflected years of battling the deadly scourge found everywhere from the loveliest sea islands to New York penthouses to Iowa farm towns to L.A. slums. "Doc will run the tests. If he's clean, then maybe he had an accident and some scum wandered by and cleaned him out. Anyway," he clapped Max on the shoulder, "sorry to screw up your evening. Thanks for helping us out."

Annie loved many aspects of their old-new home. Since she and Max had moved into their restored antebellum house, she'd especially enjoyed the golden pool of sunlight that flooded through the east windows of their master bedroom, especially in summer. They slept with the windows open, even though Texas-bred Annie was quick to hike up the air-conditioning in the daytime to combat the sticky, humid heat. The house had been designed to capture the night's offshore breeze. Since Franklin House had ample surrounding land and no neighbor near enough to glance through their windows, the shutters were flung wide with nothing to impede the rosy early-morning sunshine.

Usually, Annie woke to the distant sounds of Max in the kitchen downstairs. Yesterday he'd made pineapple coffee cake and an omelet with fresh spinach and Parmesan.

This morning he stood on the balcony in his boxers, but there was no aura of a man joyfully greeting the day.

Annie rolled up on an elbow. "Max?"

Slowly, he turned and walked to the bed. He sat down

on the edge, took one of her hands, his expression somber. His face softened. "Good morning, Mrs. Darling. Did you know you're beautiful even with your hair tangled and no makeup? In fact," he smiled, "you don't need makeup." His free hand smoothed back a lock of hair, traced her jawbone, lightly touched her lips. "Beautiful Annie. Sometimes that's all I see. But then there are mornings like these," the darkness in his eyes spoke of summer days when they had feared their life together was done, "and I know I can count on you. I have to go see Click's family. You'll come, too, won't you?"

Broward's Rock was always beautiful, even when marred by squalor. A breeze stirred Spanish moss in the live oak trees, some of the silky silver-gray tendrils brushing rusted hulks of old cars. Honeysuckle running amok half-hid a ramshackle shed, scenting the air as sweetly as expensive perfume. Two ruby-throated hummingbirds hovered over clusters of bright orange, trumpet-shaped creeper flowers twined in a drooping, barbed-wire fence.

A wooden shack, weathered to dull gray, appeared deserted. The porch sagged. Two treads were missing from the front stoop. A porch swing dangled from one chain. Flies crawled on a discarded fast-food container. The only sounds were the caw of crows and the whirr of insects.

Annie ducked from a cloud of flies. "Are you sure this is right?"

Max gestured toward the rural mailbox at the edge of the rutted road they'd followed. "The numbers match." He shifted the cooler on his hip and took a big stride to the porch that creaked beneath his weight. He reached the screen door. The front door was open to dimness within.

"No bell." He knocked, a firm bang that sounded overloud in the silence.

Annie cautiously gripped a splintery railing and pulled herself past the missing steps and onto the porch. "Where is everybody?" When someone died, people came. Family. Friends. Church. Neighbors.

Max banged again.

Steps sounded. Heavy, slow, shuffling steps. "Yeah." A big man, a very big man, perhaps three hundred pounds, stood on the other side of the screen door. He was shirtless. Blue shorts hung beneath a bulging belly. He brought with him a smell of beer. In the dimness of the interior, he was hard to see, but he looked unsteady. One hand gripped the doorjamb.

"Mr. Garvey, I'm Max Darling. We met last year at the Haven summer program night."

There was no response and no change of expression in the drooping face.

Max was somber. "I taught Hubert how to sail. I'm very sorry about his death. My wife and I brought some food."

Garvey was slow to answer. Finally, he gestured. "You can take it next door. Miz Peebles is looking after everything." He pointed vaguely to his left. "I got the day off." He blinked again. "Thank you." It was as if he drew the words from a long-ago memory. He turned away.

They walked in silence away from the house. "So much for that." Max sounded resigned. "I wanted to ask him if everything had been the same lately with Click. I doubt he'd know or care."

Annie nodded. "Drunk."

"Yeah. Do you suppose Click's little brother is in there? I'll ask Billy to check." They followed a dusty path that disappeared around the honeysuckle-shrouded shed. "I'll talk to some of Click's friends at the Haven, see what I can find out."

Annie hurried to keep up with his long strides. "Find out about what?"

Max's look was a mixture of uncertainty and determination. "His death appears to be accidental, but there has to be a reason why his pockets were emptied. I want to make sure there's no drug connection at the Haven. He was a good kid. But even good kids make mistakes."

On the other side of the shed, the difference in properties was the difference between despair and joy. They faced the backyard. A vegetable garden groaned with plenty, snap peas, corn, cucumbers, squash, and watermelons. Four boys knelt in the heat, digging out weeds between rows. They looked dusty and sweaty.

A tall, thin black woman stood on the back porch of a recently painted white frame house. She held a tray with big glasses of lemonade and a plate of cookies. "Snack time, boys." She came down the steps and carried the tray to a trestle table beneath the shade of a live oak tree.

Three of the boys scrambled up and ran, pushing one another, laughing, though they were careful not to trample any of the vegetables. Lagging behind was a little boy who shot them an anxious look as he climbed up on the bench.

The woman, crisp in a starched housedress, walked toward Annie and Max, her expression polite but reserved.

Max looked at her inquiringly. "Mrs. Peebles?"

She nodded, folded her hands, and waited.

"Mr. Garvey sent us over. He said you are taking care of everything for Hubert."

Her lips folded for an instant into a thin line. "Somebody

has to. I spoke to the preacher. The neighborhood's taking up a collection. We'll manage."

"We brought some food." Max held up the cooler.

Her face softened. "That's mighty nice. People have been real kind. Ms. Hughes came this morning from the Haven. She thought a lot of Hubert. How did you know Hubert?"

"I volunteer at the Haven. I'm Max Darling. This is my wife, Annie."

She smiled, her face softening. "I've heard about you, Mr. Darling. My granddaughter Samantha's told me about you."

Max looked eager. "Were Samantha and Hubert friends?"

She gestured toward the picnic table. "Hubert was older. Samantha's the same age as Hubert's brother Willie. He's the little one. The one not laughing. Arlen sent him over this morning. He knows I'll take care of Willie. Like I did Hubert. Their mother was my friend."

Max looked toward the dejected little boy who slumped against the table, his face tight with misery. "Mrs. Peebles, I'd like to talk to Willie for a minute."

Her smile disappeared. "Why?"

"He might know why his brother went to the nature preserve yesterday."

She folded her arms. "Any rule on this island a black boy can't go to the nature preserve?"

"It seems a funny place for him to go."

Her face folded into stern lines. "I don't need you to paint me a picture, Mr. Darling. You got it in your head Hubert was mixed up with something wrong, something hidden. I can tell you that isn't true. I know boys. I've had a passel and raised them. One of mine went bad, sold drugs. He's in prison now. You know when they're younger than Hubert if that's the way they're headed. I'm tired of a young black man dying and everybody thinking he had to have done something to deserve it. Arlen told me Hubert fell from the ladder on the viewing platform. Anybody can have an accident. As for talking to Willie, asking him about Hubert, that would just upset him more. I got Willie helping my boys in the garden. I'm going to get him good and tired and let them play in water from the sprinkler after supper and then Willie can sleep in with my Sam. As for Hubert, I can tell you Hubert was the same yesterday as every day I ever saw him, smiling at me and asking if he could help carry anything into the house. Willie sat on my back porch all yesterday afternoon, waiting for Hubert to come home. Hubert had told him he was going to take him on a shopping trip. But Hubert never came."

∴ *Three* ∾

THE HAVEN BUILDING had once served as a small
school on the north end of the island. The school had been
closed and abandoned after World War II. James Frost, an
ornithologist, retired to Broward's Rock in the 1960s and
bought the dilapidated structure along with a nearby home
and barn. He restored the building for use as a studio. He
began an informal association with the island high school,
teaching summer classes on local birds. His favorite was
the anhinga, and a carved black anhinga with its distinctive
webbed feet perched atop the gable. He was a widower, his
only son killed in the Battle of the Bulge. When Frost died
in 1984, he bequeathed his home and property, including the
studio, for use as a center for island youth. Under the leader-
ship of two dynamic directors, the Haven had added several
small structures, paved an outdoor basketball court, and
graded a field for football and soccer. A pier poked out into
a good-size lake rimmed with cattails. Construction was
almost complete on a new gym provided by Booth Wagner.

As Max's Jeep curved around a stand of pines, Annie
pointed at the anhinga, glistening with a coat of new black

paint. "Laurel once said I reminded her of an anhinga." She managed not to sound resentful. Almost.

Max looked stunned, but rallied quickly. "I'm sure she meant it as the highest compliment. Anhingas—" even Max was occasionally at a loss for words, "—anhingas," he said manfully, "have spectacular orange beaks." He eased the Jeep to a stop near the old school building that held the main office.

Annie nodded encouragement, waited expectantly.

"Anhingas, well, they swim like fish. So do you," he concluded triumphantly. He popped out of the car with the air of a man who had surmounted a difficult challenge. At the front steps, he looked up in admiration at the glistening black bird. "After all, anhingas were Professor Frost's favorite birds."

Annie gave the carving a jaundiced glance and followed him inside.

Children worked on crafts in one room. Two burly teenage boys sweated in a vigorous Ping-Pong game. In the wi-fi nook, most of the worn beanbag chairs were occupied.

Jean's office door was open. A ceiling fan stirred hot air. The old building didn't run to air-conditioning. The room was small, perhaps twelve feet by fourteen, space enough for a worn wooden desk, two metal filing cabinets, and a couple of straight chairs. She held the phone, her face anxious. ". . . Everybody's welcome this evening. The reception begins at seven thirty and the program will start about eight thirty. We'll have free popcorn and Kool-Aid. Yes. Please come. Thank you." She put down the phone and looked at Max with wide, staring eyes. "Have you heard about Click?"

Annie had felt sorry for Jean yesterday. Now, she felt a quick liking. The director faced the loss of her job, but her first thought when she saw Max, whom she had begged to help her, was about the dead boy, not her own plight.

Max nodded. "Yes. I want to talk to you about him. May we come in?"

"Of course." She glanced wearily around the room, tried ineffectually to straighten some papers.

They stepped inside, and Max closed the door.

"Everything's kind of a mess." Jean looked overwhelmed. "I've got to get things tidied up. Larry Gilbert—he's one of the directors—called to say he was doing an inspection this morning. He said it's his responsibility to report on the buildings and grounds at the board meeting next week. We've got a leak in the boys' bathroom and I can't help it that the plumber didn't do a good job. And somebody broke the padlock on the prop shop near the outdoor stage." She glanced at Annie. "Nothing's messed up, thank God. Everything is where it should be for the show tonight. That would've been the last straw. Of all mornings for him to come—" She broke off. "Anyway this morning's bad. And now the awful news about Click. Please sit down. I know those chairs aren't very comfortable."

The wooden chairs were rickety. Annie felt a splinter snag her skirt.

"Click was a nice boy. I don't know why it's always the nicest people who die young." Jean choked back a sob, looked embarrassed. "It's just . . . everything's too much." She took a deep breath. "Anyway, it's awful about Click. We're going to gather down at the lake at ten thirty—everyone who wants to come—and say good-bye to him. Anybody can speak out, say what they remember or why he was special. I brought roses from home," she pointed at a vase thick with pale white blooms, "and everyone can throw a rose in the water for him. You're welcome to join us."

Max's reply was swift. "We would like to come."

Jean's eyes were bleak. "I have trouble believing he's gone. Why, he was going to check out some things on my computer this morning. And the police say he died in the nature preserve. I can't imagine why he went there. He never much liked being outdoors. I tried to get him to play some sports, but he was always too busy with video games or his laptop."

Max asked quickly, "Why do you suppose he went to the nature preserve?"

The director shrugged. "I guess there had to be a reason. But he hated to be hot."

Max looked somber. "Maybe he was meeting someone and he didn't want anyone else to know."

The director's expression was puzzled. "Why would he do that?"

Max was blunt. "Drugs."

"No." Her reply was swift and certain. "Not Click." A sudden smile touched her face. "A girl maybe. He was really starting to be interested in girls." The smile fled. "But he wasn't into drugs. I can tell. Great big eyes."

Annie knew what Jean meant: dilated pupils. She might not have the vocabulary, but she had street smarts.

"Acting funny. Talking like your tongue is thick. Too much money." She hesitated, then said, "Booth has plenty to say now about how unqualified I am for my job, but I can keep my mouth shut. We had a problem a few months ago. Nobody but the board knows. There was one of our kids, I tried hard to reach him, get him to go into treatment, but I didn't have any luck. The police set up a sting. He's gone now. Nobody's on drugs here. Whatever gave you that idea about Click?"

"He was found dead—maybe an accident, maybe not—in

an isolated place where nobody goes on a hot July afternoon, except maybe a stray tourist. It was a tourist who found the body and called 911." Max looked somber. "The police asked me to come and see if I could ID the body because he was wearing a Haven friendship bracelet. The police may not have released this information. Click's pockets were pulled out. No ID, no billfold, no cell phone. Somebody took that stuff. So, my first thought is what could bring a kid to an isolated spot and get him killed. There's one easy answer: drugs."

"Not Click." Jean spoke with finality. "As for his pockets, somebody came by, somebody who didn't mind robbing a dead boy. Not that he would have had much. Anyway, Click wasn't into drugs. You may think I don't know what's going on. Why don't you talk to Click's friends. They can tell you what's what. Click hung out with Darren Dubois and Freddy Baker. You are welcome to talk to any of the kids. Eden Conway likes everybody. She pretty much knows everything that's happening."

Outside in the sunshine, Max looked thoughtful. "Sometimes three's a crowd. Why don't you wander around, talk to some of the girls. I'll take care of Darren and Freddy."

Annie grinned. "I get it. Guys talk to guys. That's okay with me. It might even be a couple of degrees cooler inside." She walked back up the steps and reentered the building.

Max strolled around the grounds. He heard a boy's raucous shout. "Hey, Darren, bet you can't make it over the hump."

Max turned and headed for a stand of willows.

A new thirty-foot climbing wall, also a gift from Booth Wagner, was near the site of the new gym. Simulated concrete bulged like a granite overhang on a mountain peak. A half-dozen kids watched as Darren, almost six feet of lean and muscular strength, moved crabwise toward the steepest part of the overhang. Stringy blond hair waved in a brisk breeze. He was shirtless. Muscles rippled across his tanned back. He clung to one projection, then another.

Max opened his mouth to yell, closed it. This was no time to startle him.

Darren's right hand edged higher, seeking a hold. Maybe he was sweating. Maybe he misjudged. His hand gripped, then slipped. For an instant, he flailed with that hand, wavered against the rocklike surface, then his fingers closed on a prong.

The boys below were silent, staring upward. One of them clutched the nearest boy's arm in a tight grasp.

Darren's breathing was labored.

Max moved forward. Maybe he could get up there, help him . . .

In a rapid ascent, as if propelling himself with determination, Darren went fast, hand over hand. He surmounted the bulge, and, in a moment, stood shakily on top. He was breathing fast, his face red. He called out in ragged bursts, "I did it, dudes. You got to pay up. Five bucks each. I made it up without the—" He saw Max, broke off.

Now Max yelled. "You signed the contract like everybody else." Max's voice was hard. "No climbing without the safety harness. What do you think you're doing, Dubois?"

"I guess I forgot." Darren's tone was insolent. He moved a few steps, grabbed a thick line, and dropped safely to the ground.

Max strode toward him, ready to lay down the law. Then he saw Darren's red-rimmed eyes. Beneath the bravado was

misery. What do you do when your best friend is dead?
Maybe you fling yourself up a wall, make it tough, make it
hard, make it where you can't think.

"You heard about Click?"

Anguish burned in those red-rimmed blue eyes. "Yeah."

"I'm sorry."

"Yeah." Darren started to turn away.

"Darren, has everything been okay with Click lately?"

Darren stopped, frowning. "Okay? Yeah. Same old Click.
All he did was work. He was always telling me I needed
to shape up, follow the rules. What good did following the
rules do him? He's dead." Darren's voice was angry.

Max knew he couldn't hold him, mustn't hold him. He
shot out one last quick question. "Why did he go to the
nature preserve?"

Darren shook his head. "Man, I don't get it. It's the last
place he'd go." His face crumpled. "It's the last place he
went." Tears glimmered in his eyes. He turned and ran.

"I like your drawing." Annie smiled at Eden Conway, a
sandy-haired teenager with big glasses, freckles, and a
friendly expression.

Eden pushed back a stray curl from a mop of sun-
bleached hair. She glanced at the sketch pad, added another
dark circle to the raccoon's tail, and smudged the dark mask
around the eyes. "Thank you. I wish I could do better. See,
I don't have the paws right. They should look like they have
little fingers."

"Your raccoon's face is perfect."

Eden looked pleased. "I've worked on the mask all week."

"Do you come to the Haven a lot?" Annie glanced around
the art room. Kids of all ages drew, painted, modeled clay,

and made posters. She expected some of the posters would be in evidence tonight at the talent show.

"Every day. I work in the kitchen at lunch and I make a little money. My brothers and sisters are here and I keep an eye on them."

"Ms. Hughes said you know everything going on at the Haven."

"Most things." Eden was matter-of-fact. "I talk to every-body."

"You knew Click Silvester."

"Oh." Eden's voice was sad. "That's awful. Click was kind of clumsy, but who'd think he'd fall off a platform?"

Clearly no one at the Haven suspected Click's death to be anything other than accidental. Annie didn't want to start a brush fire of gossip. "Eden, I'd like to ask you something on a confidential basis. Will you please not tell anyone?"

Eden looked wary. "How about my mom?"

"That would be fine. And the idea may be crazy. But Max and I are worried. Could Click have been mixed up in drugs?"

"Nope." Eden was firm but understated, dealing politely with a grown-up's foolishness. "Click's dad died of a drug overdose and his uncle's a drunk. Click was always warning the other kids about drinking and drugs."

Most of the intent faces in the video room belonged to boys. Max spotted Freddy Baker sitting cross-legged on the floor beneath a whirring ceiling fan.

"Hey, Freddy."

Freddy looked up. He clicked off a DS and came to his feet. He was scruffy, scrawny, and usually hyper. His nor-mally cheerful face was solemn. "Hi, Max. I talked another couple of guys into coming to the sailing class. Can I show them how to rig the sail?"

"That would be great." Max knew Freddy, who was small for his age, was thrilled to find a sport where his agility paid off. A tenth-grader, Freddy was a head shorter than most of the guys his age. "Hey, Freddy, I hear you were one of Click's buddies."

"Yeah. I *was*." He spoke as if the past-tense verb was strange.

"Had you talked to him lately?"

Freddy's face was abruptly stricken. "Like yesterday. He was pumped. He was so excited about tonight I thought he'd bust."

Max packed away his last worry about drugs. Kids into drugs didn't get excited about talent shows.

Freddy's lips quivered. "He told me he was going to have a special part that nobody knew about. He said it was a big secret. Now he's not going to be here." Brown eyes stared at Max, seeking help. "He's not anywhere."

Max shaded his eyes as he walked outside, seeking Annie. The mid-morning July heat washed over him. He glanced at his watch. If it was this hot a little after ten, the air would be baking by afternoon. He waved at several kids he knew. Encouraged by his talk with Freddy, he felt more confident the Haven remained a good and safe place for young people.

Max surveyed the grounds. Kids played soccer. A half-dozen fished from the pier. Max was suddenly alert. Larry Gilbert, who looked summer-comfortable in a blue polo, white slacks, and dark sandals, stood near the tennis court, taking a photo with a digital camera. The net slacked in the middle and had a hole at one end.

According to Henny's report to Annie, Larry's vote might be ripe for the picking. Larry sold insurance and dabbled in various businesses. A first-rate tennis player, he was active on the social scene as a divorced bachelor. Several single moms had made a real effort to snag him, but he avoided commitments. He once told Max, as they cooled off with a Tom Collins after a tournament, women with kids were damned expensive and he'd rather spend money on stamps. He proudly described his collection, which included a three-cent Hawaiian missionary stamp and a 1918 Inverted Jenny. When Max failed to indicate the proper awe, Larry turned to Dale Swenson, who regularly took first in the club championship, and they plunged into a discussion of rare stamps and auctions.

Max had intended to drop by Larry's office this afternoon, but approaching Larry here made their contact more casual. He called out, "Hey, Larry," and walked swiftly across the hummocky ground to the tennis court.

Perspiring, his bony face flushed from the heat, Larry Gilbert looked up. Deep-set brown eyes were sharp as a hawk's. "Hey, Max, hotter than a griddle out here." Dark hair curling from sweat, Gilbert jerked a disdainful thumb at the court. "I know they don't play much when it's this hot, but that net's a mess. I'm out to look things over before the board meeting next week. I have to say there's a lot that needs improvement."

This wasn't exactly the conversation Max had hoped for. "It's a big property, Larry. Hard to keep on top of everything. On the positive side, we're flooded with kids. Enrollment's up by about a third this summer. Considering there's no air-conditioning, that shows how popular the programs are."

"In a bad economy, a bunch of them are probably just here for the free lunch." The board member's frown was dark. "May be getting some undesirable elements with that." He jerked his head to the west. "Somebody broke into the prop shop near the stage. The hasp holding the padlock had been pried loose, and the door was wide-open. I had Jean check things out. She said the door was fine yesterday. I looked it over and nothing seems to have been touched, but she was pretty vague about what's kept in the shed. I told her we need to have records of everything. I can see why Booth's ready to fire her."

Max felt a sharp disappointment. There was no hint in Larry's voice of any strain between him and Booth Wagner.

"The kids like her." Max tried to sound casual.

"Yeah." Larry wasn't impressed. He eyed Max with curiosity. "I hear she's buttered up to you. I wouldn't have thought she would impress you. I'd think you'd want somebody more high-class for the job."

"I like a director who cares about kids. Like Jean. And naturally, she's concerned about her job. As you know—" (word gets around in a small town) "—I'm lining up support for her. A lot of folks are impressed with the pleasant atmosphere she's fostered. She had no idea that Booth fabricated a résumé for her. She had given him her actual résumé and that will be presented to the board."

Larry raised a questioning eyebrow. "A day late and a dollar short, I'd say. It will all get sorted out next week. Now, I need to check out the kitchen." He looked unhappy. "Damn, it's going to be hot in there. Oh well, the sooner I get in there, the sooner I'm out of here. Good to see you, Max." And he turned away.

Max looked after him. Should he gamble, make a direct appeal for Jean?

He almost took a step after Larry.

A bell-like tone rang.

Jean Hughes stood on the front steps of the main building, striking a triangle chime. She called out in her strong voice: "Come to the lake. For Click."

Annie opened a box of Jan Burke's new title in the storeroom. Annie was grateful to be back in her happy bookstore. Everything was as it should be at Death on Demand: sunburned readers, the occasional careening toddler with a tired mother in full chase, her intrepid clerk Ingrid Webb calm and cheerful. The bookstore's normalcy helped distance her from the memory of long-stemmed white roses floating on green water and a good life cut much too short.

Ingrid stood in the doorway, looking at a sheet of paper. "A book club from Bluffton wants to make this a mystery year and has asked for a list of suggested reading."

Agatha rubbed against the cardboard box. Annie petted the silky fur, evaded sharp teeth. "Has Agatha eaten?"

Ingrid eyed Agatha with wary amusement. "Of course."

Annie sighed. Keeping Agatha slim was an ongoing battle. "Maybe a little more salmon." She picked up the cat and carried her, green eyes gleaming, to the coffee bar. She spooned out additional food. "Did they say what kind of mysteries?"

Behind the counter, Ingrid expertly whipped out two cappuccinos with an extra dollop of whipped cream for Annie. The coffee bar featured mugs decorated with mystery titles. "Famous." Her tone was laconic. She handed Annie a mug emblazoned with *Rehearsals for Murder* by E. X. Ferrars. For herself, she chose *Peril Ahead* by John Creasey.

"No more said than done. I assume they are buying the books from us?"

At Ingrid's nod, Annie rattled off, "*The Adventures of*

Sherlock Holmes, The Circular Staircase, The Murder of Rog—"

The phone rang. With a glance at Caller ID, Annie broke off to answer. "Hi, Laurel."

Her mother-in-law's husky voice thrummed sadness, like a low guitar chord. "The situation is desperate." There was indistinguishable noise in the background.

Annie sat up straight, cappuccino and famous mysteries forgotten. "Where are you?" Annie envisioned flames spiraling skyward or an armed intruder and Laurel locked in a closet.

"Where hearts overflow and all things are known. Oh, if it weren't so sad, I would suggest this motto be emblazoned on the plate glass of beauty shops everywhere." In a more practical voice, she added, "At Beatrice's." Beatrice Kingsley's beauty shop had been on Main Street, if not since time immemorial, for a good long while. "Annie, I have discovered Jean's heartbreak . . ."

Max welcomed the coolness of his office after the sweltering mugginess at the Haven. He felt somber, wishing he could have better helped Darren and Freddy as they struggled with sorrow. As for Click's presence in the nature preserve, that might always remain unexplained. Max was pleased there seemed to be no likelihood Click had been involved in any way with drugs. His fear for the Haven could be dismissed. But Jean Hughes's problem remained. There was a chance he might be able to make a big difference.

His intercom buzzed. "Got what you asked for. File name Prentice."

"Thanks, Barb." Max swung to his computer, clicked the file.

PAULINE PRENTICE

Retired English teacher. Single. Sixty-three. A native of Charleston who came to the island as a young teacher and never left. She lives quietly, though reputed to be well-to-do. Local gossip has it that she inherited several million dollars from her late brother, a Chicago lawyer who never married. Henny Brawley taught with her and says Pauline is the epitome of rectitude, charming in certain milieus, especially those favoring demitasses and antimacassars, and totally lacking in humor, commenting once that Mark Twain seemed to champion disrespect for authority. Duh.

Max grinned, attributing the editorial comment to Barb.

On the Haven board, Pauline serves with an attitude of noblesse oblige. Her reaction to Jean Hughes's appointment has been one of disdain. Henny Brawley believes Booth engineered Jean's appointment not only for the convenience of having his mistress on the island but with the express purpose of irritating Pauline, who clearly finds him boorish. Pauline treats Wagner civilly but coolly.

Max frowned. He thought the chances of Larry Gilbert supporting Jean lukewarm at best. As for Pauline Prentice, she'd opposed the original appointment. Why would she change her mind?

Max reread the dossier. He pulled the phone near and tapped a number.

Henny Brawley answered on the first ring.

Max gave a silent thank-you for cell phones. Most people were never out of touch.

"Hey, Max." Henny's voice was warm. "I've had a lot of calls in support for Jean."

"That's great, but, as you know, it comes down to five votes. Tell me about Pauline Prentice and rectitude."

Henny spoke with thought and deliberation, concluding: ". . . Always fair. There's a chance."

"Thanks, Henny. See you tonight."

With a decided nod, Max dialed the international number. He needed for Pauline Prentice to switch her proxy from Booth to Henny or Frank. It was that simple. Then there would be three votes for Jean, two against her.

A polite voice answered and replied that Signorina Prentice was in residence and a moment, please.

While Max waited, he pictured a line of cypresses lining a dusty road to an Italian villa. He glanced at his legal pad: Pauline Prentice's villa . . . ten kilometers from Florence . . . overlooks the Arno Valley. It was almost noon here. Around seven there.

"Hello." The high, clear voice was formal.

"Miss Prentice, this is Max Darling on Broward's Rock." He had met her at several Haven functions. "I'm a volunteer at the Haven. Last spring I spoke with you about the sailing program. I'm calling now about the board meeting next week."

"Yes?" She was courteous, but reserved.

"I'm sure you are aware that Booth Wagner wants the director fired."

There was a faint sound that might have been a disdainful huff. "Mr. Wagner told me that he deeply regrets his unfortunate sponsorship of a woman clearly unqualified to be the director. I made my position clear at the time."

"Henny Brawley is convinced that Booth proposed Ms. Hughes for the job because he knew you would object to her background and he wanted to score off of you because you apparently find him less than charming."

Silence.

Max continued, hoping she didn't cut the connection, but very likely she was not only honorable but averse to rudeness. "Miss Prentice, it is true that Jean came to the island because she thought he loved her. However, Booth had told her he was separated from his wife. After she came and discovered that he was lying, she broke off with him. Moreover, she had no idea he had fabricated a résumé for her. She gave him her true résumé." Max felt as though he was dropping the words into a well so deep there wasn't even a faint echo of a splash. "She admits she doesn't have the administrative background for the position, but she plans to take some accounting courses online. Frank Saulter has offered to help organize her office. On the plus side, attendance at the Haven is up by a third. The kids like her. A lot."

"Why have you involved yourself in this controversy, Mr. Darling?" Her Charleston accent, smooth and mellow as bourbon, didn't soften the sharpness of her question.

"Ms. Hughes asked me to help her. My wife and I," Max wanted to be sure this was understood, "feel that she deserves to keep the job. This morning my wife and I went to the Haven . . ." Max quickly described Click's death and his own efforts to be sure no drugs were involved. "Ms. Hughes was very helpful and confident there is no drug problem. She organized a farewell to Click at the lake. I think you would have been proud of her effort."

Silence.

Max cleared his throat. "Henny says you are fair."

"That is gracious of Henny. Pray tell me. Does she intend to vote for Ms. Hughes's reappointment?"

Max tried to contain his excitement. He kept his voice even. "She will vote to renew Jean's contract, as will Frank Saulter."

"Chief Saulter, too." There was the faintest warming of the glacial voice. "In that event, I shall notify Mr. Wagner that I am rescinding the grant of my proxy and that my proxy will be exercised by Mrs. Brawley in support of Ms. Hughes."

Max was on his feet and striding to the door, a gunslinger's swagger, as he punched his cell. "Hey, Annie. Meet me for lunch at Parotti's. I've got great news." He clicked off. This news had to be presented in person. If he had a trumpet, he would blow it.

∽ *Four* ∾

ANNIE LOVED STEPPING into Parotti's Bar and Grill. Summer or winter, sunny or gray, Parotti's never failed to please. When Annie first came to Broward's Rock, Parotti's had been down-at-the-heels even though always clean and with the best home-cooking on the island. The heady smell of live bait, sawdust sprinkled near the open coolers, beer on tap, and hot grease pleased customers who came for food, not ambience. However, when bristly chinned (long before it became fashionable) Ben Parotti, partial to bib overalls, met the ladylike owner of a mainland tea shop, Miss Jolene, romance blossomed. Now clean-shaven Ben was spiffy in Tommy Bahamas casual wear, and Parotti's offered quiche as well as fried and grilled fish, blue-and-white checked cloths on the tables, and carefully situated fans to diminish the rank reek of bait.

Ben moved to greet her. "Got flounder so fresh it could swim to the table. Max is already here. Wants his grilled."

Annie hurried to their favorite table near the 1940s juke-box. She dropped into her chair and smiled at Ben, who never bothered to offer them menus. "Fried flounder deluxe with a side of guacamole." Annie's Texas roots appreciated this recent addition to the menu. The resulting meal would be blissful: flounder perfectly crisped, hot fresh French fries, heavenly hush puppies, and guacamole with just the right amount of lemon.

Max's order, grilled with cole slaw, was no surprise, nor was the chiding frown he gave her.

She gave him a bland smile. "If God had intended for all food to be grilled, He wouldn't have invented grease."

As Ben headed for the kitchen, she leaned forward, eager to hear Max's news before she shared her own. She always took happy over sad if she had a choice.

Max turned two thumbs up. "Jean's job is safe. We have the votes. Henny, Frank, and, thanks to an international call successfully placed by yours truly, Pauline Prentice. Here's what she said . . ."

Annie listened with delight. "That's absolutely wonderful. Because," and her smile slipped away, "I have news, too, and it isn't good. Laurel called me from Beatrice's. Beatrice volunteers at a hospice. She does hair for people who are terminally ill." Annie took a deep breath, remembering the sob Jean had muffled as she spoke of Click, saying, "I don't know why it's always the nicest people who die young." Now Annie understood that raw emotion. "Jean's younger sister lives with her. Her name's Giselle. She has terminal cancer. She's dying. She's twenty-four."

Annie's voice wobbled. Hot tears burned her eyes. She knew that kind of death. Her mother, sweet and kind and funny and bright, had died much too young, when Annie was in college.

Max reached across the table, took her hands in his. "I didn't know." His face folded in a tight frown. "Don't you suppose Booth knows? He brought her to the island. He had to know something of her situation."

Annie looked grim. "If he knows, he's an even bigger jerk than we thought."

Ben was at the table with their plates. He served them, refilled their tea glasses, but remained standing by the table. "Guess your ears have been hot today."

Max stopped with a forkful of flounder midway to his mouth. "Somebody talking about us?" His tone was easy, but his blue eyes were intent.

Ben shifted the tray under his arm. "Everybody who's anybody downtown comes here for coffee around ten. Not that I eavesdrop on customers, but when they're all talking loud and fast and I'm bringing coffee and serving up Miss Jolene's fresh turnovers, I can't help overhearing. That's why," he spoke with quiet pride, "I know what's up on the island. And it sounds like you got everything set for a big bust-up tonight at the Haven. Jed Maguire—"

Jed Maguire owned Maguire's Drugstore. Annie played tennis with Jed's wife, Aileen.

"—said everybody's talking about the phone campaign you got going to honor the Haven director but some people aren't sure about Miz Hughes in the job, much as they like you. The mayor, you know sometimes he don't seem to cotton to you much, Max, he's laying bets that you come a cropper. Frank Saulter took him up on it, said he'd back you over Booth Wagner any day. Frank plunked down a twenty and said he'd take five-to-one odds. I would of bet too but Miss Jolene don't hold with gambling. I don't even buy lottery tickets anymore."

Annie would have jumped up and hugged Ben, but she knew his craggy face would turn crimson.

Max grinned. "Drop by tonight. There may be some fireworks after the talent show."

"Wouldn't miss it." For an instant, Ben's usual aura of geniality faded. "That Booth Wagner's getting too big for his britches. He came up on the bridge the other day when I was making the run to the mainland and told me to goose the *Miss Jolene*, she was too slow for his taste, that he liked his boats and women fast even if I didn't. I can tell you I didn't take kindly to him talking like that." Ben, who treated his wife always with great deference and respect, looked like a porcupine in full bristle. "I told him next time when he wanted to cross he could find himself some water wings. He told me he could do better than water wings. The next week Reg—" He stopped, took a breath. "Somebody—"

Annie didn't doubt Reggie Bates, owner of the island's one bank, had been indiscreet.

"—said Wagner was talking about buying a hydrofoil and it would cut the trip to the mainland in half. Why, a hydrofoil'd cost him a quarter of a million. There's no way he could make a profit. But he'd put me out of business. 'Course, anybody can boast." But Ben's voice was thin. He gave an abrupt nod and swung away toward the kitchen. Annie poked a salted French fry into a mound of peppered ketchup. "A quarter of a million dollars because Ben blew him off?"

Max squirted lemon on his flounder. His face was thoughtful. "If money's no object and spite is your aim, anything's possible."

"It doesn't seem rational." Annie shivered. Was spite a strong enough word for the misery Booth seemed willing to inflict upon those who in any way opposed him?

Max looked past Annie at the door. "Speaking of the devil . . ."

Booth Wagner stood just inside the door, his gaze sweeping the room. As always, he looked on top of the world, golden ringlets tight as a Viking's helmet, freshly sunburned, likely from golf, and island-casual in his favorite attire—a loose Hawaiian shirt, white slacks, and sandals.

His eyes stopped at their table. With a satisfied smile, he walked toward them.

Annie tensed. "He looks like a hammerhead moving in for the kill." She always pictured sharks with let-me-eat-you smiles.

Max gave her a reassuring look. "We've got the hole card."

He started to rise as Booth reached the table, but, without asking, Booth pulled out a chair, dropped into it. "Word's out that you're in Jean's camp." He shot an appraising glance at Annie. "Have you ever heard about other women, honey?"

Annie laughed though she would have liked to slap him once. Hard. "You're the expert."

"Pretty good." His laugh rumbled, but his eyes glittered. "Anyway," he leaned back, tilting the chair, looking big and amused, "it's real nice that you two are working hard to show appreciation for Jean. 'Course, it won't do any good."

Max was direct. "Numbers don't lie, Booth. Three votes to your two. If you can count on Larry."

"Yep." Booth's tone was admiring. "I got to hand it to you. You've got three votes. Pauline sent me a fax. It was clever of you to call her. Just out of curiosity, the old bitch loathes Jean. How did you persuade her to change her vote?"

"I pointed out how much attendance has increased, and she found it interesting—" Max thought this was a fair interpretation of Pauline's silence as he spoke, "—when I told her that you arranged for Jean to get the job because you thought it would offend her."

"You should have seen Pauline's face the first time she met Jean!" Booth's wide mouth spread in a delighted smile. "Priceless, as they say. Not surprised she'd go your way. If there's anyone she cottons to less than Jean, it's me." He shoved back the chair, towered over the table, big, burly, and commanding. "The question's moot now. We'll have to start a search for a new director."

Annie looked at him sharply. He sounded utterly confident and, even more maddening, amused.

He radiated confidence. "See you tonight."

Max came to his feet. "Hold on. The vote is next week." But Max had the expression of a sailor who sees an approaching torpedo.

"Oh. By damn. I forgot to tell you. Dumb old me. Jean's announcing her resignation tonight." Booth's false consternation ended in a belly laugh. "Be real nice for her to get the good send-off you've put together. Everything works out for the best, doesn't it?"

Annie glanced at Max's set face. He was driving too fast. She braced against the door as the Jeep squealed around a curve. "If he's right," Annie didn't have to define the pronoun, "there's no hurry."

Max glanced at the speedometer, eased his pressure on the gas pedal. "He's too sure of himself. Somehow he's forced her to quit. I have an ugly feeling that whatever he's done, we can't change anything. But I'm going to try."

Leaving the Jeep in a swath of shade from a huge pittosporum shrub, Annie hurried to keep up as Max strode across the dusty ground. Annie glanced toward the lake.

Shouts sounded as racing kayaks swerved around a marker and headed for the dock. The lake was the same and yet so different from that moment when they stood on the dock and gently threw roses in Click's memory into still, green water.

Inside the old wooden building, they found the director's office door open but the room was empty and the light off. As they turned away, a chunky young woman with frizzed brown hair, small gold-rimmed glasses, and a serious expression stepped out of a side room, her arms full of plastic ukuleles.

Max lifted a hand in greeting. "Hey, Rosalind, we're looking for Jean. Annie, this is Rosalind Parker. She's a college intern this summer. Rosalind, my wife, Annie."

"Hello, Max. I'm glad to meet you, Annie." Brown eyes looked at them worriedly. "The little girls—" she glanced at Annie, "—the girls five to nine are first on the program. Actually nobody can really play the ukulele. But they're cute as can be in grass skirts. Of course," she was quick to add, "they have their T-shirts and shorts on underneath."

Max smiled. "Everybody will love them. Where's Jean?"

Rosalind's eyes rounded. Her lips parted in an O.

Max looked at her sharply. "What's wrong?"

Rosalind clutched a ukulele that tried to slip free from her stack, and the strings thrummed. "Jean's gone for a while. Can I help?"

Annie felt a jolt of concern. The intern's distress was obvious. Something was wrong.

Max was direct and demanding. "Gone where?"

The strings thrummed again. Rosalind looked miserable. "I'm not supposed to tell anyone. But you're her friend. Everyone knows how you're trying to get the board to keep her. Jean's wonderful. She didn't go to college so I hear the board wants to get rid of her, but all the degrees in the world don't give someone a good heart." Her face was flushed and her voice shook. "Now everything's falling apart for her. She got a phone call just before lunch and she came out of her office and her face was gray, like dirty sand. She went home to have lunch with her sister, but she hasn't come back. She never takes this long. I'd go after her, but I can't leave here. Someone has to be in charge and there is so much to do with the program tonight and we're going to practice the alligator act in a few minutes. It's the cutest thing, we've used tape that shines in the dark on green cloth, and when the alligators come on stage, the lights go off and you see these wavy stripes and everybody chants a poem I wrote: 'On the night when alligators prance, Abby Alligator got the first dance. With a wink and a happy glance, grab a partner and take a chance.'" She beamed.

Max seemed at a loss for words.

Annie said quickly, "I love it."

Rosalind looked pleased and proud, then worry drained her face of eagerness. "So I can't go and see about her but someone should." She looked at them hopefully. "She looked dreadful. Maybe her sister got worse. She's really sick."

"Where does Jean live?"

Rosalind gestured vaguely to the west. "She and Giselle have that lovely little cottage on the marsh. There's a really nice path through the woods. It only takes a few minutes."

Annie was accustomed to the nicely blacktopped paths in the more manicured parts of the island, where scrub had been cleared. She was always wary of venturing into woods that were, as she explained to Max, too close to nature. Nature in the maritime woods included alligators, which might be fun subjects for a dance but filled Annie with awe, plus snakes both benign and dangerous. She kept a wary eye for copperheads seeking respite from the sun in mounded leaves that had drifted across the narrow path. They brushed through ferns. Mosquitoes whined and birds chirped. A redheaded woodpecker drilled into a pine.

Ahead, a bright opening beckoned to the marsh.

Faintly, then more clearly with every step they took, poignant above the chirps and buzzes and rustling branches of the woods, came the unmistakable sound of a sitar. Annie caught her breath, recognizing "I Have a Dream." She knew that music, knew it well. ABBA had been her mother's favorite group.

As they came nearer the sunlight, as they had a view of the marsh and a cottage with a shaded porch, as the music rose and swelled, Annie saw two figures, one clearly unaware of scrutiny.

Max jolted to a stop. Annie reached out, gripped Max's arm. They stood in silence.

On the porch, a young woman, her complexion almost translucent, curled in a wicker chair. She was covered, despite the heat, by a red-and-white patchwork quilt. She listened to the evocative, hopeful, mystical lyrics, nodding, a sweet smile giving life to a face clearly nearing the end of earthly existence.

Out of sight of the porch, hidden by the fronds of a weeping willow, Jean watched her sister. It was only when the song ended that Jean turned and walked heavily toward the woods, head down.

She didn't look up, obviously knowing the path well, and walked without noticing or caring into the dim tunnel made narrow by encroaching fronds and vines and ferns.

"Jean." Max's voice was gentle.

With a quick-drawn breath, Jean's head jerked up. She stopped and stared with eyes reddened from weeping. Her face reflected a misery that made the dusky tunnel seem darker, the heat heavier, the whirring of the insects ominous.

Annie held out a hand, wishing she could ease the pain that tormented the director. Knowing that was impossible, she offered a hand to hold, a human touch that said: I'm sorry, I care, I wish it could be different.

Jean's lips trembled. Slowly, she reached for Annie's hand, clung.

Annie hadn't known what she was going to say and then she spoke from her heart. "My mother died of cancer."

"Giselle," Jean's throat worked, "has a month or so at most. That's what the doctor said. Maybe less."

Max was gentle. "Is that the call that upset you?"

Jean blinked as if awakening. She seemed to become aware of her hand clinging to Annie's and loosed her grip, stepping back a pace. "Oh." Her gaze focused on Max. "I guess you talked to Rosalind. No. I've known about Giselle for a while." Her voice was dull. "Booth called me." She folded her arms across her front. "I asked you to help me, but there isn't any help. I'm sorry I put you to the trouble. I should have known nothing could be done."

"There's lots to be done. Max did it." Annie stepped forward. Everything in life was attitude. Jean had to shake free of defeat. "Max has the votes to save your job. You can fight Booth. You've got friends."

Jean didn't even bother to shake her head. Her face told the story. She was done, through, finished. "I'm sorry I involved you. I've put you and so many people to trouble. I didn't mean to do that. I'll resign tonight." Her voice was thin and flat, as if every word took extreme effort.

Annie started to speak, but stopped at Max's quick head-shake.

Max's face was thoughtful. "What has he threatened?"

A monarch butterfly fluttered near the tiny bright orange flowers of a butterfly weed. The movement caught Jean's eye. "Everybody loves monarchs. Giselle knows the butterflies by name and which plants they like. She can see butterflies from the porch. You see," and her tone was confiding, "the porch is her favorite place. She's cold all the time. Even now when it's so hot. She sits in a chair wrapped in one of Mama's quilts and looks out at the marsh. She says the marsh changes all day, every minute there is something new to see and everything is alive. The porch means everything to her. That's why I have to do what Booth wants."

Max's face folded in an angry frown. "What does Booth have to do with Giselle on the porch?"

"Oh, everything." She gave a ragged laugh. "I was dumb. You know I always thought I was savvy when we lived in the city. I knew when some guy was hitting on me and was bad news, the worst kind of news. Nobody could scam me. Then Booth came. He was rich and polite. When he told me about the Haven, I pooh-poohed it at first. I said nobody would hire somebody like me and he told me the board wanted somebody who'd come up the hard way like I had and could understand kids who didn't come from ritzy homes. Sure. I understood that. He persuaded me I had a chance. He said all he could do was offer my résumé and maybe it wouldn't pan out. See, I thought that meant it was legit. I was just one of a bunch of applicants so I didn't even really hope. And then it seemed like such a miracle when he came and told me I was hired. Oh, it doesn't matter now, all the lies he told. But the worst lie was the cottage."

Annie gestured toward the clearing. "What does Booth have to do with the cottage?"

Jean rocked back on her heels. For an instant, hatred burned in her eyes. "He told me the cottage came with the job, no rent or anything. When I came to the island, he had me sign a bunch of papers. He said they didn't amount to anything, I didn't need to read them, just stuff like I promised to stay a year and I agreed not to accept any gifts or extra money from anyone—he said that was to protect the Haven from people trying to get kickbacks—and then there was one for the cottage and he said I was agreeing to leave it in good condition."

She watched the monarch, spoke in a monotone. "Booth owns the cottage, not the Haven. The paper I signed was an agreement to move out on demand. With one week's notice. Today he gave me one week's notice. But he said if I resigned, I could stay in the cottage for three months. That's time enough." She swiped at her eyes to wipe away tears. "Oh God knows, that's time enough."

"You don't have to stay in the cottage. Maybe he'll get the cottage, but Max has the votes to keep your job for you." Annie was furious. "We'll help you move." Annie's eyes glinted. "It won't cost you a penny. We'll get our friends to help. We'll line up a convoy of pickups and—"

Jean was shaking her head. "I can't move Giselle. We don't have anywhere to go. Even if we did, I won't move her. That kind of excitement would kill her. Oh, I know," there was a sob in her throat, "she's dying. But I don't want to steal a day or an hour or a minute away from her. She loves the porch. In Atlanta, we lived in a little cramped dark apartment and there was no way for her to be outside unless I took her in a wheelchair. Now she sits on the porch and listens to her music and watches the marsh. The music lifts her up and she forgets that she's dying or maybe the song gives her peace and she knows she can cross the street when the time comes. I'd kill to keep her on that porch."

Annie pushed the button to start the dishwasher. Their early dinner had been solemn. Usually they laughed and talked, each interrupting the other, glad to be together, eager to share, often dissolving in laughter, sometimes sparring but always with good humor. True, they were polar opposites in some ways. Annie's Puritan ethic valued work. Max extolled the ideal of the Renaissance man. He was much more interested in dabbling here and there than tethering himself to a task. Beneath his frivolity, however, was a man who always kept his word.

Annie hung up her apron. Usually she looked forward to their evenings, a stroll on the beach, dancing at the club, working on an intricate picture puzzle. Max was so much better than she at turning a piece upside down and slotting it into sky or ocean. Sometimes Dorothy L., determined to engage Max's attention, snagged a necessary piece and refused to part with it unless offered a kitty treat.

Annie bent down, petted the fluffy white cat. "Later, sweetie. We have to go out." Annie felt dull with dread. They had to go to the Haven and pretend everything was all right and help Jean maintain her dignity.

Annie stepped out onto the back porch. In the spring and early summer the garden was glorious with banks of azaleas, red and pink and cream. Now bougainvillea and hibiscus bloomed. Calla lilies were majestic at the pond. She and Max loved sitting in their wooden rockers and watching their own small pocket of heaven.

This evening, as the sun hovered just above tall pines, he stood at the porch railing.

She came near. "There's nothing we can do, is there?"

"No." There was grim acceptance in his voice. "Staying in the cottage matters more to her than the job. Or anything else. All we can do is be there for her. After . . ." His voice trailed away. He took a breath. "We'll help her find a new job, a new place to live. One thing I can do is raise some money for a bonus. She's proud. She wouldn't accept money from us, but if a group contributes and we make it clear that the bonus is in recognition of her work at the Haven, I think we can persuade her."

Annie nodded. "Henny will help."

Max slipped an arm around Annie's shoulders. "We'll ask Henny to be in charge. It will definitely be a group effort and how much any one person contributes will be confidential."

Annie knew Max would contribute the most, but he understood pride and independence.

Annie felt a curl of sadness. Had Jean told her sister that she'd lost her job? Maybe Jean would say she was taking a vacation after this evening's program. Had Jean forced a smile, promised Giselle she would tell her everything when she returned, that the program was going to be wonderful? Was Jean walking on the darkening path toward an evening that should have been joyful and now promised nothing but humiliation and defeat?

Annie faced Max. "I hate what's happening to her. I wish we could do something to make tonight easier for her."

"All we can do is go." Max nodded toward the Jeep. "And now it's time."

∽ *Five* ∾

ALTHOUGH DARKNESS HAD yet to fall, most of the Haven grounds lay in the deep shadow of huge pines as the sun slipped westward. An old concrete pad sat where the woods curved close to the lake. The pad now served as a stage for outdoor programs. "Stage" was a generous description. The concrete rectangle was all that remained of some long-ago storage building. Between the back of the stage and the woods stood several six-foot light stands. Suddenly bright light flared. Rosalind Parker darted from behind the soft box headlights and clapped her hands in excitement. "They're working!" The illumination of the stage was uneven. Rosalind bustled to the back of the stage and stepped down. She knelt to pull a plug from a cable.

Max looked relieved. "It's always touch-and-go with the lights. But I like having the summer program outside even though we have to borrow a portable lighting system. The little theater group loans the lights to us. When the new gym is finished, the programs will be inside."

The Haven summer program had drawn a good crowd. Annie guessed there must be about seventy-five people milling around, viewing artwork, corralling excited kids, drinking Kool-Aid. Conversation was animated. Some voices spoke in the old and beautiful low-country cadence. A goodly number of other accents could be heard. Yankee twangs, Midwestern flatness, and Western drawls were common on a sea island that offered year-round sun and warmth. Forty-degree days in January beat sub-zero in Minnesota.

Jean moved from cluster to cluster, greeting, welcoming, gesturing toward various venues. At one point, Jean paused to smile at a young mother who held a squirming toddler on one hip. They stood near the steps to the old school building, clearly revealed in a bright, sharp overhead light. Jean was attractive in a pale-lime cotton knit dress and white sandals. She managed to smile though her eyes were somber. There was an aura of exhaustion about her. Thankfully, the lighting on the grounds was sparse enough that she was spared close scrutiny.

A teenage boy sidled up to Max and asked shyly if he'd like to come and see the posters that Rosalind had asked them to make for Jean.

"Go ahead," Annie encouraged. "I'm going to look for Henny before the program starts." As she strolled toward the refreshment table, Annie wondered if others were aware of a dark current beneath the surface excitement. It seemed that wherever she glanced, there were sharp reminders of the drama unfolding beneath the cheer.

First and foremost, the arrival of Booth Wagner set her teeth on edge. He walked in with a tall woman at his side and two teenagers lagging a bit behind. Annie knew his wife casually and she recognized the teenage girl as a customer who bought mostly used paperbacks. She'd never seen the boy and noticed he moved with a decided limp. Booth beamed. His wife's face was composed but not enthusiastic. The teenage girl looked tense and the boy bored. Booth had a peacock strut and clearly expected homage similar to the adulation heaped on politicians. He immediately plunged into the crowd, leaving his family behind. It was easy to follow his progress because of his height and flamboyant Hawaiian shirt, this one purple and green and orange. Booth exuded charm as he moved from group to group, shaking hands, his loud voice easily heard. Booth's boisterous laughter rose above the exuberant din of conversations and shouting kids. At one point he huddled with Larry Gilbert, clapping an arm over the smaller man's shoulders. Larry gestured toward the tennis court, almost invisible in the growing gloom. Annie felt a spurt of irritation. So what difference did a ragged net make? But the sagging net was the least of Jean's worries now.

Booth's wife and the teenagers drifted toward the periphery. Annie glanced at the back page of the program. Bright red type thanked the board of directors. Each received an introductory paragraph with a photograph. She read the tributes to Henny Brawley and Frank Saulter, whom she knew well. The paragraphs were modest and unassuming and likely had been submitted in a response to a request for material. Henny was pictured standing on the porch of her house overlooking the marsh. Frank was surrounded by kids clutching fishing rods at the end of the pier.

Larry Gilbert's paragraph was more formal and clearly written by a businessman looking for a spot of free publicity. He was grinning in an informal shot at a pancake supper, a white chef's hat on his dark hair.

She read Booth's contribution:

Booth Wagner, former CEO of multimillion-dollar Wagner Enterprises in Atlanta, brought his passion for excellence to Broward's Rock when he and his family retired here two years ago. Praised in *Fortune* magazine as a hands-on executive, Booth had energy, charm, and a can-do attitude that brought new life and energy to the Haven. Wagner believes in family values. His wife Neva, daughter Meredith, and stepson Tim Talbot are also familiar faces at the Haven.

Booth had provided a family picture. His bulk emphasized the slender athleticism of his wife. She looked cool and self-possessed. Meredith had curly dark hair, a heart-shaped face, and a shy smile. Slightly built Tim stood with arms folded, face half-turned from the camera. His brown hair was fairly long.

Annie raised an eyebrow. Family values? Was that why Booth had convinced an admittedly too credulous Jean he was in love with her and separated from his wife?

Annie folded the program, put it in the pocket of her white slacks, and scanned the crowd for Henny.

Once again a member of Booth's family caught her eye. This time she was struck by the furtive slide of Booth's stepson away from the lit area. Mack the Knife couldn't have moved with a more effective slither despite the teenager's pronounced limp. Neither Tim Talbot's mother nor stepsister appeared to notice or care as he disappeared into the gloom of the forest. Annie shrugged away a feeling of concern. He was certainly safe enough. A stray bobcat could pose danger in night woods but any bobcat with sense would be as far from light and noise as possible. If Booth's stepson wanted to hunker in the woods instead of attending a party, it was not any of Annie's business. In fact, knowing what she knew would soon unfold, she wished she could flee into the darkness.

As she shrugged and turned away, she spotted Henny near the Kool-Aid stand. Annie joined her and they hugged.

Henny, as always, looked elegant. Tonight she was crisp in a scoop-neck lemon shell and beige linen skirt. Silvered dark hair framed her intelligent face. Her brown eyes lively and interested, she pointed toward the dock. "Frank's putting on a casting clinic for kids. Have you been out to see? They've caught four catfish and thrown them back."

Annie turned to look. Her face lit up and she waved at her father and stepsister Rachel, her stepmother Sylvia, and her stepbrother Cole. When Annie turned back, Henny was deep in determinedly civil conversation with Mayor Cosgrove, who was not a favorite of either Annie, Max, or Henny. Henny's eyes glinted. "I'm sure the city council will approve the resolution since . . ."

Intent on avoiding contact with combativeness, Annie slid away and joined another circle. She sipped Kool-Aid, listened absently as Emma Clyde expounded on the state of digital publishing, and studied Neva Wagner, who stood alone near a honeysuckle-covered bower. Annie had met her casually at several country club dances since the Wagners came to the island. Neva was tall, almost as tall as Booth, but trim. A golfer, she was tan and fit. Her half-smile was automatic, but her dark eyes were somber. Suddenly, her face looked anguished, her features drooping in despair. One moment she was a stylishly attractive woman at a social gathering, composed and commanding. The next, heartbreak stripped away the social veneer, revealing misery and hopelessness.

As suddenly, Neva's face stiffened and she turned and plunged into the darkness of an arbor. She disappeared into the gloom. A moment later, Van Shelton, the recently divorced golf pro, ducked into the arbor, too. Van's sunburned face was tight in a dark scowl.

Annie was shaken by that glimpse of raw emotion. Booth Wagner's laughter boomed across the field. Annie wondered if he would be amused to know his wife and another man, both obviously upset, had slipped away from the crowd.

Annie looked to see if anyone else had noticed the twin disappearances. A few feet away Meredith stared at the arbor. Annie was dismayed to see such a cynical look on such a young face.

Suddenly, a girl ran up to Meredith, took her hand. The girl spoke quickly and pointed toward the lake.

Meredith's heart-shaped face was abruptly tense and worried. She nodded, then whirled and ran to the dock and looked anxiously about. In a moment, she started forward, her hands outstretched, her expression fearful, yet beneath the uncertainty and distress, there was an aura of tenderness as she came up to a petite, dark-haired woman with a lost look. Meredith gently took the woman's elbow.

Annie watched their erratic progress toward another stand of pines that separated the Haven from Sea Side Inn. Either the woman, who appeared to be in her forties, was ill or she had been drinking. Meredith protectively steered her charge around chattering groups. Occasionally, the woman seemed to resist. Meredith bent near and talked for a moment. Finally, they moved slowly to the path to Sea Side Inn.

Annie wondered if she would ever know the end of that story, for surely there was a story there to know. She hoped there would be a happy ending. She liked her young customer, who once shyly asked her for mysteries set in interesting places. Annie had judged her to be about fifteen and had led her directly to the shelf with some newly reissued novels by Mary Stewart, who wrote breathtaking suspense in exotic locales.

Annie waved at Ingrid and her husband Duane, spoke with several old friends, declined the offer of a kitten from a good customer. Agatha owned the store, and fluffy white Dorothy L. reigned supreme at home. About fifteen minutes later she saw Booth's daughter, returning from the inn path. The girl looked around and seemed relieved that her father was occupied with a circle of friends. Annie wondered who the dark-haired woman was and whether she was staying at the inn. Meredith strolled past the stage and slipped into the shadows on the far side. The better not to be noticed by her family?

Annie found a trash basket, tossed aside her Kool-Aid cup, and looked for Max. Soon—too soon for her taste—the formal program would begin. Had Booth arranged for Jean to make her announcement first or last? First came the swift thought. Annie never doubted Booth intended to make the night as long and difficult as possible for Jean.

A high chime sounded. "Players at the ready." Jean's voice rose above the noise of the crowded area. She held the triangle chime and beater. The glow from the light stands threw her shadow in front of her. She lifted her arm and again struck the triangle that had summoned Click's friends to the lake that morning. The tinkling sound rose sweetly above the crowd, which began to shift and move toward the rows of seats. The front rows were already full, no doubt taken by families of kids performing.

Max walked toward Annie. Though there was underlying gravity in his dark blue eyes, he smiled, and the smile said, "Good, I've found you, I love you, you're mine, come with me."

She took his hand, and they walked midway to the stage. The woods behind the light stands were now dark. Only the stage was brightly illuminated. The rows of seats were in darkness. Behind the audience, lights glowed from the front porch and windows of the main building. In between, the gloom of twilight obscured the surroundings, affording a dramatic venue for the performance.

"If everyone will please find a place. We've plenty of seats but if we need more, the older boys will get chairs . . ."

There was a flurry of movement and some of the bigger boys hurriedly set up several more rows.

Henny Brawley and Frank Saulter, along with Frank's grandson, who was visiting for the summer, slid into their row.

With a rattling drum roll, a procession marched down the center aisle, led by a teenage drummer, who wielded mean sticks. His drum work was precise and accomplished. A string of small children followed him. They banged erratically on drums of all sizes. When the procession reached the stage, the children climbed and stood in a row behind Jean. The teenager lifted his sticks and gave a final tattoo.

The audience cheered.

Jean's smile was tremulous. "Thank you, Curt. As most of you know, Curt is the drum major at Broward's Rock high school. He is volunteering at the Haven this summer and teaching a drum class. Our drummers will now welcome Booth Wagner, who would like to share with Haven families his vision of the future and formally bestow his gift of a gym which will provide recreation for all of our kids and also serve as a meeting place for the community." She turned and stepped away from the stage and was lost in the darkness behind the light stands.

Booth strode down the center aisle, calling out greetings, bigger than life, glorying in the attention.

Annie was disdainful. "Any normal person would have been waiting at the edge of the stage and stepped up to speak. Not Booth."

Max nodded in agreement.

The lights centered on Booth Wagner, blond hair gleaming, ruddy face flushed, Hawaiian shirt over-large. He faced the audience. "Welcome to the Haven's summer show."

The lights went out.

Someone tittered. A voice shouted, "Stage tech emergency."

A crack. A strangled shout. A thumping sound.

The darkness wasn't absolute, though there was as yet no moonlight. Annie blinked as her eyes adjusted from the bright light on the stage to the indeterminate darkness.

A woman screamed. Shouts rose. "Somebody's shooting . . . get those lights on . . . what's happened?"

Billy Cameron's deep, powerful voice overrode the cries and shouts. "Police. This is Chief Cameron. Stay put. Do not move. We will restore the lighting as soon as possible. Does anyone have a flashlight?"

"There are some in the office." Jean Hughes's voice shook. "I'll run and get them."

A tiny beam of light flicked on next to Max. "Coming, chief." Frank Saulter held a key-ring flashlight. He scrambled to the aisle and ran swiftly toward the stage.

The woman next to Annie tried to move past her. "My son's down there. He's in the first act. He's little. I've got to get to him."

"Please wait. The police chief's on his way there. He'll see . . ." But the frantic mother clambered past Annie and into the aisle.

Someone behind them, voice high and thin, cried, "We need to get out of here."

Billy shouted, "Stay in place. Police order."

Frank reached the stage. Billy Cameron was right behind him. Even in the narrow beam of Frank's light, there was no mistaking trouble when he pointed the flashlight where Booth Wagner had stood.

Booth lay half on, half off the stage. He'd fallen forward. Blood welled across the back of the bright Hawaiian shirt.

"Coming. Hard to see." Doc Burford's deep voice was bulldog-strong. "I'll take a look." Dr. Burford lumbered up in baggy T-shirt and khaki shorts. Dr. Burford was the island's brusque medical examiner and chief of staff at the island hospital. Burford pulled off his T-shirt, wadded it to press against the welling blood. He pointed to a shadowy figure. "You there. Press firmly."

A woman a few rows from Annie cried out, obviously close to hysteria, "If somebody's shooting, what's going to happen next?"

Lou Pirelli, one of Billy's officers, though clearly off duty in a Braves T-shirt and cutoffs, thudded to the platform.

Billy held up a hand. He didn't need a megaphone to be heard. "Stay calm. There was one shot. The likelihood is that the shooter has fled. Please do not move until we can arrange an orderly dismissal. We have a casualty and must see to the victim first. The shot came from the woods behind the stage. Officer Pirelli will patrol there to protect everyone. Do not move."

Annie gripped Max's sleeve. "Lou doesn't have a gun."

Max was reassuring. "There was one shot. Anybody planning a massacre would still be shooting." Those kinds of killings happened, at schools or churches or workplaces. The attacker never stopped with a single shot. "I want to help but we'd better stay put, do what Billy said. If we move, the people close to us will move. He's sure to have already called the station. Help will be on the way."

Henny turned and gave Annie a reassuring nod. "No one can ever be sure, but it would be odd for an attacker to wait this long to fire again. I think everyone is safe enough now."

Murmurs and cries sounded. Despite Billy's orders, figures ran toward the parking lot, people melting into the night. Beyond a hedge of pittosporum, headlights flashed in the parking lot.

Running feet thudded down the center aisle. Jean, breathing hard, flashlights in both hands, skidded to a stop only a few feet from the stage. She trained the large beams on the stage. Billy Cameron stepped forward and grabbed a flashlight. He held one, shouted to Lou. "Lou! Get a light. Check the woods behind the stage."

The chunky young officer took the other flashlight from Jean.

Neva Wagner rushed forward and stopped to look down at her fallen husband. "He's hurt. Booth's hurt." Her voice was high and shrill.

A siren wailed in the distance. The Haven was perhaps a mile as the crow flies from the police station near the harbor, but the blacktop road wound in a desultory fashion.

Shirtless, his muscular back tensed, Burford squatted next to Booth's limp body and placed one finger against Booth's neck. His face grim, the doctor looked up at Billy and shook his head. "The shot must have struck the heart.

Death from a gunshot is rarely instantaneous, but it can happen."

Neva stepped toward the doctor. "Can't you do something? Can't you stop the bleeding? Why doesn't somebody do something?" Her face was gaunt.

Annie stared at Neva. If Max—dear God forbid—lay bleeding on the ground, Annie would be at his side, holding him. Annie knew shock affected people differently. But how could Neva stand away from her wounded husband? Dr. Burford rose and walked to Neva. They made an arresting tableau in the light from the flashlights—the shirtless, powerfully built, sixtyish doctor and the rigid woman staring down in horror. Dr. Burford spoke quietly. His words were not audible.

Neva folded her arms tight across her chest. Her face was ashen.

Suddenly Meredith darted into the flash-lit area from the woods to the left of the stage. She looked at her father's body. Her face was shocked and sick and terrified.

Neva reached out to slip an arm around her shoulders, tug her away from the stage.

Meredith twisted free. She spoke to Neva, then turned and hurried away. Neva took a step after her, then stopped as her son, Tim, limped forward. He walked jerkily. He never looked toward Booth's body. He was breathing in gasps, his eyes wide and staring. Tim reached his mother, then jerked about and ran, his gait uneven, back toward the woods.

"Tim. Come back."

But he was gone into the darkness to the left of the stage.

Sirens wailed. Lights shone in the parking lot beyond the pittosporum. The sirens cut off.

Billy moved behind the stage, aimed his flashlight at the ground. He stopped, bent down. The soft-box heads on the light stands gleamed, abruptly bright and harsh. He returned and stepped onto the platform, only a few feet from Booth's body. Now his shout was stentorian. "Stand in place. This is a crime scene. Anyone moving will face charges of interfering with an officer. A roadblock will be set up in the lane. No cars will be permitted to leave until the occupants are identified and listed."

At least half the audience had left.

An angry voice shouted, "Are we supposed to stay here and get shot down?"

Another siren's wail neared and abruptly ended. A police cruiser rumbled around the hedges, turned so that the headlights were aimed across the field, affording even more light.

Billy's response was gruff. "One shot, one victim. We now have reinforcements. An armed officer—"

Officer Hyla Harrison, crisp in her uniform, moved swiftly toward Billy. Her pistol was drawn, her hand steady, her eyes checking out the shadows. Two more uniformed officers hurried to join Billy. All carried Maglites.

"—Will search the area behind the stage where the shot originated. Other officers will go row to row and take down names and addresses and phone numbers." He gestured toward the newly arrived officers. "Anyone with information regarding the attack is asked to remain to be interviewed."

Max touched Annie's arm. "I'll see if I can help. After you've given your name, go on home. Someone can drop me off later."

Annie started to protest, then in the wash of the cruiser's headlights, she glimpsed Meredith Wagner plunging onto the path to Sea Side Inn. In the lights from the stage, Meredith looked frightened, upset, fearful.

Max had already turned away.

Where was that stricken child going? Why hadn't Neva kept her near? And where had Neva's son gone? He had run in the other direction. He should have stayed. Officers were moving into the woods behind the stage.

Annie started to call after Max, hesitated, shook her head. She moved to Henny and spoke quickly.

Henny looked grave, then slowly nodded.

If it weren't for the occasional walkway lighting along the trail for the convenience of Sea Side Inn guests, Annie would have quickly given up the chase. Even so, the posts with their dim lantern tops seemed too far apart, leaving most of the path in darkness. Pine limbs made soft sighing sounds, magnolia leaves clicked, an owl hooted, shrubbery rustled. She brushed past feathery ferns, jerked to a halt at one point, heart pounding, until she was sure the log lying diagonally across the path was indeed a log and not a vagrant alligator.

She heard the faint slap of running feet far ahead.

Annie hesitated for an instant. She didn't want to intrude on Meredith's private world, but sometimes instinct urged action when the mind was reluctant. Was she driven to follow the girl because she was obviously in distress? More than likely, Meredith was seeking the woman she had earlier shepherded away from the Haven. The relationship between Meredith and the woman was not any of Annie's business, but she couldn't forget her glimpse of Meredith's face as she ran toward the path. There was more than shock or distress. There was an unmistakable imprint of fear.

Annie picked up her pace, breaking into a run. She reached the end of the path and the well-lit parking lot behind the inn in time to see Meredith dash inside a back door.

Annie hurried to the door, pushed inside. She stood in a rear entryway. Uncarpeted stairs led up. Once again she heard the clatter of quick steps.

Annie was breathing fast when she reached the second floor. She stopped, listened. Not hearing steps continuing up, she opened the door to a hallway in time to see Meredith turning at the end of the hall.

When Annie came around the corner, Meredith was knocking on a door, rattling the knob, calling out, "Ellen, it's me. Open the door, I've got to talk to you." The desperation in her voice was painful to hear. She was a child bordering on hysteria. She knocked again and again, louder and louder.

The door to the next room banged open. A plump woman clutching a squalling baby looked out angrily. "If you've lost your key, go get another one. I just got Ricky to sleep. Stop that pounding." The door slammed.

Meredith slumped against the closed door, her shoulders shaking.

Annie didn't hesitate. She hurried to her, spoke softly. "Meredith. Please let me help." She reached out, touched a trembling arm.

Meredith turned. Tears slid down her pale cheeks. She stared blankly at Annie.

"I'm Annie Darling. From the bookstore."

There was a flicker of recognition and embarrassment. Meredith wiped a hand across her wet face.

"Oh honey, don't worry. I know you're upset. Max—"

Meredith nodded. Obviously she knew Max from the Haven.

"—And I were there tonight. I'm sorry about your dad." But what odd impulse sent the girl scurrying to a woman who very likely had been drinking? Who was the woman? "Are you trying to find a friend?"

"My mom. I've got to talk to her." There was an under-current of panic in her voice.

"Of course you do." Everything now made sense. Meredith's mother obviously was the dark-haired woman with the unsteady gait whom Meredith earlier had led in the direction of the inn. Annie thought her mother was prob-ably suffering from too much alcohol. Quite possibly, she was sunk in stuporous sleep and hadn't heard the banging at her door. In that condition, she might not be much help to Meredith, but the child wanted her mother. "Look, maybe I can get a key. I know the owner of the inn."

In a big-city hotel, it would be tough, if not impossible, to obtain an extra key without proof of identity. If Annie could get the owner on the phone, she felt confident a key would be forthcoming. "Let's go downstairs and—"

"Sugar pie." The slurred voice was sweet and soft and vague.

The small, dark-haired woman came from the direction of the elevator. She dipped toward the wall, righted herself with a light push and a faint look of surprise. Her face had the thinness that comes from too much whiskey and too little food. Her face might once have had gamine charm. Now sunken brown eyes lacked focus and high cheekbones jutted. A gauzy pale blue shirt was missing a button on a three-quarter-length sleeve tab, so one cuff hung askew. Cropped beige linen slacks were too wrinkled to be fresh. Mud clung to her shell sandals.

"Sugar." She came up to Meredith, attempted to em-brace her, but it took Meredith's quick lunge to keep her upright.

The smell of whiskey cloyed the stuffy air of the hotel

corridor. She blinked at Annie. "Do I know you?" She reached out an unsteady hand.

Annie gripped thin, cold fingers, managed a smile. "I'm a friend of Meredith's."

"Oh." Her tone was pleased. "Meredith's friends are my friends."

"Ellen, where have you been?" Meredith's voice quavered. "You promised you'd stay in your room."

The smile aimed at Annie disappeared as Ellen's mouth turned down and she frowned. "Sugar, I needed to talk to your daddy." The words slid together. "Didn't want to talk to him ever again, but I won't let him keep us apart." She peered earnestly at her daughter. "Nobody can stand between a mother and her child." Tears spilled down her cheeks. "I miss you all the time. I was going to tell him what was what." She fumbled at the catch of her white straw purse, managed to open the flap, poked a hand inside. "See, I was going to—" She stopped, bent over the open purse, rooted about. "Where'd it go?" She sounded pettish. "Rufus, where are you?"

The door to the next room opened again. "Listen, people, I've got him down," the young mother whispered. "Please move along. I'm going to call the desk if the noise doesn't stop." The door eased shut with a careful click.

Meredith took her mother's arm. "Ellen, where's your key?"

"Key." Dark brows drew down in a befuddled frown. "That's not what I need. Key . . ." She patted the pocket of her slacks. She fumbled, drew out the key card. The oblong plastic slipped from her fingers to the floor. "There it is. Don't care about keys. Have to find Rufus. Had him a little while ago. Can't remember . . ." She drew her purse closer, peered inside.

Meredith scooped up the key card and swiped it. As she pushed the door open, Ellen swung and headed up the hall, head down, muttering, "Got to find Rufus."

Startled, Meredith bolted after her mother. She reached Ellen and turned her back toward the room.

Annie stepped forward, held the door open. She turned on the light, glanced into the room. She felt an instant's surprise at the uncluttered emptiness, a room that showed no signs of occupancy except for the quarter-full bottle of J&B and a single lipstick-rimmed glass on the table near the window. No clothes lay strewn about. Annie glanced at the closet, which appeared to be empty. A soiled canvas carryall sagged on the luggage rack.

"Sugar, don't pull on me." Ellen's voice was low and confused.

"Let's go in your room. You can tell me about Rufus and I'll go and see." Meredith looked her thanks at Annie, who still held the door.

In the room's narrow entryway, Ellen pulled free from Meredith. With a little murmur, she stumbled to the table and reached out for the bottle. "Need a drink." She uncapped the bottle, then looked anxious. "I have to find Rufus. I will. In a minute." With enormous concentration, she moved her hand, keeping it steady just long enough to pour a thin, golden stream of scotch into the glass. She didn't bother to cap the bottle. Instead, she clanked it to the table and grabbed the glass and began to drink greedily even before she sank onto a chair.

Meredith's quick glance at Annie was combative, defensive, despairing. "She can't help it."

"I know." Annie knew. Drugs and alcohol fasten onto some lives with the tenacity of steel hooks and the destructive poison of a scorpion. Annie gave Meredith a reassuring nod. "I'll stay with you for a while. Maybe I can help you get her into bed. Or we could order some coffee."

Ellen took a final gulp, tapped the glass hard onto the table. "Now." She slid her purse off her shoulder. "Maybe he's there. Maybe I missed him." She gave a sunny smile, confided, "Sometimes things aren't there and then there they are." She upended the bag. The contents clattered onto the tabletop: a worn billfold, a change purse, several lipsticks, a compact, a travel-size Kleenex, some dog-eared sheets of paper, a frayed plastic photo album, some lottery tickets, a bag of peanuts, a bottle of Advil, a partially empty package of Tums, two ballpoint pens, a nearly full perfume atomizer, a thin notebook.

Ellen gave a huff of disappointment. "Not there." She stood, turned, headed for the door. "I have to find him."

Meredith blocked her way. "Wait, Ellen. What is Rufus?" Her tone was patient. "Tell me and I'll look for him."

"Rufus." Her mother gave a little giggle. "My new best friend. He's the cutest thing, my little pearl-handled revolver."

Meredith stood frozen. "A gun?"

Annie's breath caught. Before she thought, she asked sharply, "Do you have a permit to carry a gun?"

Ellen looked at her reproachfully. "I thought you were a friend. Meredith's friends are my friends, but I don't like," she waggled a finger, "people who are sticks in the mud. Rules for everything. I don't follow rules." She spoke with pride and then her face sagged. "Somebody's always saying I'm wrong. I can't listen to everybody."

"When did you last see Rufus?" Annie tried to sound helpful, not accusatory.

Meredith looked panicked. "Why don't you leave now. She doesn't mean anything. Mother didn't really have a gun. She didn't."

Ellen stamped her foot. Or tried to. She almost toppled except for Annie's quick move to grab her arm. She shook free and said in tones of affront, "I don't tell lies. Rufus is my little gun and I had him in my hand—" She looked perplexed. "I guess that's what happened. I must have dropped him."

"Why did you have a gun, Ellen?" Annie kept her voice conversational.

Meredith pointed at the door. "You have to go now. This is all nonsense. She's confused."

"Meredith." Her mother was chiding. "I'm not confused. I had Rufus with me and I went back because I had to tell your father I couldn't stand any more. I had Rufus—" She stopped, blinked. "I got there and I felt kind of dizzy. I heard Booth. But the lights went out. I guess I got confused. I started back to the hotel, but I got lost." She put her hands up to her face. "Tired. Think I'll rest. See about everything tomorrow." She turned and moved heavily toward the bed and slumped onto the spread.

Meredith and Annie faced each other.

Again Meredith's young face looked old. She had seen too much this night, her father's death, her mother's drunken and perhaps sinister odyssey.

Annie held out her hand, hoping to appear supportive. "If she had a gun, we'll have to search for it." That search had to include the police.

Meredith responded harshly. "Of course she didn't have a gun." Her tone was scathing, but her eyes were terrified. "You saw her. She could barely walk. Even if she had a gun, do you think she could shoot and hit anything? Besides, she wouldn't kill Daddy." Tears brimmed. "Daddy . . ."

Annie moved to her, slipped an arm around Meredith's shoulders. "Let me get some help for you. You need to go home. Your stepmother will be frantic."

Meredith pulled away, swiped at her face with shaking hands. "That's how much you know. Neva won't care where I am or if I ever come back. Anyway, I'm staying here. With my mom."

❀ Six ❀

AT THE END of the inn parking lot, Annie looked back, then reluctantly took the path toward the Haven. As much as she disliked leaving Meredith at the inn with her obviously intoxicated mother, Annie recognized that she had no authority. Meredith had insisted that Annie leave. After all, drunk or sober, Ellen was Meredith's mother. Certainly Annie couldn't force Meredith to return to the Haven. Meredith was perfectly capable of seeking help if she felt she needed it. Moreover, she'd promised to call home and report her whereabouts. Annie picked up speed. She would alert Billy.

Annie was grateful to see the lights from the Haven as she neared the end of the path. Although there was little likelihood Booth Wagner's murderer was anywhere near, the dark woods were daunting. She reached the clearing. More lights had been rigged to illuminate the stage.

Annie stopped, her gaze held by the crimson splash of blood on the concrete, stark in the glare. More blood had spread from beneath Wagner's body as he lay half on, half off the stage, turning the sandy dirt dark. Even though Doc

Burford had been at hand and surely had officially pronounced Wagner dead, the body would not be moved until a careful record had been made. Officer Harrison recorded her observations into a videocam.

The businesslike process of investigating a crime scene was in full swing. Crime scene tape was in place, creating a square box extending twenty feet in all directions from the stage. Behind the stage, Lou Pirelli moved at a snail's pace, Maglite in hand, looking at every inch of ground. Flashlights gleamed in the woods, beams crisscrossed high in the air, illuminating the branches of live oaks and magnolias.

Most of the audience had left. Only the last few rows of seats were occupied. A somber group stood in a patient line leading up to a card table manned by Frank Saulter.

Annie felt a quick relief when she saw Max near the back rows. He carried a notebook and was apparently helping record those attending. Annie nodded approval. Billy Cameron could use every willing hand available and Max's effort freed an officer for other duty.

Billy Cameron, face impassive, stood a few feet from the card table, talking to Jean Hughes. Her shoulders were hunched, her arms held stiffly at her sides. She carefully did not look toward the body.

Annie hurried toward Billy. He needed to know about the gun Ellen Wagner claimed she had lost. More important, informing Billy would make certain that Meredith's whereabouts and circumstances were known.

Annie veered around a stake with fluttering crime scene tape. She stopped a few feet from Billy, looked toward him. "When you have a minute, I need to talk to you."

He gave a sideways glance and a quick nod.

Jean was speaking. ". . . I was behind the stage, waiting

until time to start the first act. As soon as Booth finished speaking, I was going to bring on the Golden Girls. Some of our teen girls were dressed up like . . . but that doesn't matter now. Anyway, I was moving toward the girls when the lights went out. I thought somebody had tripped over the cord. A single cord linked the light stands. The cord was plugged into a battery pack. I started to go check and I heard a crack. I didn't know what it was and then there was noise, like somebody hurt—" Her face worked. "—I guess when Booth was hit. He cried out and there was a thump."

The question was quick and sharp. "Did you see anyone?"

She looked puzzled. "It was dark."

Billy was impatient. "Before the lights went out, who was near you?"

Jean made a helpless gesture. "I don't know. The lights faced the other way. It was very dark behind the lamp stands. There were people around, but I have no idea who may have been there."

"If you can't name anyone near you," his gaze was measuring, "no one can swear that you were there."

"Maybe someone noticed me." She sounded uncertain. "I don't know."

"Did you sense movement? Hear anything after the crack?"

She flexed her fingers as if they were numb. "I heard a crackle. Maybe somebody was in the woods. I couldn't see anything."

Billy's blue eyes stared at her. "To your knowledge, did Mr. Wagner have any enemies?"

Her face was a mask of emptiness. "I wouldn't know."

Billy glanced toward the body, then back at her. "Why was he shot here?"

She was startled, then said with a flash of anger, "How would I know?"

Billy's gaze moved from the stage to the empty rows of seats and back again. "The Haven seems an odd place for murder, Ms. Hughes. A murder was committed with a gun. Why didn't the murderer meet Wagner in a private place and shoot him? Why was he killed in front of an audience?"

"I don't know."

Billy gestured at the stage and the empty chairs. "Maybe seventy-five people attended a program for the Haven's summer session. How many people knew Wagner would speak?"

"He's listed in the program." Her voice was thin.

"The program was passed out when people arrived. Someone had to know ahead of time to bring a gun." Billy was relentless. "Who knew? You. Others involved with the program. His family. Maybe some friends. That narrows down the possibilities. And there's a critical piece of knowledge possessed by the murderer. How many people knew how the lighting worked?"

One hand clutched at her throat. She looked badgered but, like a cornered animal, she fought back. "Anybody who walked behind the stage would see the cord."

"Why was he shot here?" Billy returned to the question, a dog gnawing a bone. "Would you have any ideas about that, Ms. Hughes?"

Annie felt suddenly certain that Billy Cameron was fully aware of a relationship between Booth Wagner and Jean Hughes. Billy was not only the police chief, he was actively engaged on the island. His stepson was a regular at the Haven. The burly police chief, powerful and intimidating, loomed above the director.

Jean fastened her hands together in a tight grip. "I don't know why he was shot here. I've told you everything I know about tonight. Now, unless you need me for something else, I'm going to close up the buildings and go home."

Billy was gruff. "Stay on the island, Ms. Hughes. We'll be in touch."

Billy turned to face Annie. He glanced around the grounds, checking on the progress of the investigation, then nodded at her, attentive but clearly in a hurry.

Annie gestured toward the woods. "Billy, I followed Meredith Wagner . . ."

Max stood at the kitchen counter, pouring fresh-squeezed orange juice into glasses. He wore a T-shirt, boxer shorts, and flip-flops.

Still sleepy, Annie settled at the kitchen table. The windows were wide-open and she was comfortable in her blue shorty nightgown. Despite a restless night with her mind replaying the sudden darkness and the crack of a gunshot, the morning with its bright splash of golden light, silky summer air, and Max's presence combined to make her happy. She smiled at him.

He brought her a glass of juice and a plate. "Good morning, Mrs. Darling."

She took a sip of juice, admired her breakfast. "Your sausage frittata is the best."

He gave a modest nod. "Hercule Poirot is the world's greatest detective. I am the world's greatest breakfast chef. You will note the spinach, mushrooms, and mozzarella."

Annie spooned salsa on a chunk of frittata, ignoring Max's slight wince at the unauthorized addition. "Speaking of detectives, I wonder if Billy talked to Ellen Wagner last night."

"I'm sure someone did. If she could talk." Max buttered a flaky croissant. "You said she was smashed."

Annie frowned. "I hated leaving Meredith there. Do you suppose Ellen Wagner shot him? That would be dreadful for Meredith. It's awful enough that she's lost her dad."

"Billy will be finding out about everyone connected to Booth. Last night he focused on Jean. He kept asking her why Booth was shot at the Haven." Max shrugged. "Why not?"

Annie speared a slice of papaya, her very favorite fruit. "Odd that things come in bunches."

Max looked at her inquiringly.

Annie felt an urge to reach across the table and touch his stubbled cheek. There was something to this fashion of young men letting their beards grow just a little bit, a tantalizing bristle, a not-so-subtle flaunting of masculinity. She resisted the impulse. Let the man have his breakfast in peace, his delightful, delectable, delicious breakfast. Possibly after breakfast . . . "Click died Thursday and Booth was shot last night. Of course, Click didn't die at the Haven."

Max's face creased in thought. "One of Click's friends said he was really pumped about the program, that he had a secret part. I don't understand that. How could he be on the program and that be a secret?"

"You can ask Jean." She added a tad more salsa.

Max put down his fork. "I will. But it's strange. A teenager who came to the Haven regularly and a Haven director. I wonder if Billy's realized the connection."

Annie took a final satisfying bite. "'Connection' seems too strong a word."

"Maybe Billy has a point. Why was Booth shot at the Haven? Why did Click die, too? Why would a teenager fall down from a tower and break his neck? I'm going to ask Billy if Click was clean on drugs. I have to think he was from what we learned about him. If so, his death looks suspicious to me."

"Billy's got a lot to find out." Annie started clearing the table.

Max handed her his plate. He glanced at the clock and moved to the counter and a radio. He turned the dial to an all-news radio station on the mainland. Some static crackled, but the reception was fairly good:

. . . A shocking murder tops today's news. Last night wealthy retired businessman Booth Wagner was shot at a Broward's Rock recreation center for teenagers. Island Police Chief Billy Cameron said the former CEO of Wagner Enterprises, reputed to be worth more than twenty million dollars, died from a gunshot wound. No person of interest has been named but Cameron said the investigation was proceeding. According to witnesses, Wagner was speaking before an audience at an outdoor venue when the lights went off, plunging the area into darkness. A shot was heard and Wagner was struck. He fell to the ground. By the time a doctor reached Wagner and examined him by the light of a flashlight, Wagner was dead. Chief Cameron has declined to explain how a shot fired in the dark found its mark. Any person with knowledge of the crime is invited to contact the police or to call the Crime Stoppers number . . .

Max turned off the radio. "That's another queer thing. How did someone shoot him in the dark?"

Annie filled their coffee mugs. She pictured Jean Hughes

standing behind the stage. She knew precisely where the
cord was plugged into the battery pack. Could she—or
anyone—have pulled that plug, then aimed a gun toward
Wagner and shot with any faint hope of the bullet hitting
him? What if he'd turned to look toward the darkened light
stands? Certainly the gunshot, if it missed Wagner, posed
serious danger for the audience.

"Did the lights really go out first?" Annie pictured
Meredith's mother, pearl-handled gun in hand, lifting and
aiming.

Max was emphatic. "The lights went out first. But somehow—"

The phone rang.

Max reached for the portable phone, glanced at Caller ID.
"Hey, Billy." He listened for a moment. "Yeah. Give us half
an hour. We'll be right there."

The overhead fan whirred in the anteroom of the police
station. Slender, serious Mavis Cameron, Billy's wife, who
also served as dispatcher and assisted in evidence collection,
punched a button to unlock the door to the corridor. She
waved them through the swinging gate. "He's in his office."

Billy's office windows overlooked the harbor. Five or six
fishermen were spaced along Fish Haul Pier with poles and
buckets of bait. Floppy hats shaded their faces from the sun.
Sailboats scudded in a brisk breeze. White riffs flecked the
green water. The whine of a personal watercraft sounded
like angry hornets. The eight o'clock ferry pulled away from
the dock with three blasts from its horn.

Billy was clean-shaven and his uniform crisp, but circles
beneath his eyes told of little sleep. He waved them to the
chairs in front of his yellow desk. "Appreciate your com-

ing. Okay, Annie, are you standing by your story that Ellen Wagner, Booth's ex-wife, was intoxicated and talked about a gun missing from her purse?"

"That's what she said."

"For the record, I'd like to tape what happened. Start with your following Meredith Wagner to Sea Side Inn."

Billy interjected an occasional question as Annie described the unsettling episode.

"Rufus?" He wasn't amused.

"She called him her new best friend."

Billy's heavy face showed disdain. He clicked off the recorder. "Last night Meredith Wagner refused to talk to me. She said her mother was asleep and couldn't be awakened. I went to the inn this morning. They had a choice. Talk there or come to the station. Ellen Wagner claims not to remember anything about last night. Meredith Wagner says her mother didn't have a gun, she was just being silly and her mother didn't feel well."

Annie shook her head. "Meredith's protecting her mother." Her voice was sad. "Are you looking for the gun?"

"An intensive search in the woods started at daylight and we are poking around in the lake. The muck and weeds are too thick to try and drag a net."

Max leaned forward. "Speaking of guns, Billy, how did somebody shoot him in the dark?"

Billy's face was unreadable. "That information is confidential. In regard to Meredith Wagner's interview, she said everybody knows that you and Max were trying to help Jean Hughes keep her job and that her father intended to get Ms. Hughes fired."

Max's brows drew down. "So Annie made up a story about a gun to divert interest from Jean? Is that what you think?"

For an instant, Billy-their-old-friend broke out of his police-captain mold. "Nope. Annie keeps her fiction in her store. She heard what she heard. Sure, Meredith Wagner's lying her head off. However, her mother may not remember anything if she was as soused as Annie indicated. As for the gun, the problem with drunks is they can see everything from big pink rabbits to little pearl-handled pistols. Maybe Ellen Wagner started off from the inn with a gun in her purse, ready to wave it at her ex-husband. Maybe she wished she had a gun and presto she imagined a gun in her purse, even if there wasn't. Lou Pirelli's on the phone, calling people who stayed around long enough last night to be listed as present. He's trying to find out if anyone saw the ex-wife." Billy picked up a coffee mug, took a drink. "That's another frustration. Probably half the people got the hell out before we were able to calm them down. Lou's asking approximately where people sat and whether they knew anyone in the row. We'll probably have a couple of dozen more names by the time he finishes. But it's like trying to catch eels. Anyway, I get the picture about Meredith and her mother last night. It's easy to see the kid is scared, which means the gun may exist. Still," and his face reflected a man figuring from a base of knowledge, "it took a good shot. Most drunks have trouble walking, much less shooting."

Max looked at Annie. "Was she that drunk? Was she drunk at all?"

Annie looked thoughtful. "She appeared to have trouble walking when I saw her before the program started."

"Maybe she was playing drunk, from start to finish." Max leaned forward. "How does that fit for size, Billy? Stone-cold sober, Ellen Wagner decides to kill him. She acts like she's intoxicated when she arrives at the program to scope everything out. Then later, how hard is it to slur her words and hunt for her little gun? Think about the spot she's in. She probably intended to claim she never left her room at the inn after Meredith brought her back. Then she finds Meredith and Annie in the hall. What's she going to do? Maybe she's clever. She decides to convince Annie she's drunk. She underlines her innocence by prattling about Rufus."

Billy leaned back. "We're looking at her. We're looking hard."

Max gave a wry grin. "Now I'll be the devil's advocate. Ellen Wagner may look suspicious, but I don't see how she could have any connection to Click Silvester. I think it's strange that Click dies in a presumed accident Thursday afternoon and Booth Wagner gets shot during a program at the Haven Friday night, especially," and now Max sounded grim, "after Click told one of his Haven buddies how excited he was about the program. Click said he was going to have a secret part."

Billy looked surprised. "What are you implying? That Click knew somebody was going to shoot Wagner? Hey, everything we've turned up says Click was a straight arrow. The tox tests found him clean as a whistle."

Max frowned. "Why did he fall down those steps?"

Billy shrugged. "Accidents happen."

"Click wasn't an outdoor guy. Why was he at the preserve? Who pulled out the pockets of his jeans?" Max flipped up one finger at a time as he made his points. "Why was he super-excited about the program?"

· Billy's smile was tired but genuine. "Kevin was excited, too. Hey, they may be teenagers and mostly try to act cool, but it's still a big deal to be in a program. There's nothing weird about a kid being excited."

"Why did he say his part was secret? I'll ask Jean. Maybe she'll know."

Billy was abruptly somber. "That may be the easiest question she'll answer all day. Tell me about the mess at the Haven."

Max's blue eyes narrowed. He looked thoughtful.

Billy persisted. "Yesterday at Parotti's, you and Annie had a set-to with Booth Wagner. Tell me about it."

Annie felt caught in a bubble of tension. She and Max and Billy went back a long way, through good times and bad. Billy's honesty and determination to do his duty as he saw fit had saved Max from a murder charge. That same honesty now made him the man on the other side of the desk, determined to gain information from them that they were reluctant to provide.

Annie sat on the edge of the chair. "Billy, you know—" And her eyes reminded him of dreadful August days that had looked so black for Max and Annie. "—Things can be made to look bad for people."

"I understand what you're saying. You and Max have tried to help Jean Hughes. Obviously, you like her or you wouldn't bother. That's fine. But she's one of the people I'm looking at. She was upset with Wagner. She was there. In fact, she was in a good position to have fired that shot." Billy tapped his pen on a legal pad. "So if you spoke to Wagner about her yesterday, I want to know." He looked at Max.

Max nodded. "I'm sure you're aware that Wagner wanted her fired."

"Frank filled me in."

"However, I'd lined up the votes for the board meeting next week to keep her as director." Max's tone was relaxed. "Booth heard about it. He came to tell me that the question was moot, Jean had agreed to resign."

Billy waited. He looked like a man expecting an explanation.

Max remained silent. His expression was pleasant but unrevealing.

Billy's eyes glinted. "What happened then?"

"Annie and I went out to the Haven. We spoke with Jean. She confirmed Booth's statement."

Billy gave a huff of impatience. "Come on, Max. One day she's fighting to keep her job. The next, she gives up, agrees to resign. There has to be a reason for her about-face."

Max shook his head. "It would be better if you asked Jean directly."

Billy's eyes narrowed. "I'll ask her. Right now I'm asking you what caused her change in plans."

"Her sister is ill. I believe she decided to take time off to be with her."

Annie knew he had picked his words carefully. As Henny Brawley had once told her, "There are many ways to tell the truth." Max was telling the truth, but nothing in his manner hinted at the anger and confusion and despair attendant upon that calm statement. They had told Billy the truth but not all of the truth. Only she and Max had heard Jean's despairing cry in the dim tunnel in the woods, "I'd kill to keep her on that porch."

Billy was insistent. "Why did you and Annie get mad?"

Max raised an eyebrow.

Billy made an impatient gesture. "One of my officers was eating lunch, told me you looked like you wanted to break a chair over Wagner."

"I didn't want to see Jean leave the Haven. She's done a good job."

"Why did Booth want her fired?"

Max shrugged. "I wasn't in Booth Wagner's confidence."

"You must have some ideas. You must have seen his actions as unjustified." Billy's gaze was intent. "Otherwise, why were you helping her?"

Max smiled. "That's easy, Billy. I was helping her because I thought keeping her at the Haven was best for the kids. I'd lined up support on the board. I hoped she'd reconsider her decision to resign. That's the extent of my involvement."

A tiny smile tugged at Billy's lips. "That's your story and you're sticking to it."

The two old friends looked at each other in complete understanding.

Billy glanced down at a file. He no longer smiled. "Jean Hughes was there. In fact, she was very close to where the shooter stood. She had opportunity. She appears to have a motive. I'll be talking to her."

Sunburned vacationers milled around the marina. Annie avoided a couple on a tandem bike and hurried to the board-walk. The harbor wasn't quite as full as usual in July, evidence that the economic downturn had affected the rich as well as everyone else. Still there were yachts of prodigious size, sailboats, motors boats, and cruisers moored at slips.

Annie's practiced eye judged the boardwalk to be nicely filled with tourists and, of course, a goodly number would find their way to Death on Demand. Inside, she paused for her customary spurt of joy, the smell of books, the moth-eaten raven above the beaded entrance to the children's section, the bright covers on the New table, and Agatha preening on the cash desk before an admiring customer.

Ingrid, thin, brisk, and efficient, was hard at work, giving Annie a swift nod as she led two middle-aged ladies down the center aisle. "All of the Patricia Wentworth Miss Silver mysteries have been reprinted by Hodder & Stoughton in

England and we import them." Ingrid gestured to Annie to take over at the cash desk.

Annie checked out two customers, each with a hefty stack of books. There were the usual suspects, Alexander McCall Smith, Janet Evanovich, John Grisham, Mary Higgins Clark, Robert Crais, C. J. Box, Diane Mott Davidson, James Lee Burke, and Laura Lippman, but there were also fresh names, wonderful writers all, Mary Saums, Dorothy Howell, David Fuller, Charles Finch, Megan Abbott, Christopher Fowler, Patricia Briggs, Deanna Raybourn, and Donis Casey.

Annie bagged the books, handed the customers their receipts. "A good day to read on the beach."

As they left, she wished she could go to the beach with her new Margaret Maron title, a sun hat, and a cooler with chilled shrimp and cold, very cold, Heineken. Maybe this evening, she and Max would take their sand chairs and set them up in a tidal pool. She loved the little pools left between sand ridges as the tide flowed out. She was ready to immerse herself in a tale where she knew justice would prevail. In the midst of this cheerful daydream, she became aware of the clunk of purposeful steps coming from the coffee bar. She looked up.

Emma Clyde, her pink caftan swirling about her, gestured imperiously. The island's famous mystery author was always commanding. Today her sapphire-blue eyes held an impatient glint. Lines denoting intelligence seasoned with a touch of belligerence seamed her square face.

Emma stopped in front of the cash desk, clapped her stubby hands on the counter. "We've been waiting for you."

Emma turned and marched toward the coffee bar, obviously assuming Annie would follow.

Of course, she did.

Rebuffing Emma was a pleasure to be enjoyed only in her dreams. However, she was somewhat surprised to find her mother-in-law and Henny comfortably settled at a large table.

Annie couldn't help inquiring: "What are you doing?"

Emma pontificated, "As Marigold observes, 'Even with the best will in the world, the authorities lack intuitive gifts.'"

Annie restrained herself from noting aloud that Marigold Rembrandt wasn't real. She was the figment of her author's imagination. Quoting her, therefore, was not persuasive.

Emma gave a benign smile. "I am between books."

Annie translated: focusing on Booth Wagner's murder was much easier than plotting a new book.

Annie looked at Henny. Her old friend and the island's greatest mystery enthusiast also prided herself on her deductive powers but she was thoroughly grounded in reality.

Henny exuded determination. "We may be able to discover information that will be helpful. Sometimes people won't talk to the police. I want to be sure the kids are safe at the Haven. I asked Billy if an officer could keep an eye on things. He said Officer Harrison will be on duty during the hours the Haven is open."

Laurel's husky voice was firm. "Giselle Hughes should be able to die in peace."

Annie blew a kiss to her mother-in-law.

Laurel's blue eyes glowed with affection and appreciation.

Emma, never one for sentiment, cleared her throat. "Enough of this lollygagging around. Let's get to work."

∿: Seven :∿

ONLY A FEW cars were parked in the Haven lot. Two
police cruisers claimed shady spots near some pines. Max
edged the Jeep into the dimness below a towering live
oak. He punched down the windows before he turned off
the ignition, leaving the keys in place. He didn't worry
about his car being stolen. Since the Jeep didn't come with
water wings, a thief's only escape from the island was via
the ferry. The Jeep would be hot when Max returned, but
minus the furnace effect of closed windows. A gentle breeze
rattled palmetto fronds. Moist July heat enveloped him. Cicadas thrummed. Crows cawed.

He wanted to know more about Click Silvester and his
excitement over last night's program. Why would his part
be secret? Of course, Billy had a point. Many of the kids
who came to the Haven had little chance to publicly shine.
Maybe Click's eagerness for the program was that innocent.
Still, Max had a gut conviction that Click Silvester had
been murdered. Everyone knew Booth Wagner had been
murdered. Sure, coincidences occurred. Once Max had run
into one of Laurel's ex-husbands (a Brazilian) in the British

Museum. But two deaths in two days with a common link to the Haven rubbed him wrong.

He swung out of the Jeep and moved fast. Jean Hughes could have the information he needed. As he came around a sweet-smelling pittosporum hedge, he saw her across the open ground, standing near the stage. She could be looking at the stage or at the lake, the murky green water shimmering in the sunlight. Or she could be watching the searchers wading in the muck near shore. Standing beside Jean was Marian Kenyon from the *Gazette*. A few feet away, Darren Dubois watched every move of the officers.

Max strode toward the lake and the onlookers. If Billy discovered Booth's threat to dispossess Jean and her dying sister of the cottage, Jean Hughes would surely become the chief suspect. And reasonably so.

Why then did Max feel strongly that she was innocent?

Because the murder had been well planned: a weapon brought, sudden darkness without warning, the unexpected shot.

He felt a tiny spurt of wry amusement. Jean's main failing as a director was her slapdash approach to records and lack of administrative skills. Nobody doubted her empathy for kids and ability to encourage them.

His amusement was succeeded by cool reasoning. Booth Wagner's murder at the Haven made the recreation center the focus of the investigation. Jean Hughes might be disorganized, but she was nobody's fool. If she had planned to murder Wagner, she would have taken great care to commit the crime somewhere other than the Haven.

In response, Billy could point out that she didn't know until Friday that Booth had the power to force her and her sister out of the cottage with only a week's notice. If she didn't announce her resignation at the program, Wagner would evict them. That left very little time to plan a murder.

Max squinted in the sunshine. If Billy was right, Click's death the previous day was irrelevant. But if Click's death was connected to Wagner's murder, that could mean the decision to kill Wagner was in place by Thursday. Then an even stronger argument for Jean's innocence could be made. She would not have approached Max on Thursday, asked him to intervene for her, thereby sending ripples of knowledge across the island that she had a motive to wish Wagner dead. If she intended to murder Wagner, she would never have asked for help or made a stink about losing her job. She would have acted like the job was no big deal, she was ready to move on. If she knew he was going to be dead, her job was safe. In fact, Jean's public attempt to fight her ouster likely suggested the Haven as a murder site.

Billy saw Wagner's death at the Haven as a link to Jean. Maybe the site was chosen because Jean was a perfect ten as a suspect.

Jean stood with shoulders hunched, head bent forward, her posture in striking contrast to her casual summer appearance—bright orange hibiscus on a loose cotton top, flared white slacks, and white sandals. Next to Jean, the *Gazette*'s star reporter held a notebook and wrote furiously. Marian's dark hair was stirred by the wind. Bony and thin, dressed in her usual slapdash fashion—a wrinkled blue blouse and baggy brown slacks—she looked alert and eager.

In the lake, Frank Saulter in hip waders gestured to a companion searcher, a thin officer in his late twenties with a blond ponytail and sharp features. The two men, moving clumsily and heavily, mud sucking at their boots, came together.

Max came up beside the women. "Marian."

The reporter gave him an abstracted nod.

"Jean."

In profile, Jean's rounded face was heavy, her makeup too bright.

There was the sound of a splash, an exclamation from Frank.

Henny Brawley added a final pencil stroke to her sketch of the Haven grounds. Henny was stylish in a navy scoop-neck blouse and white linen slacks. She looked absorbed in her task, her intelligent face thoughtful.

Annie admired the drawing. With an economy of strokes, Henny had created a sharp black-and-white drawing of the woods and lake. Pines, live oaks, magnolias, and wax myrtle grew behind a portion of the outdoor stage at the Haven. The stage was bordered two-thirds by woods, one-third by the lake.

Emma's stubby forefinger tapped the medium-weight sheet from Henny's fourteen-by-seventeen-inch sketch pad. "The force of the shot toppled him forward. The shot must have been fired from the woods behind the stage."

Golden hair cut in a winsome pixie style, dark blue eyes kind and thoughtful, Laurel Roethke was a vision of loveliness, not an unusual state for her, in a green-striped blouse with white cuffs and a pleated white cotton skirt. She bent to look over Henny's shoulder. "Your sketch brings that dreadful moment back, Henny. Emma, as always, you see the important fact." Her tone was admiring.

Annie glanced at her mother-in-law. Kindness was good, but Emma didn't need encouragement. Emma was obnoxiously self-confident. As for her sleuth, Marigold Rembrandt, her confidence bordered on egomania.

True to form, Emma said grandly, "Therefore, as Marigold would be quick to point out, the critical area is obvious."

Annie recognized Emma's tone. She was in the hectoring mode favored by her red-haired sleuth when superciliously addressing the hapless Inspector Houlihan. *The Clue in the Queen's Tiara*, Emma's newest title, was Death on Demand's current bestseller. Millions of readers adored Marigold. That number did not include Annie, who found Marigold as enchanting as mildewed socks. The necessity to mask her instinctive recoil plus maintain good relations with her bestselling author forced Annie to an excess of bonhomie.

"What would Marigold do?" Annie heard the faint undercurrent of sarcasm in her voice.

Laurel's glance chided Annie. Henny masked a grin with a slight cough.

Emma was oblivious. She gave Annie an approving nod. "That is just what I was asking myself."

Annie concentrated on pouring steaming milk into espresso cups. She added different extras to each serving—whipped cream and cinnamon for Henny; shaved chocolate for Laurel; a tablespoon of brandy for Emma; and, for herself, a little bit of everything, including a double shot of caramel. As she placed the mugs on the table, she took pleasure in the mystery titles inscribed on each one: *What Did I Do Tomorrow?* by L. P. Davies for Laurel, *All Is Vanity* by Josephine Bell for Emma, *Scene of the Crime* by John Creasey for Henny, and *Try Anything Once* by A. A. Fair for herself.

The Lithesome Ladies, a private nickname for Henny and Laurel since they'd instituted a weekly and very popular tai chi class at Death on Demand, awaited with great deference Emma's reply to her self-asked question.

Not feeling deferential, Annie took solace in her delectable, multiflavored cappuccino. A whipped-cream mustache nicely disguised a sardonic expression.

"Marigold at once pinpointed the wooded area." Emma's voice rose in triumph. "Marigold immediately asked: When the lights came on, were Jean Hughes, Neva Wagner, her son Tim Talbot, or Booth's daughter Meredith observed in the vicinity of this rectangle? Marigold, in her trenchant way, describes this as the Rectangle of Interest." That stubby forefinger measured a rectangle that encompassed the area directly behind the stage and the space between the woods and the first twenty rows of chairs on the left side facing the stage.

Annie wouldn't deny that the clever author had posed an excellent question. However . . . "You can add two names."

For an instant, Emma looked pettish, then she graciously nodded, the detective queen welcoming additional information.

Annie described Meredith slipping away to the inn and her mother, Ellen, possibly intoxicated, possibly not, arriving in the hallway and the search for a gun, which possibly existed, possibly not.

On her sketch pad, Henny drew the wooded area between the Haven and the inn.

Laurel beamed at her daughter-in-law. "So brave of you, sweetie. I know how you feel about alligators."

Emma flicked Annie a look of disdain. "If you don't feed them, they aren't a problem."

"Unless someone else has fed them," Annie said stiffly. It was a constant worry for islanders that tourists, either unwittingly or deliberately, tossed food to alligators, teaching them to associate food with humans and making them more likely to attack.

Henny warmly rushed to Annie's defense. "Anyone with sense worries about alligators."

Emma thumped the table, clearly bringing the meeting to order. "That's one name. The second?"

Annie recalled with sharp clarity watching Neva Wagner disappear into the gloom of the arbor to be followed very soon by the club's golf pro. "Van Shelton."

Laurel nodded in agreement. "Dear Van, wearing his heart on his sleeve. I've been playing a bit more golf than usual these days." Her tone was bland.

Annie kept her expression bright and interested. She wondered if Max was aware that his mother had been spending quite a lot of time with a new assistant pro, darkly handsome Johnny Rodriguez. All, of course, to improve her game. Whichever game she was, in fact, playing. Johnny's enchantment, despite his youth, came as no surprise. Johnny, of course, was single. Laurel had standards. Of course she did.

Laurel smiled a bit dreamily, then said briskly, "Annie's quite right. I've seen Van with Neva and there's no doubt in my mind there is a strong attraction there." Her gaze was limpid with innocence. "I have rather a sense of these things."

Emma's lips twitched. Henny studied her sketch.

Henny wrote below her drawing: *Jean Hughes, Neva Wagner, Tim Talbot, Meredith Wagner, Ellen Wagner, Van Shelton.* Her dark eyes were thoughtful. "Larry Gilbert and Booth were at each other's throats a few weeks ago. Apparently they got over their tiff, but I'd be interested to know what caused the fury." She added Larry's name. "Maybe Larry might know if anyone else was mad at Booth."

Annie sipped her cappuccino. "For all we know, Booth had a bunch of enemies, all lurking in the woods behind the stage."

Emma's smile was pitying. "As Marigold emphasizes to Inspector Houlihan, it is necessary to think matters through."

Annie's eyes glinted. Someday the old harridan was going to go too far. The implication was that Annie's intellectual capabilities were minimal.

Emma proclaimed, "We can confine our suspects to those present at the program. The news stories in the *Gazette* quoted Jean Hughes." Emma flipped open a folder to reveal several small clippings. "There was no mention of Booth's involvement in the program. Therefore, only those with a connection to the Haven or someone close to Booth would have been aware that he was scheduled to speak. Moreover, the crime required knowledge of the terrain."

Annie accepted defeat. "That's what Billy thinks, too."

"So," Emma demanded, blue eyes gleaming, square face hound-dog eager, "where were these people when the lights came on?"

Annie pointed behind the lamp stands. "Jean Hughes was right there. We know she was standing behind the stage."

Henny drew a box with the letters JH behind the stage.

Emma's glance at Annie was dismissive. "We will each speak in turn." She pointed at Laurel.

Annie would have liked to ask Emma when she was elected emperor of investigations, but a tête-à-tête with an alligator would be more pleasant than confronting Emma.

Laurel's classic features were suddenly sorrowful. "Oh, I won't forget his face. Poor dear little boy. Tim Talbot came running, as well as he can with that shorter leg, toward his mother. Of course, the shock was horrible for everyone, but he appeared devastated."

Henny nodded at the drawing. "Show me where he was."

Laurel reached across the table and tapped a spot not far

from the stage. "He was near the woods. He was breathing hard."

Henny placed a box enclosing the letters TT not far from the woods behind the stage.

Emma was brisk. "Did you see anyone else on our list?"

Laurel's blue eyes narrowed in thought. "Neva hurried up to the stage. She was alone. It was later that Tim ran toward her."

It was a matter of dispute, but finally there was a consensus that Neva had also come to the stage from the left.

Henny placed a box with the letters NW in the space between the woods and the far left seats.

Emma nodded at Henny.

Henny's eyes narrowed in thought. "Larry Gilbert walked down the center aisle toward the stage. I suppose as a director he felt he should take charge. He certainly looked shaken." Henny drew a box with the letters LG and placed it in the center aisle toward the back.

Emma looked at Annie.

Annie tried to re-create that first moment when the lights came on. Her gaze had been held, as was surely true of almost everyone there, by the shocking view of Booth Wagner's crumpled body and the men clustered near him. But yes, she had seen Neva coming from the left side, that critical area near the woods that must have harbored the murderer. "I'm pretty sure Meredith Wagner came from the left side, too."

Henny added MW to the area left of the stage.

Annie concentrated. "Meredith ran up to the stage and saw her father and then she turned and ran back into the crowd. A few minutes later I saw her heading toward the path to the inn." Annie felt sure that Meredith had plunged into the crowd, seeking her mother. Not finding her, she had set out for the inn. "Did any of you see a petite woman with dark hair who might have been unsteady on her feet?" If indeed Ellen Wagner had been drinking. "She had on a gauzy blue blouse and terribly wrinkled beige slacks. She looked frowsy."

No one had seen Ellen.

"Van Shelton?" Emma inquired.

None of them recalled seeing him when the lights came on.

"We know he was present. Now we need to discover everything we can about our probable suspects. We will divide our investigation—"

Ingrid came down the central aisle, holding the portable phone. "Hey, Annie, sorry to interrupt. It's Rachel and she says she desperately needs to talk to you."

Frank Saulter's pitchfork came up out of the dark water, pulling up a sodden bundle of cloth. The second officer used his pitchfork to steady the mass and prevent it from slipping back into the green water.

"Hold it, right there." Marian lifted her Nikon D3, snapped several shots.

The men ignored her call and squelched their way to the bank. Frank heaved the slimy mass forward to slop onto the grass.

Marian was on her knees a few feet away. She made a face. "Nasty. It stinks." But she kept snapping.

Jean moved nearer the crime scene tape, craned her neck to see. An assortment of muddy objects, obviously products of the search, lined the bank in a neat row, a rotted bicycle seat, pop cans, pieces of Styrofoam food containers, a broken putter, a rusted Hannah Montana lunch bucket, and a broken wooden chair. Even at a distance of twenty feet, the stench of lake-bottom muck was rank.

Max moved nearer, his nose wrinkling at the smell.

"Hey," the thin-faced officer shouted, swinging his pitchfork. "Watch out." Like a batter's splintered bat, the pitchfork spun away from him, disappeared in the water.

Oozing out of the reeds, a muddy-brown water moccasin, mouth agape, white lining showing, was poised to attack.

Darren gave a shout. "I can get him if you need help." His narrow face was eager.

Max wasn't surprised that Darren saw a cottonmouth as no problem. In a minute, he'd talk to Darren. He still had some questions for him.

Marian was scrabbling backward faster than a sand crab. "I get no hazard pay. Somebody kill that thing."

Frank's right hand dropped out of sight, screened by the hip waders. In a swift, controlled movement, he lifted his hand holding a police forty-five and fired. The venomous snake's head disintegrated. Frank holstered the gun, studied the water, took a couple of steps, and eased his hand down into the water. He pawed and found the pitchfork. He pulled it up, ignoring the water streaming from his arm. He was casual when he turned to the shaken officer. "Let's take a break. See what we've got." He nodded toward the bank.

The sharp-featured young officer was pale under his tan. His eyes darted nervously as he clambered through the reeds to the bank.

Farther out in the water, Frank lifted his booted feet with effort to lumber through the mud. He nodded toward Jean, lifted a hand in greeting to Max and Marian. As he came up out of the water, mud and reeds clung to his waders. He carried the pitchfork to the mucky black mass they had tossed onto the bank. "I'm curious about this thing. The cloth doesn't look like it's been in the water long." Frank tugged and teased with the tines to unfold the material. Exposed was a ball of felt that wasn't altogether sodden. Again Frank worked patiently. A soggy foot-long feather poked into the air.

Max was startled. The felt looked like a squashed, old-fashioned highwayman's hat adorned with a now-bedraggled but once-decorative feather.

Marian was as close as she could get, camera trained. "Great shot."

Jean stood on tiptoe. "That looks like our Puss-in-Boots hat and cape. I wonder if somebody got them out of the shed. I'll have to—"

"Ms. Hughes." Billy Cameron's voice came from behind them.

The police chief had arrived unnoticed by the group at the lake. His blond hair glinting in the sun, Billy was big and impressive in his uniform. His expression was stern, a cop at work.

Jean turned to face him, drawing in a sharp, startled breath. In the unforgiving summer sunlight, she was haggard, makeup splotchy on her face. Her blue eyes were wide and strained.

"Captain." She drew herself up, gestured toward the stage. "I'm glad you've come. I wanted to ask if the stage could be cleaned up. I've kept the kids in the clubhouse or on the far side of the lake." She looked strained. "Except for Darren—" She glanced to her left. "Oh, he's finally gone. I'd asked him to leave and he said he would in a little while, but he wasn't a little kid and blood didn't bother him. Anyway, we don't have many here today. I guess their folks are scared. But I sure would like to have that bloodstain removed." She looked faintly sick. "It isn't right for kids to see."

Marian turned, lifted the camera, took several shots of the darkly stained cement. "Vince probably won't use these."

Billy glanced toward the stage. "Chief," Billy always used his old title as a courtesy when addressing Frank, the former chief, "please hose off the stains when you finish checking the lake. And thanks for helping us out."

Frank nodded. "ASAP."

Billy glanced at the collection of trash on the bank. "Anything interesting?"

Pointing with the pitchfork at the dark cloth, Frank was laconic. "Funny thing to be wadded up and thrown into a lake. I thought maybe there was a gun in the middle. Instead, it's a fancy hat. Makes no sense."

Jean looked uneasy. "That may be one of our costumes. Thursday night somebody broke into the shed where we keep our props and stage supplies."

Billy nodded. "I'll take a look at the shed. First," he pulled a small notebook from his pocket, "I want to go over your actions last night." He pointed at the stage. "Please stand where you were when the lights went out."

Marian sidled close, camera now dangling from the strap around her neck, a pen poised over her notebook.

Jean turned stiffly toward the stage. In bright sunlight, the black splotches of the dead man's blood were ugly and mesmerizing. She averted her gaze from the stains. She gingerly edged beneath the crime scene tape. Behind the stage, she stopped nearer the dock than the woods.

Marian lifted the camera.

Billy waved her back. "No shots here."

Marian's raspy voice was loud. "First Amendment, Billy."

Billy ignored her, stared at Jean. "When the lights went out, did you move?"

Jean gestured at the light stands. "I thought someone had stumbled over the cord, pulled the plug out of the battery pack. I took a step or two, but there was a cry and the sound of someone falling. I stopped. Someone shouted—"

Almost the instant the lights went out, Frank Saulter had flicked on his key-ring flash and moved fast.

"—That they were coming with a light. I waited."

Billy moved quickly, stepping over the tape.

Jean's frightened eyes never left Billy's face.

Billy pointed at the black cable lying on the sandy ground. The plug was now pulled out of the battery pack. The plug lay in the sunlight, only a few feet from where Jean stood. "You made no effort to get the lights going." Although his voice was uninflected, the flat statement sounded accusatory.

"I was frightened. I knew something was wrong."

Marian was taking notes, her bright, dark eyes intent.

Billy looked dour. "You're in charge." His tone was tough. "There's an emergency. Your first instinct should have been to restore light. Why didn't you move to the plug?" His eyes were steely. "Maybe the answer's simple. You weren't standing there." He pointed at her feet. "Everyone was listening to Wagner. No one noticed what you were doing. You could have moved behind the stage," he took a few steps and stood over the battery pack, "and pulled out the plug." He moved fast until he was directly behind the stage. "You stood here with a gun and shot him in the back. You got rid of the gun," he gestured toward the lake, "and hurried back here."

"I didn't." Her voice trembled. "I swear I didn't."

Billy swung away from her, pointed at the metal shed that stood about fifteen feet away. "The shed was broken into Thursday night." Again it was a statement, not a question.

Jean looked puzzled. "The hasp holding the padlock had been pried loose. One of the boys found the door standing open Friday morning and came and told me."

"Let's take a look at it."

Max and Marian followed as Jean and Billy walked to the shed.

Jean displayed the twisted remnant of the hasp with the now-useless padlock still in place.

Billy gestured at the shed. "I'd like to see inside."

Jean pulled the door open. "I'll see about a new hasp next week. With the program, I didn't have time to take care of it yesterday and nothing seemed to have been bothered."

When the door stood wide, Billy turned on the light. The shelves were packed with props, light filters, spotlights, paint cans, and assorted odds and ends. "You said there might be a costume missing?"

Jean eased past him, walked past a row of trunks, stopped at the next to last. She knelt and pulled up the lid. She pointed at a sheet of paper pasted to the interior of the lid. "The costumes are listed. See. Number five. But they get out of order. I'll look through the trunk."

Jean lifted out, one at a time, Abe Lincoln's top hat, a Viking breastplate, Daniel Boone's fringed leather shirt, Robin Hood's green tunic and shorts, an Eskimo fur, a samurai robe and vest and sash with a soft hat, a Harvey rabbit, a Japanese kimono, and a half-dozen more costumes. Finally, she began to replace them. Then she stood and looked toward Billy. "The Puss-in-Boots cape and feathered hat are gone."

She joined him in the doorway, shaking her head. "I don't see why anybody would steal a costume and throw it in the lake. I suppose that's what happened. Maybe one of the kids wanted to dress up in the hat and cape and then got scared and tossed everything in the water. Anyway, it's a relief to know there was some reason why the shed was broken into. It doesn't seem important now."

Max glanced at Billy and knew they both suspected a very clever use for the cape and cavalier hat. In the darkness behind the lamp stands, a murderer—man or woman—could easily be disguised with the cape and hat. Who would notice one more costumed figure?

"Was anyone scheduled to play Puss-in-Boots last night?"

"No. Or we would have noticed sooner that the costume was missing."

Billy nodded, his face thoughtful. Then he reached into his pocket. "I am serving you with a search warrant for your office, Ms. Hughes."

∻ *Eight* ∻

ANNIE FUMBLED IN her purse for scratch paper. She found a grocery list, turned it over, and wrote: *Not to worry. I'm with Rachel. She wants to show me something in the woods.* Annie wasn't sure what her stepsister hoped or feared. Rachel's explanation had been disjointed in her impatience to get started.

Annie tucked a note beneath the driver's windshield wiper of Max's Jeep. If he came out to the Haven parking lot and saw her car and didn't find her anywhere, he might be concerned. She tossed her purse in the trunk.

"Annie, hurry. Tim's probably there by now." Rachel gestured toward the woods. Thin as a whippet, with a narrow, intense face that hinted at the haunting beauty she would become, today she looked drenched in misery, reluctant yet committed. "Maybe everything's okay. But he looked so strange. Come on," she tugged at Annie's hand, "stay behind me and don't make any noise."

When they reached the dim opening in the fern-choked thicket, Rachel stopped, plucked her cell phone from her pocket, turned it off. She looked over her shoulder. "Make sure your cell phone's off."

"I left my purse in my trunk."

Rachel nodded and sped ahead.

Annie hurried to catch up. Rachel was a good ten feet in front of her, stepping softly on pine straw at the edge of the narrow path.

The caw of crows, the baking late-morning heat, a whirr of gnats, the flutter of ferns as they brushed past them, the smell of damp earth, the mixed scents of lavender lobelia and wild hibiscus and honeysuckle, the dreamy *Green Mansions* dimness of the path hidden from sunlight by overhanging branches, the ever-present fear of snakes were part and parcel of summer in the deep woods. As she followed her stepsister deeper and deeper into the dusky and isolated forest, Annie felt caught up in a strange and unnerving quest.

Abruptly, Rachel stopped, a hand held up in warning. She bent forward, shoulders hunched, listening.

Not far ahead came thrashing sounds.

Annie stiffened. Wild boars still roamed remote woods. With pointed ears, black bristly hair, and sharp tusks, the feral pigs were fast and dangerous. Annie squinted at the path in the dimness, seeking their distinctive muddy tracks. They often rolled in mud to cool off from summer heat.

Rachel made a tiny follow-me gesture and sidled around a curve.

Annie took two quick strides. She saw a welcome shaft of bright sunlight and knew a clearing lay ahead.

Rachel, her body taut, peered from behind a saw palm. Annie slid up next to her.

Tim Talbot, his thin face glistening from effort, sweat patching his T-shirt, worked furiously, pulling apart a bale of hay, pausing every so often to shove a hand into the pocket of his shorts.

"He's digging out the bullets." Rachel looked shaken.

The livid scar looked angry on Tim's sweat-sheened cheek. His fingers scrabbled at the hay. He stopped, sneezed, wiped his face. Dust and sprigs of hay swirled as he gouged and ripped.

Rachel's soft whisper was anguished. "If it was all right, he wouldn't, would he?" She gripped Annie's arm. "I saw him shooting at cups last week. He'd drawn a face—" She looked sick. "—With yellow hair on each cup. He blew them apart."

Despite sweat sliding down her back and legs, Annie felt chilled. She stared at the small clearing, her eyes searching. She didn't see a gun or any kind of weapon. She bent close to Rachel, scarcely breathed as she spoke, her words a ghost of sound. "Go back to the Haven. Get Max. I'll wait here."

Rachel twisted to answer. A twig snapped underfoot.

Tim's head jerked up. He looked like a startled fawn, dark hair lank on his face, lips parted. A pulse quivered in his throat. He gazed around the clearing in a frenzy, seeking the source of the sound. Abruptly, grunting with effort, he pushed at what remained of the bale, shoving the ragged bunch of hay behind a resurrection fern. He dropped to his hands and knees, frantically sweeping the remainder of the bale into the undergrowth.

"I can't stand this." There was a sob in Rachel's voice. She pulled away from Annie, bolted into the clearing. "Tim, don't be scared. It's just me and my sister. We want to help you."

Annie pushed past a scratchy frond of a saw palmetto. Alert for any threat, she watched Tim, ready to push Rachel to safety, ready to scream for help though she knew they were deep in an unfrequented wood.

Tim came to his feet, panting. His eyes were wild, his hands clenched. He was disheveled and desperate. "I don't need any help. Leave me alone."

Annie understood Rachel's pity. Yet, she remembered Laurel's words—"Oh, I won't forget his face"—when the lights came on after his stepfather's murder. Annie spoke and the words were there without thought or planning. "What have you done with the gun?"

Tim stared at her with glazed, dark eyes. His face was ashen. He glanced toward the not-quite-hidden mound of shredded hay. "I didn't . . . I didn't . . ." He backed away from Annie, jerked around, and ran toward the path.

Rachel took a step toward the trees. "Tim, please come back."

The only reply to Rachel's call was the dwindling sound of his running steps.

"A search warrant?" Jean stared down at the paper in her hand. Her eyes widened in shock. "Why did you get a warrant? I don't mind if you look in my office. You're welcome to see everything."

Billy was looking especially stolid. "The warrant makes the search official." He turned away and walked toward the main building. Marian Kenyon was right on his heels.

Jean looked at Max. "What does he think he's going to find?" Her voice was uneven. She brushed back a strand of blond hair with a shaky hand.

Max tried to keep his expression relaxed, but he knew Jean was in trouble. To obtain a search warrant, Billy had convinced the judge that there was probable cause that incriminating evidence would be found. "We'll find out."

When they stepped into the main building, Mavis Cameron waited in the hall outside Jean's office. Mavis, who also worked as a crime scene tech, held an oblong metal box and wore latex gloves.

"Go right in." Jean pointed at the open door to her office. She looked both scared and angry.

Max thought her anger was a sign of innocence.

Marian glanced in the office, then took two quick steps to confront Jean. "Ms. Hughes, you came to the island as a protégé of the murder victim. How long had you known him?"

"I don't—"

Max interrupted. "Ms. Hughes is cooperating with the police investigation and will not discuss the matter at this time."

Marian gave Max a combative glance. She sidestepped him. "Ms. Hughes, can you suggest why Mr. Wagner was killed here at the Haven?"

Jean's shoulders slumped. "I don't know. It's a nightmare. It still seems impossible, the lights going out and a shot."

Marian's bony face squeezed in inquiry. "How many people knew that he was scheduled to speak at the program?"

Jean looked in turn perplexed, thoughtful, and stunned. "I suppose a lot of people could have known."

Marian was unrelenting. "His bio was in the program, but there was no indication he would speak. You were listed as emcee."

Jean abruptly exploded. "What are you saying? Everybody who knew him would know he'd be on the stage. He always bulled his way into the middle of every event."

Marian studied Jean for a moment, then turned away to look into the office.

Billy sat behind the desk. He, too, wore latex gloves. He pulled out the center drawer, placed it on the desktop.

Mavis lifted the lid of a cardboard box near the door.

Jean paced back and forth in the hall, arms folded tight across her front.

Max was uneasy. Some fact unknown to Jean and to him must have prompted the search. Max felt sure that Billy was looking for something specific.

Jean looked from Max to Marian. "I didn't have anything to do with Booth's murder." Her voice was shaky, but determined. "There can't be anything in my office connected to the shooting."

Marian wrote in her notebook.

Jean gave a sigh of relief. "So, I don't care what they find." She seemed to take comfort in her own words. Some of the panic seeped from her eyes.

Max hoped she was right. Was Billy looking for the murder weapon? Killers did odd things, but Jean would have been an incredible fool to have hidden the gun in her office. Max spoke quietly. "While we have a minute, I wanted to ask about Click Silvester. Freddy Baker said Click was really excited about the program. He said Click told him he had a secret part."

Marian took a step nearer. "That's the kid who died in the nature preserve." Her dark eyes were sharp and intent. "What's his role in the program got to do with the Wagner kill?"

Jean looked perplexed. "Click wasn't on the program."

In Jean's office, Mavis eased files out of a middle drawer in a cabinet, bending to look inside.

Max persisted. "Click told Freddy he had a special part, but it was a secret. Click was really excited and couldn't wait for Friday night."

Mavis refilled the middle cabinet, pulled out the bottom drawer.

Jean's shoulders lifted and fell. "Maybe Freddy was talking about something else."

Max recalled his conversation with Freddy. According to Freddy, Click was excited about the program. Max jammed his hands in his pockets. That made two odd aspects to Click's death. The first was his presence in a nature preserve. The second was his excitement about a program in which he was not scheduled to take part.

Maybe both could be explained. Maybe he went to the nature preserve on a dare or somebody had persuaded him it was fun to see the birds in the rookery. Maybe he was excited about the program because somebody was going to include him in a skit even though he wasn't officially part of the program.

Neither explanation satisfied Max.

Marian's angular face was creased in a puzzled frown. "Come on, Max. What's the connection between the kid's death and Wagner's murder?"

"Chief!" Mavis's voice was sharp.

They all turned to see Mavis staring into the bottom drawer.

Billy was beside her in an instant. He bent down, looked, nodded. "Hold on." He retrieved a rod from the forensic case, poked it toward the back of the cabinet, carefully eased the rod up.

A roll of tape wobbled on the rod. Billy moved the rod until he held both ends. The tape balanced in the center of the metal piece. He rose and came out into the hall.

"What is this, Ms. Hughes?" He was still expressionless, but his eyes were cold and measuring.

Jean blinked in surprise. "Phosphorescent tape. We cut strips to mark spots on the stage when props are moved in the dark. But it shouldn't be in my filing cabinet. I didn't put it there."

Billy's gaze was steely. "Where should the tape be?"

"Oh." It was as if she suddenly understood, as if a piece of a puzzle slotted into place. "The phosphorescent tapes are kept in the shed. On the middle shelf toward the back on the left side. Whoever broke into the shed must have taken that roll and put it in my filing cabinet. But that doesn't make any sense."

Marian barked, "Chief, was the tape—"

Billy made a sharp gesture. "Later." He stepped toward Jean. "Ms. Hughes, I am taking you to the police station for questioning."

She lifted a hand to her throat. "What does that mean?"

"It's necessary to ask you more particulars about last night. And about your relations with Mr. Wagner."

Marian bounced on her feet. "Is Ms. Hughes a person of interest?"

Max stepped forward. "Ms. Hughes has a right to counsel."

Billy's jaw tightened. "You are not licensed to practice law in South Carolina. Ms. Hughes is not being charged. Her cooperation is requested in a murder case."

Max was pleasant. "That's fine. However, for any formal talks with the police, Ms. Hughes has a right to counsel of her own choosing." He turned to Jean. "I suggest that we contact Handler Jones on the mainland. It's unlikely he will be available until Monday morning." Max looked at Billy. "Since you would like to have Ms. Hughes's *cooperation*," Max emphasized the noun, "I suggest she make herself available at nine a.m. Monday morning at the police station."

Billy's expression remained stolid, but irritation flickered in his eyes. He stared at Max.

Max continued to look affable, knowing the outcome hung in the balance. Was Billy ready to formally announce Jean as a person of interest? Or was he suspicious but aware there were many other avenues he had yet to explore?

Finally, Billy gave a short nod. "Nine a.m. Monday morning."

Annie put out a restraining hand. "It won't do any good for us to go after him. He won't listen to us." She felt Rachel's arm tremble.

The last sounds of running steps, the rustling of broken twigs, the crackling underbrush faded away, leaving them in hot, green silence.

Annie looked at the evidence of Tim's frantic efforts to destroy an intractable bale of hay. There was a sense of darkness in the bright clearing, of passionate feelings and inimical acts.

Rachel's eyes glistened with tears. "He's scared."

"I know." Tim's fear had been as real as the straw that littered the ground. Annie pointed at an edge of the hay bale that wasn't quite hidden in the underbrush. "You have to tell me, Rachel."

Rachel pulled away, stood with her thin shoulders hunched. "I'd kind of made friends with him. He was like a dog somebody had kicked. I could tell by the way he acted rude that he hated the way he had to walk and the scar on his face. Kids looked at him with their eyes real big. They didn't ask what happened, but anybody could see something bad had happened to him. When he came to the Haven, he kept to himself, played computer games and never looked up. A couple of times, I showed him some silly pictures I'd drawn and we got to talking. I knew he was unhappy."

Annie understood. Several years ago, Rachel had been a suspect in her mother's murder. Rachel had known sadness and mourning, loneliness and despair. That dark experience had made her sensitive to misery in other lives.

Annie wanted to wrap her arms around Rachel, tell her that everything was going to be all right. That's what she wanted to do. She couldn't make that promise now. Everything might very well be as wrong as it could be for Tim Talbot.

Rachel shivered despite the heavy heat. "I followed him Monday morning. I'd just got to the Haven on my bike. I saw Meredith hurrying ahead of him to the gate. Tim parked his bike next to hers, then he looked around, like he was making sure nobody was paying any attention to him. He didn't see me. I was over by a big hedge. When Meredith was out of sight, he got back on his bike and pedaled as fast as he could toward the woods, the path you and I took. I thought—" Rachel paused to draw a quick breath "—he didn't look right. I thought something was wrong. After a minute, I went after him."

Annie reached out to take Rachel's hand. Dear Rachel, with her generous heart, always ready to be kind.

"I know what life's like when everything's bad." Rachel's dark eyes were huge with remembered pain. "I didn't know if I could do anything, but I couldn't pretend I didn't know something was wrong. That's why I came after him, but when I got here," she pointed at the saw palmetto where she and Annie stood and watched Tim claw at the bale of hay, "I was afraid he'd be mad that I'd followed him so I didn't say anything. I almost turned and went away, then I stayed to watch. He put the bale on top of that big log. He drew faces on some paper cups and put them against the hay. He pulled out a package. When he unwrapped it, I saw a rifle. He was over there on a tree branch." She gestured about twenty feet from the log. "He shot at the cups. He hit each one. I was scared, like maybe it would be better if he didn't know I was there, so I slipped away."

Once before Rachel had followed a boy because she sensed despair, and put herself in deadly danger. Annie felt the emptiness that comes with knowledge of what could have happened.

Tim and his targets and a man shot dead. "Where was the gun hidden?"

Rachel hurried to the shrub and brushed away a covering of leaves.

"Careful." Annie joined her. "If you find anything, don't touch it. Maybe we'd better leave everything as it is."

Rachel rocked back on her heels. "There are the plastic bags. He kept the gun wrapped in them."

Rumpled black plastic lay limp on the ground, several pieces of duct tape visible. "What kind of gun?" Annie knew her voice was slightly higher than usual.

Rachel turned up her hands. "I don't know. It looked like those guns at the fair when you shoot at the little metal ducks."

There had been a gun. The gun was no longer there.

As the front door to the Haven shut behind Billy and Mavis, Jean Hughes looked bewildered. "What's such a big deal about a roll of tape? What difference does some stupid tape make? I don't think much of him as a policeman. He'd be better off trying to find out who was mad enough to kill

Booth. A lot of people hated him." There was a vindictive hardness to her voice.

Max stared at her. Didn't she understand the significance of Mavis's discovery or was she pretending ignorance? "*Phosphorescent* tape." He emphasized the adjective.

"I don't care what kind of tape it is. Anyway, I've got to hurry." She glanced at her watch. "I always go home for lunch at a quarter to twelve. Rosalind will see to locking everything up. The Haven closes at noon on Saturdays." She turned to leave.

Marian was a bloodhound cornering her quarry. "X marked the spot."

Jean paused, blinked at the reporter. "What spot?"

"Booth's big brawny back, baby. You know, where he got shot." Marian's voice quivered with excitement. "That has to be how the killer nailed him when the lights went out, a bright patch of phosphorescent tape on his shirt. So far, Billy's kept that information quiet, but that's the only reason he could care about the tape in your office. Oh wow, I can see the lead now: 'Stage tape made murder victim a marked man.'"

Max admired the murderer's cleverness. Before the program began, someone greeted Booth, clapped him on the back, or, in the crush of the crowd, came up behind him, and pressed the adhesive side of the tape to the shirt. A swath of tape likely would not be noticed against the background of Booth's bright Hawaiian shirt. Had the tape been spotted, Booth would have lived another night. But no one noticed the green tape against the purple, green, and orange pattern, so Booth Wagner died. Probably the existence of the tape hadn't been noted until the bloodied shirt was examined at the morgue.

"Oh." Jean's eyes rounded in surprise. "You mean some-body used the tape to find him? Well," she looked relieved, "then the police have to find out who broke into the shed. I certainly didn't have to do that. I have keys. It doesn't mean a thing that the tape was hidden in my office. I keep my door open. Anyone could have put the tape there."

Marian eyed her speculatively. "Including you, Ms. Hughes."

Max knew Marian was right. "Jean, you're due in Billy's office Monday morning. You need to hire Handler Jones. He's a first-rate criminal lawyer. I'll call him for you."

Her nod was perfunctory. "Maybe you're right, but I can't deal with anything right now. Besides, I don't have money for a lawyer. Anyway, I'm running late. I have to get home to Giselle. With everything that's happened, she'll worry if I'm late." She reached into the pocket of her slacks, frowned. She patted her back pockets, then darted into her office, scrambled through several drawers in her desk. "I thought I left my cell phone in here." She grabbed the land-line receiver, started to call, put it down. "I don't want to call anyway. It's too hard for her to get to the phone. I've got to hurry." She rushed into the hall.

Max strode after her. "Don't you understand? Billy Cam-eron may arrest you Monday morning. You said there are a lot of people who hated Booth."

Once again Marian was right beside them, alert, pen poised.

Jean was at the front door, looking back in irritation. "I'm late."

"Jean, I need to know everything you can tell me about Booth. Let's go to Confidential Commissions." He wanted a quiet place with no interruptions. The time when he and Jean could talk might soon be past.

Her face twisted in anger. "I hate thinking about Booth. I hate talking about him."

Max shook his head. "You don't have a choice."

"All right." She was impatient. "Whatever you say. I'll come to your office after lunch. I have to leave now." She hurried to the door and pushed through.

"Hey, wait a minute," Marian cried.

By the time Max and Marian stood on the steps, Jean was running.

He knew she would arrive at the cottage, flushed, heart racing, to be close to her sister, who had so few heartbeats remaining. There was no mistaking Jean's priorities: Giselle first; anything and everything else, including a suspicion of murder, pushed to the corner of her mind. Yet the time with her sister that mattered to her above all else might soon be taken away.

Marian's eyebrows arched. "Lunch is more important than being a murder suspect. What gives?"

"Jean's sister isn't well." His tone was level, but he saw Marian's quick glance. He knew the reporter would dig up the whole story. He hesitated, then decided to gamble. Marian as an ally was much to be preferred to Marian in full investigative mode. "Her sister has terminal cancer. Maybe a couple of months. Maybe a few weeks. Jean has little thought for anything else. I know she wants to be helpful to the investigation. I'm going to help her organize what she knows about Wagner for the police."

"Just two good little citizens, right?" Marian looked amused.

"Right." He'd put out the best spin possible for Marian, but he was worried. Jean needed a lawyer, and she needed one now. And there was still the mystery of Click, why he had died in the nature preserve and what he had looked forward to on Friday evening.

Max turned to reenter the building.

Marian trotted right alongside him. "Where are you going?"

"I want to talk to Darren Dubois."

"Who's that?"

"A friend of Click Silvester's."

"You keep bringing up the Silvester kid." Her glance at him was sharp. "Is there a connection between the kid and Wagner?"

"I don't think so. But Click's death seems wrong to me. He told one boy he had a big part on the program Friday night, but it was a secret. Jean says he wasn't on the program. I want to see if he told Darren anything about it." He checked several rooms.

Marian chattered, "Hey, maybe the kid thought there was going to be a fake hold-up. Maybe he knew someone was going to play pin-the-phosphorescent-tape-on-Wagner. A practical joke."

When Max poked his head in the art room, Rosalind Parker bustled up to him. "Ms. Hughes isn't here right now. May I help you?"

"We're looking for Darren Dubois."

Rosalind shook her head. "I think he was watching the police at the lake. Jean told the kids to stay away, but nobody tells Darren anything. He does what he wants to do and then he gives you that charming grin and you can't stay mad."

When they came out into the bright sunshine, Max looked toward the lake. He shook his head. "I saw Darren earlier, but he left."

Marian was wry. "Not your morning, Max. Jean blows you off and the kid splits."

"I'll call around."

"Good luck. Let me know if you get anything out of him. Maybe we can do a little trading." She turned to leave, then said quickly, "Hey, something's up." Marian's husky voice brimmed with excitement. "Here comes the chief and he's moving fast."

Max looked across the field. The police chief was indeed moving fast, heading straight for the lake and the police standing on the shore.

⌁ *Nine* ⌁

PIECES OF WHITE Styrofoam lay on the ground near the tree trunk where a bale of hay had served as the backdrop for Tim Talbot's targets. Metal glinted in the sunlight. Annie picked up a stick, edged aside Styrofoam to reveal a shiny fishing weight. Obviously, Tim had given a good deal of thought to his makeshift firing range. The weight held a cup steady while he lifted a gun to shoot. This evidence of planning made her feel queasy. She poked at the remnants of a cup, saw bright yellow markings. She knelt, edged pieces together with the stick, felt sure she stared at pieces representing an image of Booth Wagner.

Annie was grateful for the weight of hot sunshine pressing down on her, a wonderful antidote for chilling thoughts. She came to her feet and turned to Rachel. "Please. I need your cell phone."

"Who do you want to call?" Rachel's tone was sharp.

"The police." She met her stepsister's pleading gaze.

"Do you have to?" Rachel's face drooped. She held a handful of hay, crumpling the dry grass in her hand.

Annie nodded. "Tim was shooting at targets that looked like his stepfather."

Reluctantly, Rachel placed the phone in Annie's hand.

"They were just cups. Oh, I should have come by myself." Then, with quick contrition, Rachel said, "I'm sorry. I didn't mean that. I'm glad you're here. Anyway, maybe that old gun is around here somewhere. Just because he didn't wrap it up, it doesn't mean it's not here."

Annie clicked on the cell and punched the number, wishing she could agree, wishing she thought it even a tiny bit likely that Tim had dropped the rifle somewhere near, but the crumpled garbage sacks with remnants of tape indicated the gun had customarily been carefully wrapped to protect it.

Rachel grabbed more hay, kneaded the pieces in her hand. "I'll bet Tim came today to hide everything because he thought it looked bad."

As indeed, Annie thought, it did. She pushed away the memory of Tim's pale face, the scar bright and angry, and the despair in his dark eyes. "This is Annie Darling. I need to talk to Chief Cameron. I have information that may be connected to Booth Wagner's murder." She took no pleasure in her words.

Marian Kenyon reached the lakeshore first, trained her camera on Frank Saulter, who knelt on the bank. He pulled a ballpoint pen from his shirt pocket and slipped the pen inside the trigger guard of a small pistol. As he held the gun aloft, water streamed out of the short barrel. The pearl handle glistened in the sunshine. "A thirty-two."

Marian clicked several shots.

Billy bent near, studied the gun. "Bag and tag it. And keep looking."

Marian's question came quick and sharp. "Is there a possibility that is the Wagner murder weapon?"

Billy was ponderous. "The weapon was found in proximity to the crime."

Marian snapped, tight as a terrier's teeth on bone, "Was Wagner's death caused by a thirty-two-caliber slug?"

"The ballistics report is part of the investigative record."

"Is the search for the murder weapon continuing?"

Billy turned away.

Marian stood, hands on her hips, and called out loudly enough for Billy to hear, "I'm on my way back to the office. Looks like the story might read: 'Although police discovered a pearl-handled thirty-two-caliber revolver in the lake near the stage, the search of the lake continues. Chief Billy Cameron declined to reveal whether the caliber of the gun that caused Wagner's death had been determined.'"

Rachel scuffed the sandy dirt with the toe of her tennis shoe and watched the police officer pull out the remnants of the hay bale.

Annie remembered Coley Benson from the high school choir. He had a magnificent tenor voice. He was the newest member of the Broward's Rock police department. He'd majored in criminal justice at Armstrong State. Billy Cameron had been delighted to welcome him home.

It seemed odd to see Coley in a police uniform instead of a choir robe. Now his strong brown hand delicately plucked at the straw. He held up a tiny piece of metal that glinted in the sunlight. He gave a slight shake of his head and stood. "I'll take this along."

Annie was startled. "I thought you'd bring the crime van, pick all of this up," she pointed at the straggle of straw and crumpled garbage sacks, "for crime scene evidence."

Coley looked surprised. "It's maybe a misdemeanor to set up a target in public woods. The chief might talk to him, but right now he's too busy with Mr. Wagner's murder."

"You picked out a piece of a bullet." Annie was puzzled. "Can't it be checked against the bullet that killed Booth Wagner?"

Coley waved a hand in dismissal. "This," and it was his turn to point at the remnants of the bale, "was used for practice with a twenty-two. The bullet that killed Mr. Wagner was a lot bigger than that."

Annie watched Rachel pump away on her bike, dust spewing from beneath the wheels. Rachel's dark hair streamed behind her and Annie thought of a bird in flight, soaring and serene. The relief both she and Rachel felt upon Coley's calm pronouncement was tinged by a feeling of foolishness.

Even though Annie usually opted for genteel mysteries, she knew a fair amount about guns. It would require enormous skill and a huge amount of luck for a twenty-two slug to kill at a distance of twenty to thirty feet. She'd had the clue when Rachel described the gun as the kind used at the fair in the yellow-duck shooting gallery. But embarrassment was a small price in exchange for Tim's dismissal as a suspect. Max would tease her.

She was disappointed not to find Max's car in the Haven lot. Annie fished her purse from the trunk. She smiled as she slid behind the wheel of her new flaming-red Thunderbird, a Valentine gift. She had lots to tell him, the unleashing of the Intrepid Trio of Emma, Henny, and Laurel as well as the ignominious outcome of her detecting foray with Rachel.

She put the key in the ignition, and her cell phone rang.

"Hey, Max." She was ready to regale him with the sweaty and fruitless trek to Tim Talbot's dismantled shooting range.

Before she could speak, he said quickly, "Please bring lunch to Confidential Commissions. Jean's got big-time problems. I want—oh, here's a call from Handler Jones. I've been trying to find him. I'll explain when you get here."

Annie nudged open Max's office door with her knee, balancing a cardboard drink holder with two iced teas, a nicely hot sack with lunch from Parotti's, and her purse.

". . . Thanks, Handler. I knew I could count on you." Max put down the phone and popped up to help. He pointed at his office table. "Our places are set." The office kitchen ran to blue and yellow pottery and woven red place mats. Max insisted on eating in style even for an office lunch.

Annie dished up Veracruz-style red snapper for Max and two green chili chicken enchiladas for herself. Ben Parotti had recently expanded the menu for the island's many Latino families.

Max disdained iced tea in paper cups. He brought chilled glasses from the refrigerator in the office's tiny kitchen.

As Max described his morning, Annie pushed her plate away and began to take notes on one of Max's legal pads. When he finished, she looked at her list:

Pertinent Facts Re: Murder Booth Wagner

1. *Puss-in-Boots costume stolen from Haven storage shed, thrown into lake.*
2. *Phosphorescent tape found hidden in Jean's office.*
3. *Clear assumption tape had been placed on Booth's back by the murderer to make him a visible target in the dark.*

4. *Click Silvester told Freddy Baker he had a big role Friday night, but Jean said he wasn't on the program.*
5. *Jean to be questioned Monday morning at nine a.m.*
6. *Pearl-handled thirty-two-caliber revolver found in lake. Ellen Wagner claimed she had lost a pearl-handled gun.*
7. *Chief orders search to continue. Does this mean the murder weapon was a different caliber?*

Annie read No. 2 aloud. "That's grim."

Max shook his head. "Jean would have been an idiot to hide the tape in her own office."

Annie didn't reply. Maybe Jean never envisioned a search of her office.

Max took a last bite of red snapper. "The tape is incriminating. There's no doubt about that. Jean for sure has a motive, maybe a bunch of them. But she said she knows plenty of people who hated him. She'll be here after lunch. We have until Monday to come up with enough evidence to keep Billy from arresting her. If he puts her in jail, the worst part for Jean will be keeping her away from Giselle."

Annie was troubled. "I don't know if I have much to contribute. But," and she welcomed a reason to smile, "the Intrepid Trio is hard at work. Emma, Henny, and your mom are rounding up information on their list of suspects."

Max, too, smiled. "We can count on them to make things interesting."

Annie pulled the legal pad to her, but turned it sideways so Max could see additions:

Intrepid Trio Assumptions

1. *The shot came from the woods behind Booth.*
2. *When the lights came on, the murderer may have been observed in the area near the woods and the stage.*
3. *The murderer had to be aware that Booth was scheduled to speak.*
4. *Among those who knew he would be on stage: his wife Neva, daughter Meredith, stepson Tim Talbot, Jean Hughes. Van Shelton could have learned from Neva that Booth would appear. Meredith could have informed her mother.*
5. *Observed in Emma's Rectangle of Interest (which included the area behind the stage): Jean Hughes, Neva Wagner, Tim Talbot, Meredith Wagner.*
6. *Van Shelton, the golf pro, earlier followed Neva into an arbor. He appeared to be angry and upset. Laurel believes Neva and Van were more than casual friends.*
7. *Booth's ex-wife Ellen was present at some point.*

"I don't want to jump to conclusions. This morning I thought I had everything figured out." Annie was wry. "Laurel saw Booth's stepson right after the lights came on, and he was terribly upset. A while ago, Rachel called and wanted me to go into the woods with her, something she wanted to show me about Tim." Annie described creeping through the woods after Tim and confronting him as he frantically plucked spent bullets from the bale of hay. "He ran away, and I called the police. But it's a big to-do about nothing. He'd used cups decorated with his stepfather's face as targets. No wonder he wanted to hide everything, but he was shooting a twenty-two. Officer Benson said the murder weapon was a bigger-caliber gun."

Max nodded. "Billy's keeping quiet about the gun, but if the pearl-handled thirty-two that Frank pulled out of the lake is the murder weapon, Ellen Wagner will be the chief suspect."

A crew member hosed down the top deck of a gleaming white yacht. A cabin cruiser putted slowly out of the harbor. Pink-cheeked tourists hurried up the gangplank of an excursion boat.

Leaning on the railing that overlooked the marina, Annie breathed deeply of salt-scented air, welcomed the feel of hot July sunlight. She was turning to walk back to the boardwalk and Death on Demand when Jean Hughes, frowning and abstracted, reached Confidential Commissions. Jean carried with her an aura of sadness, the wrenching awareness of life slipping away. The contrast between Jean's face and the marina's summer cheer was a stark reminder that sunny days do not last forever and a reminder as well that even when Annie's own days were carefree and joyful, there were those burdened by pain and sorrow.

Annie pulled open the front door of Death on Demand. She took a deep sniff of the lovely mingled scents of books and coffee. She had plenty to do, unpacking backlist by Nancy Atherton, Charles Ardai, Leann Sweeney, and Jasper Fforde.

Ingrid looked up from the cash desk. Her eyes gleamed behind stylish new large-framed glasses. "Two book clubs from the mainland. We're sold out of the new Evanovich. What else is new?"

Annie looked toward the coffee bar. She didn't know whether to be relieved or pleased to see the coffee area free of Emma, Henny, and Laurel.

Ingrid needed no hints. "Rest easy. They marched out a few minutes ago, moving with both alacrity and determination. What kind of havoc do you suppose they'll wreak?"

Henny Brawley parked her old Chrysler behind a BMW at the end of an expansive circular drive. Cars were lined along both sides of the drive. A florist's delivery truck, hazard lights blinking, blocked the center of the drive opposite broad, shallow steps leading to the front veranda.

As Henny walked toward the door carrying a Saran-wrapped disposable bowl filled with fresh-cut fruit, she made two swift judgments: Booth Wagner must have been very rich indeed, for the house was an overlarge, three-story mansion in the current style of combined brick, stone, wood, and glass, and no expense had been spared in the landscaping with a profusion of roses, bougainvillea, japonica, and hibiscus.

Where would all the money go?

Henny pushed the doorbell. Often now, more often than she would have wished, she brought food to houses of mourning, but this was the first time she had done so for a reason other than friendship. If she had felt that Neva Wagner was grief-stricken, she would not be standing here. When Neva gazed at her fallen husband Friday night, she had looked pale and shocked, but there had not been the piercing pain of heartbreak in her eyes or on her face. She had exhibited neither the wild abandonment of crushing loss nor the frozen somnambulism of heartbreak scarcely comprehended.

The door swung in. The maid, perspiring a little, welcomed her inside. She had curly brown hair, a round, open face, and a harried expression. "Everyone's in the far living room, ma'am."

Henny's smile was swift. "I can see you're pretty overwhelmed right now. I'm here on behalf of the Haven board of directors. I didn't know the family that well. Let me be useful and come out to the kitchen to catch up on some of the dishwashing."

"Oh, ma'am." The housekeeper darted a glance down a wide marble hallway with inset niches holding busts and vases. "*She* might not like it."

The personal pronoun was not spoken with affection.

"Who's to know? And help is best where it's needed," Henny said lightly. "You check the living room, I'll take care of the rest. I'm Henny Brawley." She looked inquiring.

"Beth Sullivan, ma'am."

"All right, Beth, we're a team. Is the kitchen straight ahead?" Henny moved swiftly, her shoes clipping on the marble floor. She had no trouble finding the huge kitchen and stood for only a moment to appraise the stainless steel Bosch appliances. Everything was of the best quality. The counter next to the double sink was piled with dirty dishes. Henny opened cupboards, found a lovely Limoges bowl, and filled it with the fresh-cut fruit. She placed the bowl on an island with other food gifts. Then she moved to the sink, ran water, and began to rinse soiled dishes.

Beth hurried in and out, bringing more dishes, carrying out freshly filled plates and bowls. She flashed a shy, thankful smile each time at Henny.

Henny wedged a few more glasses in the dishwasher. She found detergent beneath the sink, filled the dispenser, and punched start.

Back with another tray, Beth heaved a tired sigh. "Ma'am, you saved my life. If you don't mind, I won't tell Mrs. Wagner you helped out in the kitchen. I told her you came for the Haven and brought fruit. Is that all right with you?"

Henny dried her hands. "That's fine. Why wouldn't Mrs. Wagner want anyone to help in the kitchen?"

"Oh, she's very fancy. Everything is always la-di-da." Her dark eyes were disdainful. "You've got me caught up now. Would you like some iced tea?"

They settled at the center island on tall stools. Orange slices and fresh mint garnished the glasses.

Henny chose her words carefully. She spoke in an inviting, confidential tone. "Murder is dreadful, but I understand Booth and Neva didn't get along very well. I suppose that makes it much easier for her. Or much harder."

Beth looked around to be sure she wouldn't be overheard. "I'd say no love lost. She moved into her own room a few months ago and you know a marriage is on the rocks when that happens. She's been white as a sheet today, but I don't think she's wasting any grief on him. She's a lot more upset about her son than she is Mr. Wagner being dead. The kid's been kind of nuts since the murder."

"Was her son especially fond of Booth?"

Beth squeezed the orange, took a huge gulp. "I needed that. She's run me ragged today. She treats me like I'm a robot, punch a button and watch me go. 'The stairs down to the lower den aren't clean.' 'I found dust in the laundry room.' 'Master Tim doesn't like cinnamon on his toast.' As for Master Tim, he's kind of weird. Master Tim, that's what I'm supposed to call him, it's Master Tim and Miss Meredith. I've worked for a lot of families, but I never had to call kids 'master' and 'miss' until here. Anyway, Master Tim's scared out his mind. He kept screaming out in his sleep last night and she was up and down with him. But he wasn't the least bit fond of Mr. Wagner. Master Tim could hardly stand to be in the same room with him, anybody could tell that."

Laurel reminded herself to keep her thoughts on her goal, though it was difficult with dear Johnny so near. How lovely to be a woman and how enchanting to have such an attractive man pressing close. He was such a help with her follow-through. Such a gorgeous young man . . . This was not the moment for thoughts such as these, however.

". . . If you turn your left wrist a little more, that will add loft to the ball." He was lithe and athletic. Dark curls framed a matador-handsome face that reminded Laurel of Spanish grandees.

Laurel looked up, her lips curving into a smile. She knew she was at her best on a sunny summer afternoon, her hair a shimmering gold, her dark blue eyes softly glowing, her lips inviting.

Johnny Rodriguez took a deep breath.

Laurel understood. She gave a tiny shake of her head. "It is hard sometimes to focus on the game."

"Your wrist . . ."

"Someone told me that poor Van has had the hardest time lately keeping his mind on golf. Someone told me he was furious with Booth Wagner." She arched golden brows in delicate inquiry.

Johnny looked appalled. "Who's talking about Van?"

"Oh, everybody." She was charmingly vague. "You know how interested people are in love affairs."

"Look, it isn't how it looks." He was quick to defend his boss. "I mean, he and Neva were through. It was making him crazy. See, she broke things off because of this prenup agreement. I mean, she and Booth were kaput and had been ever since the kid got hurt. She was feeling pretty grim and Van was really nice to her and he thought they could work something out. I mean, he got it in the gut from his ex-wife. She took up with a drummer and walked out on him. But if Neva tried to get a divorce, she wouldn't get anything and she'd lose health insurance and her kid still needs another couple of operations. So, it doesn't do any good for Van to be mad. She had to make the choice and she stayed with the money. Seems to me, he's better off. If a woman wants money more than she wants love, that's a lousy deal for a guy."

Laurel murmured, "Life can be so difficult." Of course, death sometimes made everything simple. Possibly it had occurred to either Neva or Van that Booth's death made certain Neva would receive whatever had been due to her under the prenuptial agreement. Likely the agreement provided nothing if she left him for another man. "Now, show me again," she moved closer to Johnny, "just how do I turn my wrist?"

Emma Clyde was pleased that the crime scene tape had been removed, indicating the area had been searched and was now open for its customary use. Her square face creased in a grim smile. Customary use would not have included a further search by a noted mystery author. However, that was her intention and she felt confident that she would make deductions and quite possibly realize information missed by all others. After all, she and Marigold had encountered much knottier challenges in their eighty-six books and counting.

Emma walked briskly to the stage. The blood had been washed away. Eyes narrowed, she re-created in her mind the moment before the shot rang out. Booth Wagner faced the audience straight-on, big, burly, self-confident, a showman enjoying his domination. Had he turned either to the left or right? She shook her head. The shot had propelled him forward, because he landed facedown. If he had turned, he would not have fallen as he did.

Emma jumped into Booth's mind as the lights went out. She often jumped into character's minds, the prerogative of a writer. Why hadn't Booth turned to see about the lights? Her smile became even grimmer. Arrogance. An assumption that rectifying stage miscues was the work of underlings. It wasn't for him to bumble about in the dark. He would wait, calm and in charge, until the momentary blackout ended. But when the lights came on, he was dead. That lack of movement afforded the murderer time to move after pulling out the cord from the battery pack.

Emma climbed onto the stage. Here was where Booth had stood. She marched forward, came to the back of the stage, stepped off. The four light stands were still in place. Emma walked to the battery pack. She looked at her watch, followed the second hand as she estimated the time between the cessation of light and the sound of the shot. Not more than nine seconds. Much can be accomplished in nine seconds if planned in advance. She reached down as if yanking the cord loose. She hurried to the woods and looked back at the stage. Of necessity, the shooter had to be able to see Booth, so the murderer had gone no farther than here. She moved into that unknown mind. Possibly the murderer had night-vision goggles. Somehow Booth had been visible. She lifted her hand.

If Jean Hughes committed the crime, she had then returned to her place near the stage. If another hand held the gun, it was essential for the shooter to get away from the area.

Emma turned toward the trees. A few steps and she was out of sight from the stage. Then light had been needed. A small pencil flash would have sufficed.

She surveyed the trees. Not that live oak. A rope would have been necessary to reach the fork of the trunk. Her gaze moved. A satisfied smile lifted her lips. With a decided nod, she walked out of the woods and strode toward the Haven building.

* * *

Jean Hughes was unsparing. "I was too late smart." Pale and composed, but with haunted eyes, she faced Max. "I should have known that a man like Booth wouldn't really care for somebody like me, a singer in a second-rate jazz club. Always before, when guys gave me a rush and told me they weren't married, I asked around. I didn't ask around about Booth until it was way too late. I was a fool, but everything was so awful with Giselle getting sick that it seemed wonderful to have Booth be so kind and thoughtful. I guess I wanted to believe in happily ever after. He was good-looking and rich and charming. Did you know he could be charming?" Bitterness twisted her face. "He didn't care about me. He used me to get back at the people on the board who dared disagree with him. So much for having dreams."

Max heard the pain. He made an abrupt gesture. "Don't give up on life, Jean."

She managed a tremulous smile. "People like you and Annie prove not everybody lies. And Giselle . . . Do you know how brave she is? I could never be that brave. She's dying and she smiles. She thinks of me. She tries to make me feel good. She's always thought that I was wonderful. I don't know how she could, but she does."

"She knows you." Max's voice was gentle. "She knows you are good and kind. That's why the kids at the Haven love you."

"The kids." There was a depth of sadness in her tired voice. "I didn't know when I came that I'd care the way I do. There's Mickey, who isn't quite right. He's stiff and can't look at you. But I got him to painting the sun and now every day when he comes he goes straight to the art room and he fills pages with suns and they're as bright as gold. Sometimes he smiles. He brings me a sun painting every day. There's Willamae, who loves everybody and everybody loves her. There's Bud. He's always angry. I got one of those punching dummies, you know, you blow them up and they have a heavy base and you can knock them around. I asked Bud if he'd like to have some boxing gloves. He thought about it and then one day he came and said, 'Yes,' and every day he goes to the dummy and he hits and hits. There are the fun ones and the sad ones. I want things to be good for all of them. Most everybody will probably be back by Monday. I called Mr. Gilbert, told him I may have to take some time off. If I get put in jail. He was real nice, even though I know he didn't want me back. He said maybe everything will work out. Anyway, I told him Rosalind can take care of things just fine. She's done a great job this summer. She's another good person like you and Annie and Giselle. I got to hold on to knowing about good people to keep me from being so upset about Booth. See, when I got to the island, I was working hard to try and learn everything I needed to know. I didn't even realize at first that I wasn't seeing much of Booth. And then maybe it was only after a week or two, I found out he and his wife were still together. I didn't know what to think. I have a friend, a guy I knew at the club. I'd helped him out when his daughter was sick. Anyway, he's a private detective. I asked him if he'd find out what he could about Booth, but I didn't have much money. Ben said he'd be glad to and it wouldn't cost me a cent. I told him I didn't want to take up his time, but he said he could find out a bunch in no time flat." She reached into her purse, pulled out a manila envelope. "He found out a lot. You can have his report. I found out more than I ever wanted to know." She pushed back her chair, stood. "Now, I got to get back to the Haven."

Emma nodded at Officer Harrison.

"Morning, Mrs. Clyde." Hyla Harrison was crisp in her

uniform. As always, her demeanor was that of a careful, thorough, thoughtful cop.

"Good morning, officer. Everything going all right?"

"Just fine, ma'am. I'm keeping a close eye on everything."

Emma nodded approval and strolled around the side of the building. She stopped to watch a vigorous volleyball game. The middle hitter on the north side spiked the ball into the opposite court for a kill. As a player darted out to pick up the ball, Emma held up a hand. "Your attention, please." Her deep voice was at its most stentorian.

Obediently, the players turned to look.

"Your game can resume in a few minutes. However, I need assistance. I'm here on behalf of Miss Jean." Emma would have hotly insisted that she spoke accurately. Any effort made to solve the murder of the Haven board member would benefit the Haven and therefore its director, so Emma's actions were being taken on behalf of Jean Hughes, whether she knew it or not. That her listeners would assume she came to them as an emissary from Jean Hughes simply demonstrated how easily a statement could be misconstrued. "Which one of you is the best tree climber?"

Every player immediately claimed to be best.

Emma nodded gravely. "I see. Since all of you are equally expert, it will have to be a matter of chance. I am thinking," she glanced over the possibilities, "of a number between one and twenty. Whoever comes nearest will win."

The numbers rang out.

Emma immediately pointed at a tall, skinny teenager who hadn't yet grown to fit his huge hands and feet. "You win. What's your name?"

"Craig." His sunburn couldn't compete with the flush that stained his face at what was clearly unaccustomed attention.

"Very well, Craig. Follow me." She pointed toward the woods behind the stage. "The rest of you can come, too. But mind now, only cheers, no jeers."

At the edge of the woods, she arranged the players in a semicircle. "All right, Craig." She pulled a pair of gardening gloves from her capacious purse. She handed them to him. "I don't want you to leave any fingerprints as you go."

Craig's blue eyes glowed as he pulled on the gloves.

Emma pointed. "Climb that magnolia." The magnolia was huge, with several limbs low to the ground. Clusters of blooms scented the air. "Look for signs that someone has recently climbed the tree: scuffed bark, bent limbs, snags of thread. Be careful not to disturb any markings you see." She glanced toward the stage, judging distance. "When you get up about twenty feet, hunt for anything that might be left in the tree. If," and now she was emphatic, "you find anything, anything at all that doesn't belong in a tree," her voice grew louder, "do not touch it. Shout down to me, and I will tell you what to do."

Craig scooted up the tree with ease.

A dark-haired girl folded her arms in disdain. "Who'd hide something in a tree?"

Leaves rattled above them. "Hey, lady," glossy leaves framed Craig's face as he held aside a thick branch to peer down, "there's a twenty-two rifle stuck in the crook between two branches."

⌣ *Ten* ⌣

THE WHITE-HAIRED OLD lady's softly wrinkled face was a picture of gentility and kindness. She beamed at Annie. "I'm visiting my granddaughter and I am so excited to find your store. I just can't get enough of books like these."

Annie beamed in return. She picked up the first book, expecting perhaps one of Susan Wittig Albert's *Cottage Tales* from the Beatrix Potter series. Her eyes widened as she added up the total for *Walking the Perfect Square* by Reed Farrel Coleman, *Shadows in the White City* by Robert W. Walker, *Down River* by John Hart, *Summer of the Big Bachi* by Naomi Hirahara, and *Five Shots and a Funeral* by Tom Fassbender and Jim Pascoe. As she bagged the books, she took another quick glance at Whistler's mother. The old dear probably drank her whiskey neat from a shot glass.

In the lull that followed the departure of granny-who-likes-'em-rough-and-tough, Annie leaned on the counter and absently doodled on a Death on Demand scratch pad with a logo of a silver dagger with a drop of blood at the tip. Agatha jumped up and batted at her hand.

Annie reached out cautiously to pet her mercurial cat. "Sometimes you're nice and sometimes you're not." Niceness held sway for the moment. Agatha remained quite still, head lifted to be stroked. Annie petted as she glanced at her not-so-aimless drawings, a row of cups each bearing the facsimile of a face. Yet Laurel had emphasized how stricken Tim Talbot appeared shortly after the murder of his stepfather. But as Agatha's namesake once observed through Tommy Beresford in *Partners in Crime*, "Very few of us are what we seem."

The telephone rang. Annie glanced at Caller ID, lifted the receiver. "Hi, Marian. Who's your favorite mystery writer?"

Marian gave an impatient whuff. "This is no time for a survey. Rita Mae Brown. I can't get enough of Mrs. Murphy and Pewter."

Annie shook her head. Marian was one tough broad who covered murders with a quip and a curse. So she couldn't get enough of Brown's detecting cats. Go figure.

"Not to interfere with literary matters, but I'm in a rush. Max gave me some good info this morning. I always do payback. He must be out picking daisies. I got no answer at Confidential Commissions or his cell, so when you see him tell him I picked up an interesting nugget at the cop shop. I checked the crime reports and guess who called in a little while ago about a 'burglary,'" Marian's tone was skeptical, "of a forty-five pistol plus a box of bullets? Neva Wagner. She claims somebody broke a lock on the bottom drawer of Booth's desk. Doesn't know when. Admits they don't keep the house locked. Could have been anytime. No one had been in his office since Friday night until she went in this morning. So now we got a missing forty-five and a found thirty-two. Interesting, right? Thought Max would want to know. Got to see a woman about a cat. Joke." The connection ended.

Annie suspected that Max had checked his Caller ID and chosen not to answer and interrupt his time with Jean Hughes. She made quick notes on her pad. Max would be very interested, but maybe she was most interested of all. Once she had been assured that Tim had shot at his targets with a twenty-two but Booth died from a larger-caliber bullet, Tim's desperate flight had puzzled her.

A black paw whipped through the air, knocking the pen from her hand. Clicks and clacks marked Agatha's progress down the center aisle with the pen. Annie didn't mind. She had finished writing. She looked at her questions:

1. *What caliber gun caused Booth's death?*
2. *Why was Billy refusing to reveal information about the murder weapon?*
3. *In the clearing, when Tim was asked about the gun, was he thinking about the forty-five stolen from his stepfather's desk?*
4. *Shooting at cups with Booth's image obviously meant that Tim hated Booth. Why?*
5. *Max seemed convinced that Click Silvester was murdered, too. Was there a connection between Tim Talbot and Click Silvester?*

"A version of cat lacrosse back here. I think Agatha's winning." Ingrid sounded amused. "Do you need your pen?"

"She can keep it. Ingrid, there's someone I need to see. Do you mind if I leave again?"

Running the bookstore alone on a July weekend afternoon was akin to being the little Dutch boy with his finger in the dike.

Ingrid's response was quick and good-humored. "Not a problem. But maybe you can bring me back a Dr Pepper. I know we've got fancy fruit teas, but I have low tastes."

". . . Please ask Darren to call Max Darling." Max gave his cell number, then hung up. It was never very satisfactory to leave recorded messages. Max's face folded in a frown. He'd keep calling. Maybe Jean could suggest the names of Darren's friends. Maybe Click's "secret" role in the program was irrelevant. Maybe Click died in an accident. Maybe not.

Max picked up the PI report Jean Hughes had brought. He skimmed background information, Booth's hometown, college degrees, success as an entrepreneur in Atlanta. The personal information held his interest. Ellen became involved with an aspiring writer she'd met in a playwright group at a local bookstore. Shortly after the Wagners divorced, the writer moved to New York. By himself. Ellen's best friend said that Booth gave him a hundred thousand dollars to drop her. She said, "Booth was such a rat. He didn't care about Ellen, but he was furious that she'd leave him for someone else." They had been married for fifteen years. Neva was Booth's secretary. She was a widow with a nine-year-old son. Booth and Neva married a year after his divorce was final. Ellen Wagner lost custody of her daughter after she was charged twice with DUI. The PI picked up a news story about injuries suffered by Booth's stepson in an all-terrain vehicle accident on a Pigeon Mountain trail. An investigating officer indicated Booth had urged his stepson to go faster and the boy lost control. The vehicle rolled, resulting in a concussion, a cut on his face that required fourteen stitches, and a crushed leg.

The phone rang. Max looked at Caller ID. "Hey, Larry."

"Hey, Max. I wondered if I could drop by and talk to you for a minute. About all this stuff that's happened." He sounded dazed. "I was blown away when Jean called and said she's a suspect."

Max raised an eyebrow. Larry was a little slow if that hadn't occurred to him before. However . . . "I'm looking into some other possibilities."

"That's what she said. Anyway, I know something that maybe I should tell. I don't want to get involved, but I'll see what you think. I'll be there in a shot." A pause. "Guess that wasn't a good way to put it. See you in a minute."

Max was thoughtful as he replaced the receiver. Larry sounded uncomfortable. He'd obviously been thick with Booth in recent days. Maybe he knew something that mattered.

Definitely the PI report mattered. Max scanned the sheets and e-mailed a copy to Billy. Those bare factual bones could hold a lot of meaty resentment. As he slid the report into a folder, Max remembered Jean's farewell words. She stood in the doorway of his office, her face bleak. "You know, even if Booth didn't buy off Ellen's lover, he should have felt that he got the better of her. He married Neva. He got custody of Meredith. Ellen ended up alone and drinking too much. He should have blown off Ellen like yesterday's news. But he never forgot her. Booth hated Ellen."

Annie came around the corner of the hallway on the second floor of the inn. The corridor was cool and quiet and empty. Sun splashed through a far window. She had a quick memory of Ellen drunkenly searching her bag for a missing gun. That moment, embedded in her mind, had existed for a slight passage of time and was forever past. Annie had a sudden, eerie wonder of what else had occurred in the hallway of this old inn that left no physical impression but whose effects reverberated through time, lovers meeting clandestinely, conversations that changed minds or broke hearts or disturbed memories, a hand lifted to knock at the door, setting that person on an irrevocable path.

Would Annie's knock change lives?

She shivered. Before she could change her mind, turn and run as she wanted to do, she lifted the knocker, clacked it against its metal holder.

The door was yanked open. "Mo—" The eagerness in Meredith's heart-shaped face fled. Quick anger twisted her mouth. "You've got a nerve. If you hadn't run to the police, everything would be all right. I hope you're satisfied. They've taken Ellen off to jail. She'll be scared. I wanted to go with her. She told me to wait, she said that she'd be back, but I know she's scared. When you knocked, I thought she'd forgotten her key. Nobody else would come. Except you. And it's all your fault." Abruptly, she burst into tears and tried blindly to close the door.

Annie held tight to the doorjamb. "I'll help. In a way, that's why I've come." Helping one might hurt another, but murder could not be hidden. Tim's anguished face, Meredith's tears, which one's pain could be eased?

Meredith turned and stumbled away. Last night she'd looked fresh and crisp in a white cotton top and lavender shorts. This afternoon, the same clothes looked as though she had slept in them, as probably she had.

Annie followed, closing the door. The dead air smelled

strongly of whiskey. The beds weren't made though the covers had been pulled up. Annie stepped into the bathroom, found a clean washcloth, wet it with cool water.

Meredith stood at the window, which overlooked the parking lot and the strand of trees that bordered both the lot and the Haven. Her shoulders shook. She looked small in her wrinkled top and shorts.

Annie gently folded the washcloth into one hand. "Wipe your face. I'll get you some water."

Meredith swiped at her reddened eyes. "Can you help my mom?"

Annie spoke with total honesty. "If you believe she is innocent, then the more we can find out about who might have killed your dad, the better it will be for her."

Meredith's face brightened. "Mom wouldn't shoot anybody. She wouldn't hurt Dad."

"Why did she have a gun?"

Meredith drew in a sharp breath. "You don't understand. Ellen's kind of silly sometimes. Like a kid." The girl spoke as if she were old and understanding and awfully wise.

Annie felt a curl of sadness and wished that Meredith could be a child, thinking about dances and boys and dresses, not guns and loss and murder and her troubled mother.

"See, I can explain it all." Meredith's words were confident. "She wanted to have me home again. She got the gun because she thought it would give her courage to face Dad. Not that she wanted to shoot him. She didn't even have any bullets in the gun. She just wanted to have the gun in her purse and pretend she was like a spy going to a dangerous meeting. Knowing she had the gun would make her feel bigger." Meredith's don't-you-see-how-silly-that-was smile invited Annie to join in grown-up, kindly amusement at a child's nonsense.

But Ellen Wagner was no child.

"Anyway," Meredith waved her hand in dismissal, "she lost the gun."

Annie tried to sound positive. "Maybe she can give the police some idea where she lost the gun."

Meredith's face twisted again in worry. "She doesn't remember what happened. She really doesn't remember." Her tone was defensive. "Sometimes she has a little too much to drink when things are going bad. But the police know that Ellen and Dad," she paused, added in halting words, "didn't like each other."

Annie wasn't willing to go there. She was not going to push this child to reveal what she did or didn't know about her parents' emotional turmoil.

Annie smiled reassuringly. "Families get kind of complicated." Banal words; heart-twisting truth. "That's why I came to see you."

Meredith stiffened, her face wary.

Annie said gently, "I need to know about Tim." Did he kill your father? That's what she could have asked, but she didn't want to pose that question, not unless she felt she had no choice.

"Tim? Why?"

"Why did he hate your father?"

Meredith scrubbed at her cheek with the washcloth. "Dad was never scared about anything. He always said the world belonged to those who made it theirs." The words obviously were quoted. "He didn't ever like for anybody to be a weenie. I got thrown from a horse at camp last summer." There was an involuntary pulse in her throat. "When I got

home, Dad said I had to keep on riding. Once every week."
There was no joy in her voice. She looked surprised. "I
guess I don't have to go anymore."

"Do you like to ride?"

"I hate it. And that's kind of what happened to Tim. We
have ATVs and Dad liked to ride trails on the weekends.
Last year, Tim was riding his and Dad yelled at him to
go faster and he came up hard behind Tim and I guess
Tim got confused. Anyway, he turned the wrong way and
the ATV went off the trail and crashed. He's had to have
some operations and he has a scar on his face. He hasn't
ridden an ATV since. Dad said he had to get over it. We
were going out to ride next week. Dad said Tim couldn't
be a weenie."

But maybe he could. Now.

Max punched the number. How many places had he called
in the last hour? A half dozen at least. In the weblike way
of teenagers, each offered a likely name who might know
where Darren Dubois was. As the phone rang, a knock
sounded on his door. "Come in."

The panel swung in and Larry Gilbert stood in the doorway. Larry's angular face looked worried. Today he was
cool and crisp in a white short-sleeved shirt and tan slacks,
far different from his sweaty appearance late Friday morning at the Haven.

Max gestured for him to enter, waved at a chair, mouthed,
"Be right with you."

Larry's nod was agreeable.

Max turned back to the phone. "May I speak to Johnny
Sallis?"

"You got him." The teenage voice was very laid back.

Larry strolled to look at an orange-and-black geometric print, his back to Max and the conversation.

"Johnny, this is Max Darling. I volunteer at the Haven."

"Yeah." Supreme disinterest.

Johnny was obviously way too cool to be caught dead or alive at the youth center. Max quickly dangled bait. "You may have heard we had a murder at the Haven." Johnny might not be a big fan of the police, but it would be hard to resist a murder investigation. Television's *CSI* was a magnet for kids. "I'm trying to get word to Darren Dubois. He may be able to help figure out what happened. Darren was a close friend of Click Silvester. Click may have run into trouble because he knew too much." Max realized as he spoke that Billy Cameron might be irritated if gossip began to swirl that Click's death was no accident. Max felt a sudden determination. Maybe that kind of gossip would be a good thing. Maybe a murderer would begin to wonder how much else was known. "Darren may be in on some exciting stuff. If you see him, ask him to call me." Max repeated his cell number twice. He clicked off the phone. He looked up to see Larry staring at him in perplexity, dark brows drawn down, brown eyes intent, bony face furrowed.

Larry pointed at the phone. "Sorry. I couldn't help over-hearing. That sounds ominous. Have we got some kind of serious problem centered around the Haven?" He dropped into a chair to one side of the desk, clearly perturbed. "I'd already decided to call a board meeting next week with everything the way it is with Jean. But what's this about Click?"

"I think he was murdered." Max listed his reasons: Click's unexplained presence in the forest preserve, the oddness of a healthy teenager falling from a platform, the pulled-out pockets in his shorts, Click's excitement about his role Friday night though he wasn't on the program.

Larry appeared skeptical. "You have murder on your mind, Max. I don't remember which boy he was, but kids do funny things. Maybe he was going to meet a girl there. Maybe she stood him up. Maybe he climbed up because he was bored and had a misstep on the way down. Anyway, it's Jean who looks to be in trouble. She called to tell me she might be arrested Monday. She said you're trying to help her." He appeared plunged in gloom. "That's why I'm here." He stopped, his expression indecisive.

Max looked at him with full attention. Clearly, the businessman was struggling with knowledge of some sort. Yet he was skittish, much like a horse scenting a rattler. Max knew he needed encouragement.

"I'm glad you came." Max's tone was easy. "I was going to check in with you. You and Booth had some business dealings. You knew him well, the good and the bad. Tell me about the bad."

For an instant, Larry looked bemused. "Oh man, speak ill of the dead? I kind of hate to slam him now. Though I guess I have to go into a little background to explain why I'm here." He rubbed his knuckles against his cheek, obviously uncomfortable. "You have to understand that Booth saw most things as a big joke unless the laugh was on him. Like with his first wife. She got mixed up with this poet or writer of some kind. She was kind of a weak sister, if you know what I mean. Booth overwhelmed her. Anyway, when she left Booth, she thought she was going to marry this guy after the divorce. Booth laughed his head off when the guy took a hundred thou and beat it to New York. Minus Ellen. I mean," Larry's shrug was eloquent, "what was a hundred thou to Booth? He had the bucks to do whatever he wanted, whenever. That's how he and I got crossways. Man, was he mad at me."

Max grinned. "Did you fall for a poet?"

"Wish it had been that simple." Larry looked weary. "A friend told me about a sweet deal on a factory down in Nicaragua, going for a song. I told Booth, just one friend to another. It turned out my friend was trying to unload a loser. Booth bought the factory, and he lost a bundle. He told me he understood the deal wasn't my fault. I guess I should have known he wouldn't make nice with somebody he thought had gulled him. But it wasn't my fault." Larry looked aggrieved. "The other guy fooled me. And yeah, I picked up a little commission, but nothing to make it worth what it cost me eventually. Anyway, I thought Booth and I were still friends. About six months later, he tipped me to an Inverted Jenny stamp that belonged to somebody he knew, a woman who'd inherited it in a box of old stamps from her aunt and didn't realize what it was worth. Booth handled the deal, and I got the stamp for a half mil. One sold in an auction recently for almost nine hundred thousand so I knew I had a sweet deal. I guess if the market hadn't crashed I'd never have known that Booth had gigged me." His face hardened for an instant. "I needed money, bad. When I tried to sell, the stamp turned out to be a fake. Booth laughed his head off. That brings us up to a week or so ago. All of a sudden Booth tried to be chummy. He wanted my vote to get rid of Jean. Well, I saw my chance. I told him if he bought the stamp back at what I paid for it, my vote was his."

Max made no comment. On his legal pad, he sketched a precipice and a stick figure reaching for a rope.

Larry massaged his cheek again, slid his eyes away from

Max. "Maybe I don't come off looking swell, but I had to get the money."

Max sketched a snake. "Did you?"

Larry looked pleased. "Every penny. I told Booth I wanted the money signed, sealed, and delivered before the board met. That's why I was at his house Friday morning. He transferred the money online to my bank. But," Larry gave a heavy sigh, "that's why I saw what I saw. I wish I hadn't. Look, how bad is it for Jean?"

"Bad. Like she said, she may be in jail Monday." Max pointed at the papers spread across his desk. "If I don't come up with some credible reasons for Chief Cameron to keep looking, she's going to be in real trouble."

Larry stared at the papers. "That's what I was afraid of. I mean, I didn't mind seeing Jean fired. She got the job because Booth agreed to build the gym and it was pretty clear on what basis: Hire this woman. But to see her go to jail if maybe somebody else pulled the trigger, that's something else. I guess I don't have a choice. But I feel like a louse." He took a deep breath. "Okay, it's Friday morning. Booth asked me to come over. He told me to come on inside when I got there, that the door would be unlocked. I opened the front door and went straight to his office. Maybe I should have knocked, but it didn't occur to me. He was expecting me. Anyway, I opened the door and his daughter was standing behind his desk with the middle drawer open. She was holding a bank envelope, you know the kind they put cash in. Actually, I knew Booth kept ready cash in his desk." He stopped and shook his head. "It was like seeing a cartoon. Meredith held some bills in her other hand. When she heard the door, she swung around and if ever a kid looked terrified—and guilty—she did. I knew she was taking money on the sly. She knew I knew. We kind of looked at each other and then she started crying. She said, 'Don't tell Dad. Please don't tell him. I had to get some money. It's for my mom. She's broke.'"

Larry turned his hands over. "I don't know if I did the right thing. Maybe I didn't. I told her I wouldn't tell him. I told her to go on, that I hadn't seen her, didn't know she'd been in his office, and I was going to sit down and wait for him because we had some business, but she was invisible to me. I walked over to look at a painting, some damn ship scene. I heard the French window click. When I turned around, she was gone. The desk drawer was still open. I shut it and waited for Booth. I didn't tell him. As far as I was concerned, what was between him and his kid was between him and his kid."

Larry pushed back his chair. At the door, he looked back at Max. "I came to you because I know you'll do what's right for Jean. Try to do what's right for the kid, too."

Annie bent to pick up three folders resting on the back porch. Max balanced a grocery sack as he unlocked the back door. They almost always came into their lovely old house from the back porch.

Annie followed him into their redecorated kitchen. Annie still had that thrill of delight from the freshness of the countertops, wooden not granite, and an old-fashioned white wooden table that could seat eight. The food island did have a granite top, the better for Max when in the throes of culinary creation.

He put the sack on the food island. "How about shrimp Creole?"

"Great. I'll fix a salad in a minute. Tea?" As the tea brewed, she settled at the table with the folders. "Maybe one of the Intrepid Trio has discovered the fact that will unravel all." She kept her tone light, though she felt drained and weary. The pointer now seemed to be aimed squarely at Ellen Wagner and that argued even more misery for a child who'd watched her father die and might now lose her mother. Or was Meredith the prime suspect? Max believed Meredith's filching of money from her father's desk indicated desperation. Had Meredith been desperate enough to wish her father dead so that she would be able to take care of her mother? If not aimed at Ellen or Meredith, the pointer swung toward Tim Talbot. What would he have done to keep from taking to a trail in an ATV, his stepfather riding fast behind him?

As Max browned onions and green peppers, Annie held up the folders for his inspection. Each surely reflected its author. Emma's folder was blue. Her name adorned the cover in huge gilt letters. Of course, her name on her book covers was always a shiny gold and large enough to be read at thirty feet. Small black letters announced: closing the noose. Laurel's folder was a soft pink. On it she'd written in a looping script in bright red ink: lovers' plight. Henny's folder was plain white, the legend purple: nightmares.

Max drained freshly cooked shrimp, dropped them into the skillet, added his own homemade seasoned tomato sauce. "The rice is almost ready."

Annie put the folders aside. She stirred up Thousand Island dressing, then cut them each a quarter of crisp iceberg lettuce. Max could yearn for endive. Sometimes, especially on a steamy summer day, she had to have iceberg.

As they settled at the table, Annie read aloud the results of Emma's investigative foray. Annie was excited by Emma's discovery of the twenty-two rifle in the magnolia behind the stage. "That must be Tim's gun. Rachel and I found the plastic bags he used to wrap the rifle, but they were empty." She felt a lurch of her stomach. "If he had the gun Friday night and was up in a tree behind the stage, he must have intended to shoot Booth." What else could have been his plan? She pictured him climbing, careful with the gun, pausing to rest his leg, finding a sturdy branch. Had he sat on the branch, wrapped his good leg around it, lifted the rifle? Still, she clung to hope. "The officer said a bigger-caliber bullet killed Booth."

Max put down his fork. "Billy's keeping quiet about the gun. But maybe . . ." He pushed back his chair and retrieved the phone from the counter. He clicked on the speaker-phone. Billy answered on the first ring.

"Hey, Max." He sounded tired.

"Billy, what caliber bullet killed Booth?"

When Billy didn't reply, Max said temperately, "I know you keep a lid on information you acquire in an ongoing investigation. But the killer knows what caliber."

Billy gave a snort that might have been amusement or might have been irritation. "Right. Between us, the slug was damaged by bone. It was deflected into the heart. A lucky break for the shooter. Not so lucky for the victim. That's why he died so quickly. More tests will be run to try and determine the caliber."

"Billy, do you know enough to tell us one thing?" Annie heard the wobble in her voice, wished she didn't have a sad memory of Tim Talbot's face twisted in panic, the scar angry on his cheek. "Could the slug have come from a twenty-two?"

"Are you talking about the twenty-two Emma Clyde found? Nope. That rifle has nothing to do with the murder. But try to tell Emma that!" He sounded impatient. "I'll grant she was smart to have someone climb the tree. We checked the trees out thoroughly from the ground Friday night with flashlights and again in daylight. Problem is, the gun was balanced where it couldn't be spotted through the foliage. But we've now been over that magnolia from bottom to top and found nothing related to this investigation. Emma can't see beyond what she calls the Rectangle of Interest. If she tells me one more time that the case will only be solved when everything that happened there is revealed, I'm going to tell her to take her idea and," he drew a breath, "use it in her next book." Now he did manage a laugh. "Actually that is only roughly what I was thinking of telling her. Try to get her to back off, if you can. A text message an hour with her own creative abbreviations for *Close the Noose*." He snapped the letters, "'CLS TH NUS.' She's driving me nuts."

"I'll try." Annie knew that diverting Emma was as likely as Laurel taking vows of . . . Better not go there. "Billy, I know you're hassled, but could the slug have come from a forty-five?"

"Maybe. Maybe not. I suppose Marian tipped you about the reported theft of a forty-five from Wagner's desk. We don't know if there is a connection. We are considering every possibility." Billy clicked off.

Annie saw a silver lining. She looked at Max. "Why would Tim have his rifle there and also bring a forty-five? Does that make sense?"

Max speared a portion of lettuce. "It doesn't look good for him, even if the shot didn't come from a twenty-two. Apparently there was a forty-five in the Wagner house and now it's missing. Tim hated Booth. He blamed him for the accident. Tim's scheduled for more surgery, and every time he looks in a mirror he sees that scar. Then Booth set it up for them to go out and ride trails next week. How desperate was Tim not to do that?"

Annie shook her head. "He didn't need both a twenty-two and a forty-five." She took a second helping of the shrimp Creole. Max used just enough cayenne pepper for a flicker of heat. She picked up the pink folder. As she ate, she scanned Laurel's looping script. She knew Max was watching her, so she managed not to reveal her thoughts. Honestly, the pages crackled with fired-up libido. Laurel was . . .

Annie decided to concentrate on the message, not the messenger. Her lighthearted amusement fled when she finished. "Your mom thinks Neva Wagner dumped Van Shelton because she had a prenup that would have left her with nothing if she divorced Booth."

"Hey, Ma always gets the goods." His pride was evident.

Annie chewed energetically. That wasn't all Laurel got, but some things were better left unsaid.

Max was pumped. "The more we find out, the better it is for Jean. Billy can't ignore Tim Talbot's state of mind or a missing forty-five or an angry lover. Or the thirty-two found in the lake. Both a forty-five and a thirty-two are powerful."

Annie reached for Henny's folder. Annie read the contents aloud.

When she finished, Max looked somber. "So Tim Talbot's having nightmares." He glanced outside at the deepening shadows thrown by the pines as the sun slipped down, splashing the sky with cream, rose, vermilion, and mauve. "That has to get Billy's attention. Tomorrow we can tell him about Booth insisting Tim ride an ATV again and Meredith taking money from Booth's desk. Maybe by then I'll have found Darren Dubois."

Max cleared the table while Annie dished up fresh strawberries. She spooned a generous amount of Max's homemade whipped cream with a dash of rum.

She settled at her place. Mmm. Her favorite summer dessert.

Max stood at the counter with his dessert. "One more time. It may be the charm." He flipped on the speakerphone, punched a number.

"Hello."

"Is Darren there?"

"Just a minute. Phone, Darren." The woman's voice was relaxed and pleasant.

Max gave Annie a jubilant look.

"H'lo."

"Hi, Darren, this is Max. I've been trying to get in touch with you."

"Yeah?"

"Freddy said Click had something special planned for the program Friday night. Did he tell you anything about that?"

"Not a bunch. Something about an announcement."

Annie added another dollop of whipped cream to her bowl.

Max looked eager. "Did he explain why he was excited?"

"Excited?" Darren's voice was grim. "Yeah. He was excited. He thought he was going to be called up on stage. That's all I know for sure." The connection ended.

Max frowned at the phone. He shook his head and carried his dessert to the table. "Maybe Billy can get more out of him."

Annie ate a bit of strawberry and a bunch of whipped cream. To her, the proportion was perfect. "Why do you think he knows something more?"

Max poked his spoon toward the phone. "You heard him. He said, 'That's all I know for *sure*.' Didn't you hear the emphasis on 'sure'? That means he has some ideas about Friday night. I wish I knew why he's being so cagey."

∴ *Eleven* ∾

BILLY CAMERON TUGGED at the collar of his white shirt even though he'd loosened his tie. His suit coat hung from a coat tree. A steamy, sea-scented breeze flowed through his open office window. The ferry blasted its whistle. Ben Parotti's *Miss Jolene* was into its summer schedule of several crossings a day. In the distance, a white yacht glistened in the brilliant sunlight. Inside, the ceiling fan whirred, but the air was still hot. "Air-conditioning went out yesterday. Always happens in July." The police chief sounded morose, looked sweaty.

Annie knew Billy must have come to the station directly after church. "Have you had lunch?" She and Max had gone home from church and changed into summer casual and enjoyed a grilled-chicken salad and iced tea. A quick phone call had located Billy at the station.

"Mavis packed me a sandwich. I forgot about it. I'll get it out of the fridge in a minute." His desk was stacked with files. He looked at the paper wearily. "What have you got?" He made notes, abruptly looking sharp and intent as Annie described her talk with Meredith. "They were going to ride trails next weekend?"

Annie nodded. If Tim Talbot was innocent, this information couldn't hurt him. She wanted to believe he was innocent. Even though a twenty-two had been found in the tree behind the Haven stage, Booth had been killed by a larger-caliber bullet. But a forty-five was missing from his stepfather's desk.

Billy listened with interest as Max retold Larry Gilbert's account of Meredith and the money, but he shrugged when Max described his talks with Darren Dubois. "Get over it, Max. There's no proof Click Silvester was murdered. Maybe this Darren kid's blowing you off because there's nothing there. Guys aren't girls. They don't have to tell everything they know. If Click had a secret, maybe Darren didn't want to share it."

Max looked stubborn. "Why did Click die the afternoon before the program? Who pulled out the pockets of his shorts? What was taken? What was Click's big secret about Friday night? Why did Darren say that's all he knew for sure?"

Billy grinned. "Maybe that's all he knew for sure." Billy leaned back in his chair, the smile slipping away. "If Click was murdered, that means he knew something about Friday night and the murderer had to kill Click before Booth could be shot. Like what? You're not suggesting Click knew Booth was going to be killed. So what could the kid know? Maybe," there was a trace of sarcasm in his tone, "he saw Jean Hughes take the phosphorescent tape. Until somebody shows me a good reason why Click had to be killed, I don't buy murder. I've always liked 'Keep It Simple, Stupid.' Speaking about me," he was quick to make clear, "not you. So, KISS. What's simpler than Jean Hughes about to lose her job and get tossed from the cottage that means everything to her right now and she gets a gun and blows Booth away? She's right there at the lights. She's standing behind him when he's shot. It's important to focus on the main point. Who needed Booth dead immediately? Jean Hughes."

Annie never tired of the beach. The sturdy blue canvas umbrella offered plenty of shade. The breeze off the water made the beach ten degrees cooler than inland. They usually spent Annie's free Sunday afternoons on the beach. Annie and Ingrid alternated Sundays at Death on Demand. Annie insisted that she and Max keep to their schedule. They had done what they could do to help Jean Hughes. They—and the Intrepid Trio—had unearthed information that Billy was sure to consider. Yes, Jean was high on his suspect list, but Billy had made careful notes about Tim Talbot and Meredith Wagner. In the morning, Max would meet Handler Jones at the early ferry and Jean would have a lawyer present during her interview with Billy.

Annie contentedly smoothed on sunscreen, her nose wrinkling in appreciation of the coconut smell. She felt pleasantly soporific in the hazy heat, lulled by the recurring rumble of waves, the chirp of sea birds, and the occasional drone of a Coast Guard helicopter. She gazed through droopy eyelids at Max, wished he would relax. "TGIS," she encouraged, offering her own riff on TGIF. Actually, she loved each and every day, finding joy in godly Sunday, first-great-day-of-the-week Monday, infinite-possibilities Tuesday, organize-and-catch-up Wednesday, beginning-to-slow Thursday, think-about-it-next-week Friday, and have-a-party Saturday.

Max looked wry. "KISS."

Annie tried to sound alert, though she wanted to slip into a light nap. "Billy's got a point."

Max looked out at the green water. "I don't think so. I think everything's more complicated than Billy realizes." Abruptly, he sat up and pulled their beach carryall closer. "KISS is his mantra. I've got one, too. 'Never give up.'" He wiped his hand on a beach towel, pulled out his cell, punched a number. He waited, ended the call, punched another number, looked relieved. "May I speak to Darren, please?" He frowned. "No. I haven't seen him." Max listened, frowning. "If you'll give me directions, we'll be right there."

Dust rose in a cloud behind the car. "Maybe there's nothing wrong. His mother sounded upset, but guys get busy and forget to call home. It won't hurt to talk to her. If he shows up, maybe she'll push him to tell us what he knows."

Annie felt sticky in the T and shorts she'd pulled on. Max looked beach-scruffy as well.

The sandy road curved around a stand of pines. Max slowed as a dusky red white-tailed deer and her fawn crossed in front of the car. Occasional small frame houses, many well-kept, some dilapidated, sat at the end of rutted drives. They passed hunting cabins and a derelict apartment house with boarded-over windows.

Annie glanced at a sketchy map Max had drawn. They passed Whooping Crane Pond. On the map, a stick-figure bird was in the center of a wavy oblong. Oleanders bloomed near a mailbox with DUBOIS lettered in red paint.

A tall, slim blonde stood on the front porch of the neat gray shingle house. She hurried down the steps as they got out of the car. "Darren was going to be home in time for us to catch the two o'clock ferry. He didn't come. His cell didn't answer. Everybody I called said you kept trying to get in touch with him about Click Silvester. I thought he might be with you. You kept calling for him and now he's disappeared." Her tone was accusing.

The front door was open. Through the screen door came the faint sound of a telephone.

She whirled and ran, the screen door slamming behind her.

Annie and Max stopped on the porch, looked into the small living room at wicker furniture with cushions, a braided oval rug, a maple coffee table, a laptop computer on a card table.

She held the phone with a hand that shook. "This is Darren's mother. Have you seen him anywhere? Do you know where he is? . . . Please ask everyone to look for him. Call me if you hear anything at all." She put down the phone, darted to the screen door, held it open. She brushed back a strand of long, straight blond hair. She had wide-set blue eyes, aquiline features, and, for now, a somber gaze. "My name's Mickey. Why did you want to talk to Darren about Click? Click's dead."

Lines grooved Max's face. "He was Click Silvester's friend. Yesterday morning I asked Darren if he knew why Click went to the nature preserve."

She stared at him, her gaze never wavering.

"Darren said he didn't know. It was later that another friend told me that Click had been excited about the Friday night program at the Haven, that he was part of a big secret. Click didn't live long enough to come to the program. I wanted to know about that secret. I wanted to know if Click told Darren what was going to happen Friday night.

When I talked to Darren late yesterday, I thought he was evasive."

She stared at him incredulously. "Are you crazy? Do you think Click knew somebody was going to shoot that man?"

Max shook his head. "No. Click was excited, cheerful. Whatever he knew, he didn't expect anything bad. Click said there was going to be a big joke played that night. The man who died was known for his jokes. My guess is that Click knew about a plan that Click thought was fine, but it wasn't, and that's why he had to die."

"Click had to die?" She lifted a hand to her throat.

"I think Click was murdered."

Mickey Dubois walked to a wicker chair, slumped into it. Her face was pale and drawn. "I encouraged Darren to hang out with Click. Click was so steady. Darren can be," she twisted her hands in her lap, "a wild man. He butts up against authority. I can't tell you how many times he's done crazy things just to see if he could or because somebody dared him. His dad," she swallowed hard, "was a Green Beret. He was killed in Iraq. If he'd come home, he would have known how to handle Darren."

Annie felt the beginning of fear.

Max took a deep breath. "Darren and Click were buddies. Darren's a smart kid. Click died Thursday. Booth Wagner was murdered Friday night. Maybe Click told Darren something about Friday night and Darren was keeping an eye on somebody. Maybe he put things together after Wagner's murder."

She stared at him in growing fear. "You think Darren knows something about that shooting?"

"I'm afraid so. If Darren thought somebody killed Click, what would he do?"

She scarcely managed to speak, her voice a whisper. "He'd do whatever he thought needed to be done."

"Do you think he'd try to go after the killer by himself?"

"He might. Oh dear God, he might."

Max was brusque. "If Darren got in touch with the murderer, he put himself in great danger."

She lifted a trembling hand, pressed it against her lips. Her words were indistinct. "Something's happened to Darren. He'd call me if he could. He was excited we were going into Savannah for a baseball game." Mickey swallowed hard. "He's been counting on the game for weeks. He rode his bike downtown to take a book back to the library. There's a deposit bin there. But he hasn't come home. Darren and Click. They were always together. And now . . ."

A knock rattled the screen door. "Police."

Annie knew that voice. Officer Hyla Harrison was serious, purposeful, calm. She always spoke with deliberation. This afternoon her voice was essentially toneless, carefully without inflection. Annie drew in a wavering breath.

Mickey Dubois rushed to the door, her dangly earrings jangling.

Officer Harrison, freckles prominent on her pale face, stared forward. "Is this the home of Darren Dubois?"

"Yes." Darren's mother barely managed the word.

Officer Harrison's eyelids flickered. She spoke in a rush. "Ma'am, if you'll come with me. Your son needs you."

The Meducare Air transport lifted up from the center of the harbor pavilion park. The *whop-whop* of its engines reverberated across the boardwalk and the harbor. The helicopter rose straight up, its yellow top and white undercarriage bright in the hot sunshine. Annie thought it looked too small to hold the gravely wounded boy and his mother and medical personnel. The helicopter banked and turned, its destination acute care in Savannah.

Men in polo shirts and shorts were crowded on the deck of a docked cabin cruiser in the marina at the harbor. Officer Lou Pirelli, notebook in hand, spoke to a hulking man in a white polo and white slacks. Several fishermen waited solemnly by their bait buckets and rods on the boardwalk. Billy Cameron spoke with a man in his sixties, who gestured at Fish Haul Pier.

Marian Kenyon wrote furiously. "They ID'ed the kid as Darren Dubois."

Max watched the helicopter as it turned into a small speck in the western sky. "Yes."

"He's the one you were trying to find." Marian quivered with excitement. "Now he's been shot. Just like Wagner. I picked up the call on the scanner. 911s in a flurry from the pier around one o'clock."

Annie felt cold. They'd arrived on the beach about a quarter after one, seeking solace in the sun. By that time, Darren already lay wounded.

"I got here pronto. I've already talked to some of the guys who were fishing on the pier. Everything was cool. They had their lines out and the catch had been good, lots of yellowfin croakers and spottail bass. One guy had his boom box, said it was playing 'Sitting on the Dock of the Bay,' another day in paradise and everybody having fun. Nobody paid any attention when the kid walked out on the pier about one o'clock. He didn't have any fishing gear but hey, people walk out on the pier just to look. Paul Tucker—you know him, Max, the high school math teacher—barely noticed him, not to recognize at that point. He was just a teenage guy slouching along on the pier, but Tucker said he knew something was odd when the kid stopped and pulled some scruffy old gardening gloves out of his pocket and pulled them on. I mean, he didn't have any equipment with him, so why the gloves? Paul kept watching. The kid knelt on the south side of the pier and bent over the side like he was looking for something. In a minute he stood. He had an envelope in his hand. He was holding it real carefully on the edges. He looked real serious. That's when the shot came. One shot from the woods." She pointed at the trees opposite the pier. "Paul said everything was in slow motion. Guys yelled. Somebody shouted for everybody to get down. Paul hit the boards and his rod flipped into the water. The kid's shirt turned bloody. He fell forward into the middle rail. He banged his head hard, then flopped into the water. People started calling 911. When no more shots came, Paul rolled to his feet and ran and dived in. He found him pretty quick and pulled him up and swam to shore. Everybody helped them out of the water. He was still breathing, but he kept bleeding and the side of his head was swelling. When Doc Burford got here, he immediately had them call Meducare. Doc said the only hope was to get him quick to the acute trauma center. Paul identified him. He'd had Darren in class. Meantime, the cops arrived and searched the woods. They didn't find anybody."

Annie pictured the teenager walking to the edge of the pier, leaning down . . . "Darren must have told the murderer to put the envelope there. An envelope . . . that sounds like blackmail." What price friendship?

Max shook his head. "Click was his buddy. I don't believe Darren would protect his murderer."

Annie felt sad. "His mom said he was wild and crazy. Funny he'd wear gloves." Annie's face changed. "Why do people wear gloves?"

He looked blank. "Because they're cold or protecting their hands."

Annie looked solemn. "Or to keep from leaving fingerprints. Don't you see? Darren didn't want his fingerprints on that envelope. What if he saw something, knew something, but didn't think anyone would believe him? What if he decided to test out his idea, pretend to blackmail someone? An envelope stuffed with money and with someone's finger-prints on it would be enough to take to the police. He wore gloves because he didn't want to mess up the evidence."

Max remembered the daredevil climber and the misery in his eyes. "Wild and crazy. And brave." The gloves might well indicate Darren was trying to set a trap. He didn't want his fingerprints on the envelope. He figured anybody who paid blackmail wouldn't be thinking the envelope would ever be fingerprinted. Blackmailers don't run to the cops. But Darren was no blackmailer. He was a kid on a mission. "I suppose he thought he'd be safe if he set up the drop spot and came to get the envelope when there were plenty of people around. A sweet idea, but the killer had a sweeter one. I expect Darren made his approach yesterday. The killer probably visited the pier late last night and put out the bait. Today the killer was in the woods at one, waiting. Dar-ren retrieved the envelope, and that's when the shot came."

The tall, slender black woman stood behind the screen door of the small house, stiff and straight as a sentinel. "You don't need to come here. My boy doesn't know anything about Darren Dubois." Fear held her rigid, fear and an angry determination to protect her son. She still wore a lovely rose silk dress from church, but there was no peace in her face.

Max was amazed that word of Darren's shooting had al-ready spread. Obviously, his efforts to speak to Darren were part of a wildfire of speculation.

A German shepherd lying on the porch came to his feet and growled softly in his throat, his hackles rising.

"Thunder." Her command was crisp.

The dog stopped. He watched Max with dark brown, unblinking eyes.

"Mrs. Baker, Freddy won't be in any danger if I talk to him. Darren Dubois was shot because he threatened a killer. Darren didn't tell what he knew. The safest thing for Freddy is to answer my questions. You and Freddy can tell everyone you know what he's said. It will be obvious Freddy isn't a threat to anyone."

She slapped her hands on her hips. "How is this killer going to know Freddy's not a threat?"

Max was blunt. "Freddy isn't going to try and catch a murderer."

"Mama, please, it's Max." Freddy Baker tugged at his mother's arm.

"Frederick."

At her word, he dropped his hand and turned back into the living room.

She opened the door, stepped onto the porch. Arms folded, she stared at Max, her gaze as watchful as the shepherd's. "How can you be sure Darren contacted the murderer?"

Max understood her terror. One teenage boy dead, another in intensive care, and, according to the latest word, not expected to recover. Both were regulars at the Haven. Both were her son's close friends. She knew there was danger but to her the threat was formless, boundless, might at this moment be waiting to ensnare Freddy.

Max spoke quietly but firmly. "Darren saw something Friday night. He tried to set a trap for the killer." Max described the pier and the envelope and Darren's gloves. "We think he intended to take the envelope to the police as proof of what he'd figured out. Instead, the murderer shot him." Darren had been clever, but not quite clever enough.

Mrs. Baker regarded him stonily. "Freddy doesn't know anything about the shooting Friday night. I've been over it and over it with him. If he knew anything, he'd have told the police. I raised my kids to do what's right. As for Darren, Freddy didn't talk to him yesterday. Freddy heard about you hunting for Darren, but that's all he knew."

"I'm sure Freddy doesn't know about the murders. I want to talk to him about Click Silvester and what Click had been doing the last few days." Max hoped the question sounded innocuous enough.

"Mama." Freddy edged open the front screen. "Click was my friend." His eyes were shiny with tears. "Let me help find out what happened to him."

She took a deep breath, pressed a hand against one temple as if she had a headache. "All right. But we're talking out here on the porch in front of God and everybody. Freddy doesn't have anything to hide."

Freddy slipped through the door and stood beside his mother. Eyes huge, he stared solemnly up at Max.

Max kept his tone easy. "This isn't anything hard, Freddy. Tell me about a usual day for Click, as far as you know."

Freddy relaxed a little. "He got up and got his little brother ready to come to the Haven. They always got there in time for breakfast. Click helped his brother start his project. If Click was working, he went to the computer store. Click loved working there. Mr. Ramirez was real nice to him."

Max felt that he was grabbing smoke. Somewhere in Click's final days lay the answer to his death. Somehow, some way, Click had become privy to knowledge that he thought was innocent, but a killer knew otherwise. For some reason, Click had to die before Booth Wagner could be shot. "Did Click work Thursday?"

"I don't think he was at the shop." Freddy spoke slowly,

squinted in thought. "He said he'd been kind of scared to do a job, but he was going to get a big bonus, enough to buy a scooter, and he was going to give me the first ride on it." Tears rolled down Freddy's thin cheeks.

Max scarcely dared to breathe. Maybe a tiny ray of light was beginning to shine from behind the black cloud that obscured Click's death. "Was he getting the bonus for a computer job?" Max remembered the white cotton lining of Click's pulled-out pockets.

Freddy looked uncertain. "I think so. We'd been talking about his repair work and he said he'd been off on a private job. Click said he'd fixed everything in only a few minutes. Then he started talking about Friday night and there being a big secret at the program and how he was going to be recognized."

Cocoa brown mudflats steamed as the tide ebbed in the salt marsh. Fiddler crabs scurried, seeking algae and rotting marsh grass. Annie took a deep breath of the distinctive brackish smell. She looked out from the wooded path at the back of the lovely white cottage. This afternoon there was only the music of the low country, the chitter of birds, the rustle of cattails, the whirr of insects. The quiet figure on the back porch, again wrapped in the white-and-red quilt, sat with her chin on her hand, watching the marsh. Greenish-golden spartina grass rippled in the onshore breeze. Jean's sister exuded an aura of peace.

Annie didn't want to disturb the tranquility of that frail observer. Annie waited, hoping Jean would step out on the porch. Annie's mission was simple: tell Jean of the attack on Darren and find out if she saw Darren Friday night. Minutes slipped by. Annie almost turned to walk away. The inn was nearby. Meredith might be able to help pinpoint Darren's movements Friday night as well. But she needed to talk to Jean.

Annie walked out of the woods and onto the oyster-shell path.

When she reached the back steps, a thin face turned toward her. "Hello." The faint voice was gentle.

"Hello." Annie felt awkward and intrusive. She stopped on the second step. "I'm Annie Darling and I hoped to talk to Jean."

"Oh." The quick cry was glad and welcoming. "You and your husband been kind to Jean. Won't you come up? I'm Giselle, Jean's sister. She's over at the Haven but she hoped to be back soon. Please sit down. There's tea in the pitcher and ice in the bucket. If you wouldn't mind fixing your own glass. I don't get up and down very easily now." There was no complaint in her voice, simply calm acceptance.

"I don't want to trouble you."

The delicate face softened in a swift, sweet smile. "You are no trouble. Please come and tell me what's happening."

Moving as if in a dream, surrounded by the soft sounds of summer, Annie poured a glass of tea and sat opposite Giselle. Annie hesitated, then felt complete certainty that Giselle would be saddened by the latest violence, but would meet whatever came with calm. "Another teenager from the Haven has been hurt." Annie described Darren and the attack on the pier. "I'm hoping Jean might have noticed Darren Friday night. If we ask enough people, we may be able to find out what he did and where he stood." At some point and in some place, Darren saw something that linked a murderer to his crime. Now he lay in intensive care, gravely injured.

"I'm sorry. To be near death when you are young and well, that is a great tragedy. Jean will be upset." Giselle was suddenly abrupt. "I hope that policeman understands that

Jean would never harm a child. Never in all the world. Yes, she was angry with Booth. But Jean had worked everything out. She agreed to resign. That's what he wanted. All she cared about was keeping our place here until I leave." She spoke as if she might be walking into another room. "I wouldn't have minded if we moved. I told her that, but she made a joke of it, said she'd wanted time off and now she had it, and we'd be fine and she'd spend every day with me." Giselle leaned forward. "Don't you see? Jean was looking forward to our time together. Besides, she could never even shoot a rabbit. Daddy hunted and wanted us to be good with guns. But Jean would only shoot at a target. Once Daddy said, 'Somebody has to keep the rabbit population down.' Jean told him she would never kill a living thing, no matter what. So that policeman is silly. I know everything will work out eventually. Jean and I will be all right. She's afraid she'll be arrested and she's arranged for a friend of ours to come tomorrow. Of course, we can't complain when those families are struggling with so much sadness. I know everything will be all right eventually. Jean will be cleared."

Annie looked at Giselle and knew there was no guile in her soul. Billy would know that, too. Maybe everything was going to be all right for Jean. The right answer from Giselle could spell the end of suspicion. "Was Jean here with you at one o'clock?"

"She left to go to the Haven about twelve thirty. She wants to be sure everything is in order for Rosalind." Her voice fell. "Just in case."

Annie felt a wave of sadness. Once again Jean was a suspect with no alibi. The woods opposite Fish Haul Pier were no more than a brisk five-minute walk from the Haven.

∽ *Twelve* ∾

Two LITTLE GIRLS pumped high on swings. Three boys, one after another, flung old towels on a slide, scooted down without touching the hot metal. A stocky dark-haired man flipped burgers on a grill. A little girl pointed at a piñata swinging from a tree. A cheerful woman gave her a hug. "After we eat, Rosalie. Not long now."

Max avoided a game of tag and came up to the grill. "Hey, José. Can I talk to you for a minute?"

Sweat rolled down José Ramirez's face from the sun and the grill. He looked surprised.

Max knew José was always willing to come at night or on weekends for a computer disaster, but crashing a family birthday party might strain even his good humor. Max hurried to explain. "I'm sorry to bother you. This will only take a minute." Less than a minute if José had no answers. "I need to know what Click Silvester was working on last week."

José's quick flicker of irritation was succeeded by a look of sadness. "Poor kid. I can't believe he's dead. How could he fall off a platform? That seems crazy to me. Click didn't even like to be outside. What was he doing out in the woods?" José shook his head.

"I think he was there to get some bonus money for a special computer repair job he'd done that morning."

José frowned, put down the spatula. "Not for me."

"You weren't aware he had a private job?"

José folded his arms across his white apron with red letters proclaiming: DAD, THE WORLD'S BEST COOK. "At my shop, anything he brought in, he got ten percent of the payment. I paid him ten bucks an hour." José glanced at the grill, grabbed the spatula, and began to flip burgers. "There was one exception. He did a lot of work for the Haven. That was separate from our deal." He looked up, yelled, "Line up for burgers." As kids pressed forward, paper plates in hand, José gave a last glance at Max. "If he got a bonus for some job for the Haven, that would have been private."

The ceiling fan whirred, but did little to lessen the heat. The Haven didn't have air-conditioning. Jean's white face looked empty. "Click dead. And you say Darren may die." She jerked up her head and stared at Annie. "I don't believe Click did anything dishonest. Or Darren, either."

"Click was keeping a secret about Friday night. No one thinks Click knew Booth was going to be shot, but he knew something and we think he told Darren Dubois. It may be something simple, like so-and-so and I are going to play a big joke on Mr. Wagner. Maybe Friday night Darren wondered if the joke was still going to be played. Maybe," and she warmed to the idea, talking fast, "when the evening began Darren was just curious and he kept an eye on the person Click named. Instead of a joke, Darren saw something that linked that person to Booth's murder. But he didn't have any proof. Max thinks he was trying to get proof, and that's why he was shot."

Jean sighed. Her eyes held knowledge. "That could have happened. Darren was fearless. He liked to take chances. Once I found a rat snake curled up in the bottom drawer of my desk. Darren put it there on a dare." Her smile was trembly. "I couldn't be mad. He was impish, but always cheerful and awfully nice to the little kids."

Annie glanced at the old walnut desk. "Don't you have a drawer with a lock?"

Jean shook her head. "I don't believe in locking things up. The board got onto me about that after we had some petty thefts even though that was cleared when a certain family left the island. A kid who needed a lot more attention than she ever got. Anyway, I told the board I wasn't going to treat the kids like they were thieves. Everybody knew I don't believe in locking things up. Miss Prentice—" Jean looked inquiringly at Annie.

Annie nodded. Indeed, she knew Pauline Prentice never met a lock she didn't love.

"—Was appalled. I told her if you treat kids with no respect, they'll earn it." For an instant, Jean's lips quirked in a smile. "She didn't get it at first. Then she stared at me with eyes like a dead fish. She insisted we lock up the outer doors and the prop shed, but there are no locks inside the Haven, not in my office, not in the art rooms, not in the kitchen, and there won't be as long as I'm director." Her smile fled. "Which I guess won't be for very long. Billy Cameron thinks I shot Booth. But surely he'll know I couldn't have hurt Click or Darren." Suddenly her eyes were bright with tears. "You and Max have been wonderful to me."

Annie wished she could announce with conviction that all

would be well. Instead, she feared the net was drawing ever tighter around the Haven. Everything had a connection to the Haven, Jean had no alibi when Darren was shot, and she grew up with guns. When Billy learned that . . . Perhaps he already knew. He would have sent out inquiries about Jean.

"Why do you believe in me?" Jean's voice was shaky.

"If you'd planned to shoot Booth, you would never have come to Max in the first place. But," Annie pulled her chair nearer the desk, "we need to do what we can to help the police find the murderer." She hoped her voice was upbeat. "Did you see Darren Friday night?"

Jean leaned back in her chair, stared at the open window, but clearly she wasn't looking at the playing field. "I saw him at one point. I find it hard now to know what I remember. I was pretty upset because I knew I was on my way out, but I didn't want the program ruined for the kids. I was thinking about what I was going to say. Booth wanted me to do a farewell speech, but he didn't tell me whether I'd come first or last. I was determined to be positive. So everything is kind of a blur. I was all over the place, saying hello to people, checking on the food and drinks, helping kids with their costumes."

Annie pointed through the window at the field. "Close your eyes and think of Darren."

Obediently, Jean closed her eyes. "Darren . . . not part of the program . . . free food . . . Oh, I saw him getting cookies . . . lots of people . . . I checked the green room . . . that was a kind of holding pen near the dock . . . all the costumes were there . . . everybody pulled on a costume over T-shirts and shorts . . . later when it was getting dark . . ." Her eyes popped open. "I saw Darren moving quickly toward the back of the field. There were people still milling around, who hadn't taken their seats yet. I think Darren was following someone. You know how it is in a crowd, someone is trying to keep up and they kind of weave in and out without paying too much attention to the people around them. That's what it looked like." She shook her head in discouragement. "I don't know who he was following."

"Who else did you see?"

She looked puzzled. "I guess I saw everyone at one point or another."

Annie leaned forward. "I'm not talking about the whole evening. Who else did you see at that moment?" One name could lead to another and another until finally perhaps someone saw Darren in close pursuit of a killer.

Jean frowned in concentration, then her eyes lit. "Meredith Wagner. She was walking in the same direction as fast as she could go." Jean looked concerned. "Meredith's a sweet, sweet girl. I imagine she was looking for her mother. Meredith told me she was staying at the inn. I could tell Meredith was worried about her. When she spoke of her mother, it was as if she were talking about a child, one who needed care. I doubt if she was noticing much."

Annie smiled. "I'll ask her."

Outside a car door slammed.

Jean looked strained. She pushed back from her desk, walked to the window to look out. "The police." Her face was stiff.

Annie took a step toward her. "Would you like for me to stay?"

Jean swallowed. "That's all right. They'll want to know if I can help them with Darren."

In the hall, Annie came face-to-face with Officer Benson. He gave her a friendly nod, then walked purposefully past. He stopped in the open doorway of Jean's office. "Ms. Hughes, if I can speak to you for a moment, I'd appreciate some information about a teenager who spent time here."

"Come in, officer." Jean's voice was weary.

Annie came out into the blazing heat. She walked fast, heading for the path that led through the woods to the inn. She had an uneasy sense of events in motion. She hoped at the end of the day Jean Hughes would still be free.

Annie plunged into the woods. Despite the shade, the air was as hot as a steam bath. A bumblebee buzzed near. She waved her hands and arms. She was absorbed in fighting off insects and almost walked into the huge web of a golden silk spider. Annie caught her breath and jumped back. That's when she saw the alligator. He was nine feet long if he was an inch. Oh well, maybe six feet. But he was big and he was lying right across the path. She began to retreat. Quietly. Circumspectly. Respectfully. Oh yes, big fellow, very respectfully. Sweaty and breathing fast, she backed up, one careful foot after another. No matter that naturalists insisted Al Alligator didn't want to munch on humans. Annie had no intention of tempting the many-toothed creature. She was almost around the corner, out of sight of the black creature that could, if he wished, outrun her, when her cell phone rang. She plunged her hand into her purse, fumbled, found the phone, lifted it. "Hello." She listened then said quickly, "Don't be upset, Rachel. I'll come. Wait for me."

Even though it was Sunday afternoon, the police station was in full gear, officers in and out, Mavis at the front counter on the phone. She looked up, saw Max, gave a little head shake, and continued to listen. "Please come to the station. An officer will be glad to take your statement. Thank you."

She hung up, sighed. "Everybody in town thinks they know something and you have to pay attention. One of them might be right." She shook her head. "This caller claims a sinister-looking man came out of the woods on a bike right after the shot. For starters, I don't think she could have heard a shot that far from the pier. But it might help to find anybody who was in the woods around that time."

Max gestured toward the door to the offices. "I've got something for Billy."

Mavis looked uncertain. "He's on overload right now, sorting out everything about the shooting." She punched a button. "Max Darling's here."

There was a pause, then a gruff, "Okay."

Billy's office door was open. Sweat patched his white shirt. He was replacing the phone receiver in its cradle, his face hard and angry.

Max paused on the threshold.

Billy looked up. It took a moment for him to focus on Max. "Darren's dead. He died without regaining consciousness. Another kid dead."

Max felt his gut twist. "Maybe Annie and I should go to Savannah, help his mom."

Billy shook his head. "She's staying with her sister there. I don't think you're the right person to offer help." He looked tired and impatient. "If you've got something for me, make it quick."

Max talked fast. "Freddy Baker said Click had done a special computer job. I checked with José Ramirez. The job didn't come through his shop. They had an agreement, everything Click brought in, he got a slice. He was paid ten dollars an hour except for stuff he did at the Haven. That was separate. I think Click was in the preserve to meet someone and get paid. My guess is that Click took his money and when he turned to go down the ladder, he was maybe whacked from behind, maybe shoved. The murderer came down, made sure he was dead, then pulled out his pockets to get the money. Click was getting enough to buy a scooter. That kind of money in his pockets would have indicated something wasn't right. Click told Freddy he was part of a big joke with someone. He must have told Darren who was going to pay him. That's why Darren was watching Friday night to see what would happen."

Billy massaged one temple. "You keep tying everything to computers. Back up a minute, Max. Click told Freddy he had a special computer job. He also told him he was going to be part of a big joke at the program Friday night. Maybe," Billy spoke clearly and distinctly, emphasizing each word, "these were two different matters. One, a computer job. Two, a joke. Maybe they're connected. Maybe they aren't. Maybe it's the joke we need to find out about. As for computer repair, that brings everything right back to the Haven." He thumped the legal pad on his desktop.

"Billy," Max was insistent, "there are plenty of people with motives besides Jean Hughes."

Billy leaned back in his chair. "You're right. Adulterous wife. Her angry lover. Stressed stepson. Light-fingered daughter. Bitter ex-wife. I've considered all of them. There's not a shred of evidence to link any one of them to Wagner's murder."

"How about intent?" Max objected. "Using your stepfather's image as a target should qualify."

Billy shrugged. "The family better get him to a shrink, but his twenty-two had nothing to do with the murder. You're right about intent. Lugging a gun to the woods and perching up in a tree with a great view of the outdoor stage kind of suggests he had bad ideas. But the five-shot magazine was full. Either he didn't shoot the gun Friday night or he reloaded before he climbed down that magnolia. Under the circumstances, lights off, people yelling, that doesn't seem likely. Besides, no twenty-two bullet killed Wagner. I called Tim's mother. She's agreed I can talk to him this afternoon. I'll take the gun with me, give it to his mother, tell her he needs help. As for the others, they were at the Haven but," Billy sat upright and looked like a triumphant fisherman admiring a four-hundred-pound blue marlin, "only one person had to kill Wagner Friday night. The timing gives her away. Booth had Jean Hughes cornered. Give up the job or jerk her dying sister out of the place she loved. When the program started, Hughes had only minutes more to be the Haven director. Turns out, she's still the director and still in the cottage. When the program started, Booth Wagner had only minutes to live."

Max tried again. "Maybe the timing had to do with Click's work on a computer. Maybe that had to be kept secret before he was murdered."

Billy still looked triumphant. "Maybe. But you heard his boss. The only repair work Click did that wasn't funneled through the shop was for the Haven. You've got plenty of ideas. I've got some, too. Maybe Click was deleting something from Jean Hughes's computer that would have nailed her. Was she skimming some money off purchases? Had she sent a threatening e-mail to Wagner? We're going to check all of that out. As for the big joke, we may never know."

Her eyes like saucers, Rachel jumped into the passenger seat before Annie had the car fully stopped. "I didn't do a thing, but she was all over me, like everything was my fault. She wasn't making sense. She said I had to come and tell her where he is. She hung up on me before I could say anything. When I tried to call back, the line was busy."

Annie loved the sleepy lane where Pudge and Sylvia and Rachel and Cole lived. Comfortable houses were surrounded by live oaks and palmettos, willows and crape myrtle. The unpretentious rambling ranch house was perfect for her dad. Occasionally, she felt a pang at how much her own mother would have loved the house and how sad it was that misunderstandings could part two people who had loved each other. Her mother had died much too young. Annie was glad Pudge had found happiness. She liked her stepmother, and she especially enjoyed watching coltish Rachel grow up, sometimes coolly sophisticated, other times flustered and uncertain.

Now Rachel's dark eyes were stark with fear. "I heard about Darren. Everybody's been texting. But not Tim. He doesn't have any friends. You know how people are. Tim's kind of jerky and rude. When somebody talks to him, he always turns the good side of his face toward them. I know guys aren't supposed to be vain, but I think he minds a lot about that scar. Some of the guys called him Scarface. You know," there was a plea in her voice, "if he had handled it right, you know, said he was the original for the movie, they'd have thought he was cool." She sat hunched forward. "Can't you go faster?"

Annie picked up speed, but she slowed as she came around a curve. This was the season for visitors on bikes. The Wagner house was a Mediterranean-style mansion on the ocean. Annie didn't understand why anyone would choose to live in a ten-thousand-square-foot house, one of the largest on the north end of the island. Most of the huge homes were within the south end gated community. "Okay, Neva Wagner called you and said Tim is missing. Missing from where? Why did she call you?"

Rachel twined a dark strand of hair around one finger, talked faster and faster. "See, I'm about the only name she found in his phone. I mean, I told him the other day that sometimes if he wanted to call someone, you know, just to say how awful everything was, I liked to gripe, too. Once when he called he said wasn't it the pits to have a stepfather. I didn't tell him how great Pudge is. I mean, what good would that do? I said something like life is complicated. He said the only thing that would make his life better would be if Booth died. And he hung up. Anyway, a little while ago his mother called and asked if I'd seen him. She was real upset."

Annie turned into a drive lined by live oaks. There was a disconnect to Rachel's narrative. "Why is she upset? Had they quarreled?"

Rachel turned a worried face toward Annie. "He was supposed to come down to the living room when the police came to talk to him about the twenty-two. When he didn't, she went up to his room. She found a note. It said," she took a deep breath, " 'Mom, I'm sorry about everything.' "

Annie braked behind a police car. Several people clustered on the broad front steps of the stucco mansion. Neva Wagner faced Billy Cameron, who stood with his arms folded, frowning. He glanced at Annie's car, turned his attention back to Booth's widow.

Neva was crisply dressed in a cream silk blouse and black linen slacks and black lattice slide pumps. Her mother-of-pearl necklace matched her earrings. She was as elegant as usual, but fear glittered in her dark eyes. Despite delicately applied makeup, her face looked gaunt and pale.

Rachel grabbed and held Annie's hand as they started toward the house. Broad marble steps reflected the late-afternoon sunlight. Heat rebounded from the concrete drive.

Neva looked at them blankly, then hope lit her eyes and she hurried down the steps. She ignored Annie, stared at the girl. "Are you Rachel? Do you have any idea where Tim might be? You're the last person he talked to on his cell."

Billy joined them. His face was red and perspiring in the unshaded drive.

Rachel shot an uncomfortable sideways glance at Annie. "Tim phoned last night and asked me not to tell anyone about the gun. I had to tell him my sister called the police. He said," and her voice quivered, "he thought I was his friend, then he hung up on me."

Neva looked stricken. "If you don't know where he is, I don't know how I can find him." She whirled toward Billy. "You have to help me. He's only thirteen. He must be terribly frightened."

Billy's expression was sympathetic, but his head-shake firm. "There's no indication that your son is in any danger, or, for that matter, that he's a missing person. You saw him a little over an hour ago. He would have to be gone more than twenty-four hours for us to put out an alert."

"Twenty-four hours." Tears brimmed in her eyes. "Anything could happen to him."

"There's no reason to think he is in danger." Billy frowned. "Was your son acquainted with Click Silvester or Darren Dubois at the Haven?" His blue eyes were abruptly intent.

"I don't know those names. Who are they?" She looked

hopeful. Neva had no knowledge that two teenagers had died within days of each other, two teenagers with links to the Haven.

Rachel's grip on Annie's hand tightened.

Billy looked grim. "Click Silvester died in a fall from a viewing platform at the nature preserve Thursday. Darren Dubois died today after he was shot on Fish Haul Pier by an unknown assailant. The shot came from the woods opposite the pier. No one has been apprehended."

Neva reached out, gripped his arm, held as if to keep her balance. She flung questions at him. "Who were they? Why were they killed? What do they have to do with Tim?"

Billy looked thoughtful. "Click and Darren were regulars at the Haven. Darren was Click's best friend. Nothing can be proved about Click's death, but it is possible he told Darren something special was planned Friday night at the Haven. We believe Darren was watching someone and that he saw your husband's killer. Darren set a trap and the murderer shot him. If Tim was in contact with either Click or Darren, there might be cause for concern."

Rachel loosened her grip on Annie, took a step toward Billy. "Tim hardly knew anyone at the Haven. He never talked to anybody but Meredith or me or Mrs. Hughes. The guys didn't have anything to do with him. Besides, Click and Darren were older."

Billy's gaze was sharp. "Are you sure?"

Rachel was solemn. "Yes. I don't care who you talk to, they'll tell you the same. Half the time, Tim left right after he and Meredith showed up in the mornings. When he did stay, he fished, but he always sat by himself on the pier. Chief Saulter was real nice to him."

Billy looked relieved. "As long as there was no contact

between Tim and the dead boys, I see no reason to be concerned for his safety."

Neva wavered on her feet, her face twisting in fear. "You're telling me two boys have been killed and now Tim is missing and you won't help hunt for him?"

Billy was crisp. "Your son ran away because he didn't want to talk to the police about the twenty-two we found in the magnolia behind the stage. Or," Billy's face was grim, "his target practice. You told him I was coming and he thought he was in big trouble. You'll probably find him at a friend's house."

"But that note he left . . . I'm frightened of what he might do."

Billy was patient. "Your son wrote that he was sorry. He could be sorry for shooting at targets fashioned like his stepfather or sorry for taking that rifle to the program. It's clear that the gun found in the tree behind the stage belongs to him. His initials are scratched on the stock. Maybe seeing his stepfather killed made him sorry for wanting to shoot him. I hope so. It's lucky for him that we know a twenty-two bullet didn't kill your husband." Billy gave a short nod and turned toward his car.

Neva watched him walk away. Her face twisted in despair.

Annie understood Billy's attitude, but someone had to reassure this fearful woman. "Neva, I'm Annie Darling, Rachel's sister. We've met before." It was as if she spoke into a void. Neva stared at her with no change in expression.

Annie felt uncomfortable and intrusive. Even though they had come because Rachel was summoned, there was no place for them here. They had no help to offer, only sympathy. Neva Wagner was suffering from new shock laid upon old. Her husband shot dead. Her son's whereabouts unknown. Annie spoke quickly. "I wouldn't worry. Billy's probably right. Tim was scared. That's why he ran away. Why, he may be watching us right now, waiting for the police to leave."

Neva lifted her head, looked beyond the well-kept lawn at the surrounding woods. "No." Her voice was dull. "I would know if he were near. He's gone." She looked at Annie with anguished eyes. "He doesn't have anywhere to go."

Rachel took a step forward. "Look, why don't we call people, ask about Tim? And you can tell us where he likes to go, and we'll go look."

Annie's eyes widened. Who would go and look? Where would they look? The island was small, not more than twelve miles long and three miles across at the widest point, but there were deep woods tangled and choked with underbrush and creepers. Anyone could remain hidden for a long time. Had Tim taken any food? Was he prepared for mosquitoes and chiggers and horseflies? She pushed away thoughts of nightfall and the creatures that moved in darkness: lean, quick foxes, stealthy bobcats, sharp-hooved feral hogs.

Neva took a step toward Rachel. "You'll help me?" Neva's cry was glad. She turned to Annie, hand outstretched. Her eyes, huge and dark in her pale face, were beseeching. "I'm so frightened. Will you help me find Tim?"

∿ *Thirteen* ∿

MAX'S OFFICE WAS cool and quiet. All the lights were on, including his desk lamp, brilliant with its Tiffany shade, a Valentine's Day gift from Annie. Papers and folders were arranged atop the immense Italian Renaissance table that served as his desk. He lightly touched the silver frame of his favorite picture of Annie. He always took pleasure in seeing her blond flyaway hair, steady gray eyes, and kissable lips. His mood buoyed, he turned back to the legal pad.

Rank of suspects in terms of motive:

> 1. *Jean Hughes—Booth Wagner's death on Friday night—*

He underlined *Friday night* three times.

> *—was the only reason she kept her job and could stay in the cottage.*

There was no tomorrow for her.

2. *Tim Talbot—He blamed his stepfather for his injuries. Wagner's death meant he wouldn't be forced to ride trails again.*

3. *Van Shelton—Neva Wagner had ended their affair. Would he kill to marry her?*

4. *Neva Wagner—She had broken off her affair with the golf pro. Did she do so because she planned a murder that would set her free?*

5. *Ellen Wagner—She drank too much. She wanted her child back. She brought a thirty-two pistol to the island.*

6. *Meredith Wagner—She wanted to be with her mother. She'd stolen money from her father's desk.*

7. *Larry Gilbert—He had reason for revenge after Booth rooked him over the collectible stamp. Larry claimed they were on good terms, the money restored in return for Larry's vote to oust Jean.*

Max shook his head in disgust. It was a nice ranking as far as it went but maybe it didn't go far enough. How could he judge what mattered enough to make one of these people kill? Almost anyone would agree that Jean had far greater reason and far greater urgency to kill Booth Wagner Friday night. What if Tim Talbot's fear of riding on an ATV was all-consuming? Lovers were known to kill the unwanted spouse. Ellen Wagner had lost her marriage and her lover and her child. Meredith wanted to be with her mother, care for her mother. Larry Gilbert claimed all had been resolved between him and Booth, but murderers lie.

Max reached for Henny Brawley's folder. He read the housekeeper's revealing comment about Tim Talbot: "He kept screaming out in the night. She was up and down with him. But he wasn't the least bit fond of Mr. Wagner. Master Tim could hardly stand to be in the same room with him, anybody could tell that."

Max opened Laurel's folder. The assistant golf pro defended his boss: "I mean, he and Neva were through. It was making him crazy. See, she broke things off because of this prenup agreement."

Maybe Neva thought they were through, but Van decided she was worth killing for. Or perhaps Neva decided on murder to make sure her son would have medical care and she could marry Van.

Had Booth discovered Meredith's theft? How frightened was she for her mother's safety?

As for Ellen Wagner, Gilbert claimed Booth had bought off her lover. That was history. Had she brooded about her humiliation and come to exact revenge?

Max studied the list. Obviously, Billy Cameron considered Jean Hughes the primary suspect. The only physical evidence against her was the phosphorescent tape found in her office, but someone else could have placed the tape there. Unless Billy found a gun and connected it to Jean or discovered some other incontrovertible link, she remained one suspect among several.

Annie respected Billy Cameron's judgment. She understood that he was much more concerned about three deaths than a runaway teenager. But she could no more turn away from a desperate Neva Wagner than she could ignore the frantic cries of a kitten abandoned in a Dumpster. They were unlikely to find Tim. There were too many woods, too many hiding places.

"We'll do what we can." Annie knew she sounded doubtful. She hurried to add, "Let's look at his room, see if you can figure out what he's taken."

"That's a good idea. Then we'll know . . ." Neva trailed off. "If he didn't take anything, that would be worse, wouldn't it?"

Annie saw despair in her eyes. Neva was afraid something dreadful had happened or would happen. Was she hearing those panicked cries in the night? Billy had told her the twenty-two was not the murder weapon. A forty-five had been taken from Booth's desk. Was she terrified that Tim had carried the pistol as well as his rifle Friday night and that he still had the forty-five?

"We need to hurry." Neva turned and started up the marble steps.

Annie glanced at Rachel. "Call Max. Ask him to come. He can organize a search." She took a step, paused. "Call Henny Brawley. Ask her if she'll put together a phone bank."

Neva was almost to the front door. Annie rushed to catch up. Surely Billy would understand. He loved his stepson and his beautiful little blond daughter. If one of them ran away, as a father he would seek them. Whatever Annie brought about, a gathering of searchers, telephone calls seeking Tim, the noise and sound would at the very least comfort Neva and might help find the missing boy. In the best of all possible worlds, Tim would come home by nightfall.

Max pulled off the sheet from the legal pad, reread the questions he'd listed:

1. *What caused Tim Talbot's nightmares?*
2. *How many of the suspects could handle guns with ease?*

3. *Why did Ellen Wagner come to the island now? Why did she bring a gun? Or perhaps two guns?*
4. *Could Larry Gilbert prove Booth had transferred money Friday morning, reimbursing him for the fake stamp?*

He leaned back in his red leather seat. Tomorrow he and Barb would look for answers and who knew what else might be discovered between now and then.

The phone rang. He glanced at Caller ID and picked up the receiver. "Hi, Rachel." He frowned as he listened. "If Billy doesn't think . . . Annie promised?" Exasperation mingled with pride. Of course she shouldn't have agreed to mount a search that Billy clearly felt was unnecessary. Of course she had agreed. Annie never met a broken heart she didn't want to mend. He looked at her picture. Gorgeous. But stubborn. "Okay. I'll come."

Alcoves with Roman and Greek statuary in the marble hallway made the upper floor resemble a museum. Annie wondered fleetingly if the marble sculptures were reproductions. Or not. If the latter, Booth Wagner had been a wealthy man indeed. That kind of wealth conferred all imaginable luxuries and set him apart from ordinary constraints. If someone displeased him, he had the power to cost them dearly. He had used that power, buying off his first wife's lover, luring Jean Hughes to the island as an affront to a dignified Haven board member, bartering reimbursement for a fake stamp to gain Larry Gilbert's vote to oust Jean, keeping Neva locked in a failed second marriage.

Stepping into Tim's bedroom was like visiting an alternate universe. The room was huge, but the furnishings were modest, a maple bunk bed against one wall, a battered old walnut desk, a long Formica-topped table littered with balsa wood and model airplanes in various stages of completion and rows of metal soldiers in battle formation, some painted Union blue, others Confederate gray. Miniature cannons on a mound of dirt were trained on a Union company. Bright rock posters adorned the walls. Albums were stacked next to a CD player. A red plastic bean bag chair flopped opposite a TV set hooked up to a Wii. A scuffed baseball glove lay in the depression of the bean bag chair.

Neva looked uncertainly around, then walked to an open closet door. She stepped inside. Her muffled voice rose in excitement. "His sleeping bag is gone and his backpack." She came out into the room. Abruptly, tears spilled down her cheeks. "He took things. That means he's run away. Really run away, not just walked out with nothing. I've been so terribly frightened."

When problems loomed, Annie always felt better when Max was near. Now he stood with his arms folded in the hallway of the Wagner house, tall, blond, handsome, resolute.

Annie knew the folded arms weren't a good sign. "Can't you call on the Boy Scouts, round up a group of men and get a search started?"

Max's face furrowed. "I can't ask people to look for a boy who might be armed."

Neva took a quick step toward him. "That's crazy. Tim ran away because the police found his gun in a tree. That policeman said Tim's gun wasn't the weapon that killed Booth. Don't you see, Tim ran away because he's frightened. He isn't a danger to anyone." Her voice shook.

Max's expression was bleak. "His twenty-two didn't kill

Booth. The murder weapon was a larger caliber." His gaze at Neva was uncompromising. "Booth was killed by a gun like the forty-five that someone stole from his desk. Tim took his sleeping bag and his backpack. He could have that forty-five in his backpack."

Annie felt jolted. Max was right. They could not be sure that Tim Talbot was innocent. He'd been in the right place at the right time to have shot his stepfather and he could have taken Booth's gun. Maybe the rifle had been left in the tree because Tim had the forty-five in hand. Maybe he'd hidden the forty-five in the woods. The police search had been careful, but woods have many hiding places. Tim could have retrieved that gun.

Neva stood, eyes staring, with her hand at her throat. Finally, in a rush, she spoke, the words tumbling over each other in her haste. "Tim doesn't have Booth's gun. He absolutely does not have that gun. I took the forty-five out of the desk Saturday morning. I threw it in the ocean. I threw it as far as I could." She was sobbing now.

Max's eyes narrowed. "Why?"

Neva was angry and despairing. "I was afraid. Does that satisfy you? Tim had terrible nightmares Friday night. I went to his room and he was twisting and turning, his sheets all sweaty, and I tried to wake him up. He was crying and saying he hadn't meant to do it, he was sorry. When I got him awake, I asked him and he looked at me with his eyes all empty and he shivered and said he had a bad dream, he didn't remember, and he turned away from me." She reached out toward Max. "I swear it's true. Tim doesn't have that forty-five. He ran away because the police found his twenty-two and they were coming to the house. He probably thought they were going to arrest him. He doesn't know a bigger gun was the weapon. All he knows is that someone shot Booth and his rifle was found behind the stage. Of course he's terrified."

Max looked grim. "You'd better be telling the truth."

"I am." She met his searching gaze without flinching.

He gave a short nod. "I'll call around, see if I can get some men to meet at the harbor pavilion. We can fan out from there. It makes sense to search the north end of the island. I have a friend, Buddy Winslow, who can probably furnish some megaphones."

Annie knew that was a good idea. Buddy ran the summer beach program. "He can contact the other lifeguards."

Neva clasped her hands tightly together. "Van Shelton will help. I know he will." Her gaze was defiant.

Max knew about Neva and Van. She knew he knew. But his expression never changed and he spoke as if she was acquainted with Van only as a golf pro. "I'll ask Van to round up some golfers. I'll call Frank Saulter." Max walked to the door, paused, and looked back at Neva. "If you're lying," his gaze was unwavering, his voice grim, "someone else may die tonight."

Most of the men gathered at the pavilion on the harbor had brought Maglites. They were dressed in long-sleeved shirts and trousers and boots to protect them from mosquitoes and ticks. Max counted eighteen. The sun slipped westward and swaths of rose and purple marked the horizon.

"Thanks for coming. Here's the situation. We have a missing teenage boy. Tim Talbot. He ran away from home this afternoon because he thought he was in trouble with the police." Max hesitated, then decided to be frank. These men were giving up their evening to check out the island. He owed them the truth. "I'll try to sum it up as quickly as possible. Tim's stepfather was shot Friday night at the Haven during the annual summer program. It was later discovered that Tim brought a twenty-two rifle and hid it in the woods behind the outdoor stage."

He heard the murmurs. ". . . brought a gun . . . behind the stage . . . what's the deal . . ."

Max talked louder. "The twenty-two was later found in a tree there and proven not," he repeated, "*not* to be the murder weapon. Obviously, Tim didn't shoot his stepfather—"

Hal Fraley, a muscular firefighter, yelled, "If somebody beat him to it, why'd the kid run? Why aren't the police looking for him?"

"He isn't considered to be in danger. The police view is that he's hiding because he thinks he's going to be arrested for having the rifle there. That isn't the case. But his mother is upset, and I promised we'd try to find him. My hope is that we can cover this end of the island and use loudspeakers to let him know he isn't being sought by the police." Max had decided against a search on foot. Maybe Neva hadn't taken the forty-five. Maybe she had lied. Men driving in cars calling out over loudspeakers should not be in danger. "Buddy Winslow's got a box of loudspeakers at that first picnic table." Max pointed at the table. "All right. There's a map of the island. Here's how we'll split up . . ."

Comfortable rattan furniture with bright cushions was scattered about the terrace room. An eclectic art collection included a painted carousel bobcat on a bronze pole, a Roman jar, a gilded Portuguese mirror, a marble bust of Homer, and a Ming Lo Han sculpture. This evening, the wooden blinds were open even though it was dark outside and the patio and dunes invisible.

Annie had no trouble distinguishing the voices: Emma's

gruff rasp, Laurel's husky tone, Henny's precise diction. Henny had brought the all-important Haven phone directory.

Emma had fashioned questions seeking information about Tim's whereabouts, followed by queries about Darren Dubois and Click Silvester. So far nothing helpful had been discovered. Tim Talbot had walked out of his house and vanished.

Annie kept busy. She made calls, set up a buffet on an elegant Louis XV lacquered commode, and later arranged for Pudge to pick up Rachel and take her home. As she cleared the buffet, gathering up dishes, washing them, she tried not to worry. She had initiated the search for Tim Talbot. What if Neva had lied about the forty-five? What if Tim had that gun? Or perhaps Neva's lie was in the timing. Perhaps she had taken the gun from Booth's desk on Friday and Friday night lifted her hand and aimed and shot at the husband who wouldn't set her free.

Every so often, Annie walked from one caller to another in the terrace room. She paused, looked down, and each time received a head-shake. No one had seen Tim Talbot. Annie occasionally touched the cell phone in the pocket of her linen slacks. It was as if she reached out to Max. If she called, she would hear his voice. She clung to that sense of connection, and the little prayer in her mind ran over and over: *Keep them safe, the men looking for Tim. Let Tim be found and everyone be safe, everyone.* Too much had happened in her life and Max's to take safety for granted, not now, not ever.

Neva paced in front of the windows. Every time a phone rang, she froze and waited, her eyes enormous in a face blanched by fear. Each time there was no news and she expelled a breath and began again her nervous, driven circuit, her sandals clicking on the tiled floor.

Abruptly, Neva cried out, "He's been gone for hours. I can't bear it. I'm going to look for him." She whirled and hurried to a French door that opened onto the terrace.

The sandy road twisted and turned, deeper and deeper into the forest. Overreaching branches blocked the moonlight. The Jeep's headlights seemed puny against darkness as impenetrable as a pool of oil. All four windows were down. Max drove the barely moving Jeep with one hand, held a battery-powered megaphone to his lips. "Tim Talbot. You are not wanted by the police. Tim Talbot. You are free to come home. Tim Talbot . . ."

Every ten minutes he paused to drink some water, and then he began to call again. "Tim Talbot . . ." The megaphones had a five-hundred-yard range. Max felt confident Tim would hear the summons. Whether he chose to respond was another matter. As time passed, Max received calls from other searchers, indicating they'd driven their routes with no success.

Max reached the end of the road. He shook his head, turned the Jeep, and drove back the way he'd come, the megaphone lying in the seat beside him.

Neva stood on the boardwalk to the beach, a dark form in the creamy moonlight. She stared out at the ocean and the curling white of the breakers.

Annie hurried to catch up, her shoes thumping on the wooden planks. Waves rose and fell, the crashing sound familiar, reassuring.

Neva stood stiff and straight. "He took his sleeping bag."

Annie knew Neva held on to that fact like a talisman. "He's probably fast asleep right now. I'm sure he's perfectly all right. Maybe he feels like he's having an adventure, sleeping out under the stars." She looked up at the Milky Way and the Big Dipper, at Mars and Saturn and Venus. Untold millions of stars glittered across the expanse of sky, shining on the unlit beach with dazzling brilliance.

Neva's pale face turned toward her, the features scarcely visible. "Will they find him?"

"They'll do their best." *And, please God, may they all be safe, Max and the men and Tim, too.*

Neva gave a ragged laugh. "Do your best. That's what my mother always said. God knows I tried, but I've made so many mistakes. Poor little Tim. I didn't know everything would end like this. His dad died of cancer. Tim watched him die, getting thinner and sicker day by day. Booth was very kind. He was my boss. Two years after Paul died, Booth told me he and his wife had separated. I'd heard she was involved with someone. I should have been smart enough to see how angry he was with her. Anyway, he kept after me and he was nice to Tim. Booth was so loud and healthy and vigorous. I thought he'd be good for Tim. And good to him. We hadn't been married six months when I realized the truth. Booth didn't care about me. He married me to get back at Ellen. Someone at the office told me that word was out that I was a home wrecker. I know who put that word out. Booth. That isn't the worst thing he did. The worst was trying to make Tim 'act like a man.' I hated him then. Tim will be a fine man. He's a good boy. But he is gentle and reserved and sensitive. Nothing like Booth. The accident was Booth's fault. Tim can't run now. Or play baseball. One leg is shorter than the other. They think they can put in a rod and maybe he'll be as good as new. But it costs thousands of dollars. The scar on his face needs more surgery. Booth thought that was a waste. He said that a good scar made a man look tough. I wanted a divorce. He refused. Then I met Van. I suppose everyone thinks I'm a slut. I don't care. When Booth found out, he threatened to get Van fired. Booth said if I left him I'd have no medical insurance for Tim and not enough money to buy it. Do you wonder that I didn't care when someone shot him? I didn't know Tim was angry enough to take his rifle to the program. That breaks my heart. I should have known he was desperate. I should have done something, anything, taken him away, but he needs those operations. And now he's frightened. He's just a boy. He must think the police will arrest him and blame him for Booth's death." She looked out at the water. "Tim? Tim, where are you?" Her voice rose against the immensity of the night and the boom of the surf. "Tim, please come home, please, please, please."

Annie lifted the saucepan just as the milk began to steam. She measured and added nutmeg, cloves, cinnamon, and honey.

Max leaned against the kitchen counter, comfortable in a T-shirt and boxers. He looked tired but calm, a man who had done as he'd promised.

Annie poured his portion into a mug with a zebra-head handle. Her handle was a lioness. They'd brought home a set of six from an African safari. She remembered nights in the bush, the roar of lions, the cackle of hyenas, the odd thwacking sound of hippos, and the rumble of frogs. She had enjoyed the journey, but she had known at all times and in every place that danger was near. She felt very much the same now.

"Don't you think he would have come out if he was okay?" She cradled the warm mug in her hands.

"Tim's all right." Max was irritated. "You're as bad as Larry Gilbert. He helped me box up the megaphones and he was like a cat on hot bricks, worrying about the Haven and some kind of kid cabal. I told him that was nuts. This wasn't a matter of disaffected teenagers cooking up some weird murder. Click Silvester wasn't disaffected from anything. He was a happy, good kid who worked hard and was excited—in a good way—about the Friday night program. Darren was a daredevil, but he didn't have teenage angst. The only disaffected one is Tim Talbot and he never hung around with the older guys, plus he had a good reason to take a hike when the cops came calling. No, the central murder is Booth's and that's where we have to look for the killer. Who hated him enough to be willing to kill a teenager to clear the way and take out a second who tried blackmail? Tim Talbot doesn't fit into this picture. He's a side issue."

Annie persisted. "Why didn't Tim come out when he heard the calls that it was okay to come home?"

Max shrugged. "This isn't a kid who's willing to trust. If there's no posse with dogs out looking for him tomorrow, I promise he'll be home by dark. Look at the facts, Annie. He took a backpack and a sleeping bag. He wasn't going to walk into the ocean. If that was his mind-set, he'd have run away empty-handed. I don't have any doubt he heard one of the megaphone calls tonight. He decided to wait and see. Tomorrow nobody will be looking for him, and he'll realize it's safe to come home. In the meantime, Mrs. Darling," Max's eyes lit and he reached out his hand to take hers, "it's time we slept the sleep of the just. As in, just fell in love, just can't wait . . ."

⌒ *Fourteen* ⌒

IN HER DREAM, Annie ran through darkness, trying to catch up with Neva Wagner, whose voice rose above the roar of the surf, ". . . Please come home . . . please . . ." The shrill peal of the telephone brought her gasping to wakefulness. Heart thudding, Annie threw back the sheet.

Max's groggy voice mumbled, "H'lo."

Annie fumbled with the switch, turned on the bedside lamp.

Max's beard-stubbled face furrowed into a tight frown. "I'll come over . . . That's all right. I think you need someone there." He put down the phone. "Jean. Somebody threw something under her house. The noise woke her up. She's called the police."

Annie swung over her edge of the bed.

Max gave her a weary smile. "Go back to bed, honey. I'll take care of it." He glanced at the clock.

Annie didn't need to check the time to know they were still in the dark watches of the night, when mind and body clung to slumber. Max was not going out into the night alone. There were too many guns loose on the island.

Though her decision wasn't logical, she felt that two together was safer than one alone. She knew his response if she revealed her reason. Instead, she blinked away sleep and said firmly, "This may be a big break. I don't intend to miss any of the action."

Light streamed from the cottage windows and blazed from all four corners of the deck. Her hair tangled, Jean looked as if she'd dressed in haste—a red cotton shirt untucked from worn Levis. She was barefoot and wore no makeup. She stood on the steps, pointing.

Lou Pirelli's uniform was wrinkled, but he looked competent and wide-awake. He held a Maglite trained on the side of the cottage. In common with many low-country structures, the cottage was supported by brick pillars, which lifted the floor a good four feet above the ground, protecting it from hurricane storm surge. The wooden lattice that screened the area beneath the house was pulled ajar.

". . . I didn't leave the screen that way. Someone's pulled the lattice out. I heard the screech as it moved and then a thump. I got up and came to the front window." She turned and looked toward the woods. "In the moonlight I saw somebody for an instant before they ran into the woods."

"Man or woman?"

"I couldn't tell. It was just a dark form and then it was gone."

Lou nodded. "I'll take a look." He walked toward the dark opening beneath the cottage. He took his time, swinging the Maglite back and forth in front of him. Annie wondered if he was looking for footprints, tracks of some sort.

Lou reached the opening. He knelt and played the light beam into the darkness. Suddenly he stopped, his posture tense.

Annie started to move forward, but Max caught her hand. "Wait. There might be footprints. Traces."

She stopped. Moonlight dappled the cottage. Cicadas burred, their summer song intense. Swamp frogs trilled. It was any summer night, hot, humid, alive with noise and movement, except for the now ominous beam of light poking into darkness beneath the cottage.

Lou remained in a crouch. With infinite patience, he moved the beam of light back and forth, back and forth. Finally, he held the Maglite steady. He stared beneath the house, then clicked off the light. He rose, tucked the light under one arm, unclipped his cell phone, and punched a number. "Chief, sorry to wake you." Lou glanced at their watching faces, turned away, walked far enough toward the woods that his words were inaudible. In a moment, the call ended and he walked back to them, his face impassive. "Chief Cameron will be here shortly." Lou spoke to Jean, ignoring Annie and Max. "He will wish to speak with you. Please remain available."

Jean stared toward the opening under the house. "What's there?" A current of hysteria bubbled in her voice.

Max was abrupt. "Jean has a right to know what you found. She saw a prowler. What was thrown there?"

Lou looked at them with his cop face, remote, wary, unyielding. "Chief Cameron will handle the investigation."

Jean took a step toward the opening. Her eyes were wide with fear.

Lou barred her way. "This area is off-limits until our investigation is completed."

Annie reached out, touched Jean's rigid arm. A confrontation between Lou and Jean would only make matters worse for Jean. "Let's wait on the porch."

Jean stood taut for an instant, then nodded toward the

house. "I need to check on Giselle." She started for the back steps, then swung to look at Max and Annie. "I'm sorry to have bothered you. It's late. Please go home. I'll call in the morning and let you know what they've found."

Max smiled. "We'll wait."

Jean looked shaken. "I'm scared. Booth and Darren shot and Click dead, too. Something terrible is going on. Everything seems to be connected to me. I haven't done anything. I shouldn't have called the police."

Max shook his head. "That was the safest thing to do."

Jean stared at Lou, standing with a hand on his holster. "Was it? I don't think it's going to be safe for me." She whirled and ran to the porch and up the steps.

Annie stood, arms folded. "Whatever Lou found, it must be big or he wouldn't have called Billy."

Jean came out on the porch to check.

Max shook his head. "Not yet."

"I'll wait inside. If you want to come in . . ."

"We're fine. Billy won't be long. He lives very near." Annie tried to sound reassuring, but she saw fear in Jean's eyes.

Jean stepped back inside.

It wasn't long until headlights flashed and a police cruiser pulled into the drive, followed by the forensic van. Billy Cameron slammed out of the cruiser and walked to meet Lou at the opening beneath the house. Billy knelt and bent to look. In a moment, he stood, spoke in a low voice with Lou, then turned and walked toward them. The van door opened and Mavis stepped out, carrying an aluminum case. She wore latex gloves.

Billy glanced over the porch. "Where is Ms. Hughes?"

"She's seeing about her sister."

At Billy's nod, Lou walked to the back door, knocked.

They waited in taut silence until Jean came out on the porch. She came down the steps, stared at Billy. "I have a right to know." Her voice shook. "Someone put something under the house. What did you find?"

Billy's gaze was sharp, his blue eyes studying her. "We have careful procedures with evidence retrieval so complete information isn't available. However, the investigating officer observed a pistol, which he believes to be a forty-five, and a cell phone. Ms. Hughes, please describe the incident that prompted you to call 911."

Jean shuddered. "A gun? That's awful."

Billy pulled out a notebook, held a pen. "You say you heard a sound."

Annie thought his tone sardonic: *You say* . . . He could have begun by asking Jean what she had heard. Instead, his question implied that her complaint was false.

"I heard a screech. The hinges on the lattice are rusted. I've been meaning to oil them. That startled me. It wasn't right. It wasn't a night sound. I sat really still and listened. I heard a thump."

Billy glanced at the cottage. "Where were you?"

She gestured. "In the living room."

"The time?"   •

"When I called, it was twenty-six minutes after two. I guess that was a couple of minutes after I heard the noises. I was scared. I jumped up and hurried to the window and looked out. Someone ran into the woods. Then I ran to the phone."

Billy gauged the distance from the now well-lit opening under the cottage to the woods. "About thirty yards. You can't say whether it was a man or woman?"

"It was a shadow. That's all I know."

"Big? Little?"

"I don't know." Her voice trembled. "It was just a glimpse. I saw a dark shape and then it was gone."

He looked toward the open trellis. "Move the screen back and forth, Lou."

Lou obliged. The screech was scarcely audible above the sounds of the night.

Billy's questioning gaze returned to Jean. "It's interesting that you heard the noise."

Jean was suddenly angry. "I was in the living room. Right there." She pointed at a window directly above the pulled-out lattice. "I heard a screech and a thump. Why do you act like I'm making everything up?"

Billy's expression was stolid.

Annie reached out, gripped Max's hand. Billy didn't believe Jean. Jean obviously realized the police chief was suspicious, but Annie knew Billy very well. He was going through the motions with his questions. Billy thought the gun and phone had been thrown there by Jean and the 911 call made to create a straw man.

Max started to speak, stopped, his lips compressed.

Billy gave him a quick glance, looked back at Jean. "Can your sister corroborate your story?"

"Corroborate? It isn't a story. It's the truth." Her voice was hard and angry.

Billy was imperturbable. "Your sister is here. Can I speak with her?"

"She's asleep." Jean clasped her hands tightly together. "She was having a bad night. She's in so much pain. I gave her a painkiller at midnight. She fell asleep shortly afterward."

"Was the painkiller strong enough to sedate her until morning?"

Jean stared at him. "She hurts so much. She needed the pill."

"You say she fell asleep soon after *you*," his emphasis was slight but unmistakable, "gave her a pill that would knock her out for several hours. Then what happened?"

Jean looked puzzled. "I sat down in the living room."

"Why didn't you go to bed?"

"I couldn't relax. So much had happened. I kept thinking about Booth and Click and Darren. Nothing makes sense. I knew I wouldn't be able to get to sleep."

"Where is your cell phone, Ms. Hughes?"

She frowned. "It's lost. I've looked everywhere for it."

"When did you *lose* the phone?" His gaze was intent. His tone put the verb within invisible quotation marks.

"Yesterday." Her voice rose. "I couldn't find my cell after you searched my office." She swung toward the opening beneath the cottage. "If that's my cell phone, somebody put it there. I don't know why." Tears trickled down her cheeks. "You should be finding these things out. Why don't you look for the person who did this?"

"We'll look." Billy's voice was grim. "It's hard to find a shadow, Ms. Hughes."

Max waited on the ferry dock. The brassy rumble of the *Miss Jolene*'s horn rose above the squall of sea gulls and slap of water against the sea wall. The early-morning breeze, cool off the water, tugged at his polo. The sharp scent of seawater and fresh air gave him a needed spurt of energy. His fractured sleep had been made even less restful as images and sounds tumbled in his mind, the dark blue metal of a pistol, a black cell phone, Billy's skeptical questions, Jean's frightened face, the amplified sound of his own voice, hollow through a megaphone, the wail of a siren. He'd awakened feeling tired and dull. Breakfast and several cups of coffee helped.

The *Miss Jolene*, expertly steered into her berth, thumped against the tires lashed to the harbor wall. Handler Jones was the first person down the gangplank. The breeze stirred his chestnut hair, highlighted by streaks of silver. He was a courtroom warrior, boyishly handsome with confident, bright blue eyes. He moved like a man ready and eager for combat.

Max strode to greet him, hand outstretched. As no one knew better than he, Handler was a premier criminal lawyer, smart, bright, clever. He was as quick with a verbal punch as a prize fighter with a physical blow. He'd fought like a tiger for Max during those hot August days last summer when Max was accused of murder.

Handler wasted no time. "Thanks for sending the information." He tapped his briefcase. "I've got some ideas. If we can alibi her for either of the crimes, that may keep her out of jail."

"We need every idea you can muster." Max led the way across the boardwalk to the parking lot. "Last night they found a gun and a cell phone—hers is missing—underneath the cottage."

Annie burrowed up out of sleep and reached for the phone. Dimly, she realized it had rung and rung. She blinked at the empty side of the bed. Maybe Max was in the shower. She fumbled with the receiver but by the time she clicked the phone on, the call had ended. The clock radio registered eleven minutes after ten.

"Max?"

When no answer came, she felt the house's emptiness. She checked Caller ID. No name and not a number she recognized. The house was empty because Max had left early to pick up Handler Jones, who was coming in on the eight o'clock ferry. She amended her thought. Handler had arrived at eight. Max would have driven him to Jean's cottage, where Handler could speak with her before the nine o'clock meeting at the police station.

Annie swung out of bed, slipped her feet into thongs. She didn't bother with a robe, but hurried downstairs in her shorty nightgown. As she'd expected, there was a note on the breakfast table. Max had set her place—plate, silverware, juice and water glasses. She picked up the note:

Good morning, Mrs. Darling,
    A delicious green chili omelet in the fridge is ready for brief—very brief—warming in the microwave. Homemade salsa, as well. Also, pan dulce.
    I alerted Ingrid that you were sleeping in. I'm off to pick up Handler. I'll call when I know anything.
    Amor to my favorite Texan—Max
    P.S. Don't do anything rash.

    P.P.S. No forays to quiz suspects in remote sites. Comprendes?

Annie heated her breakfast, propped the note against the Worcestershire sauce. She was torn between amusement and irritation. He'd fixed her favorite breakfast. He had left her asleep since they'd been up so late. She loved his thoughtfulness. But did the man think she was an idiot? She had no intention of wandering in Gothic-heroine fashion onto the equivalent of a desolate moor. For an instant she had fun picturing a moor with Spanish moss and an alligator. Smiling, she shook her head. Bless Max. He wanted her to be safe. That was always the prayer for those we love. *Be safe. Be safe.*

She finished her wonderful breakfast, tidied the kitchen, and was hurrying upstairs to shower when the phone rang. She noted the number. The earlier caller had tried again. "Hello."

"He didn't come home. The police won't help." Neva Wagner's hoarse voice was dull with exhaustion.

"He'll come home by evening." Annie tried to sound as confident as Max. "My husband thinks Tim is waiting to be sure the police aren't hunting for him. When there aren't any official search parties out, he'll realize it's okay to come home. He took his backpack and his sleeping bag. That shows he was intending to hide out."

"What about those boys who were killed?" The words were sharp and jagged.

"Tim scarcely knew them." Annie was willing to rely on Rachel.

"He knew one of them. The one who fixed computers. That's the one who took care of our computers."

"I'll bet Tim wasn't even home the times that Click came to your house." Annie hoped she was right.

"I guess that's so. Tim never spent much time here. He liked to be out. I always thought that was a good thing. I didn't know about his shooting the twenty-two."

Annie had a quick memory of Friday night, of dusk falling and the milling crowd. Tim had climbed a magnolia with his rifle. His mother had ducked into an arbor near the woods. Forgetting Max's oft-repeated urging to think before she spoke, Annie blurted, "You went into that arbor by the woods Friday night."

"The arbor?" She sounded startled. "I wanted to get away for a moment. I don't like crowds."

"Van Shelton followed you. Did you talk to him?"

There was an appreciable pause. "Just for a moment."

"Was he with you when you heard the shot?"

"The shot?"

Annie waited. There had been one shot, and it had killed her husband. Neva had to know exactly where she was at that moment.

Finally, Neva spoke, the words rushing together. "The lights went out." There was remembered shock in her voice. "It seemed terribly dark. There was a pop. It sounded far away."

Annie's eyes narrowed. "So you were alone?"

"Oh no. Van and I were together. We heard the shot together."

Annie raised a skeptical eyebrow. Neva was lying. Was she protecting Van Shelton? Or was she protecting herself? "When did you see Tim?"

"I don't know. I can't remember much after that. It was dreadful, Booth on the ground and blood. Tim came and told me he was going home. I tried to stop him, but he ran away."

Running seemed to be a specialty of Tim's.

"I have to find him." Neva sounded even more distraught. "I don't know what to do."

"Stay there." Annie was firm. "He'll come home." Feeling her response was inadequate, she offered, "I'll try to find him. Where are some of the places he spends time when he's outside?"

"I don't know. He takes long walks. He likes to look for artifacts. There's an Indian Shell Ring not far from here."

Annie knew the site. Long ago Indian tribes tossed oyster, clam, and mussel shells, as well as the bones of deer, raccoons, bear, and fish, in a refuse heap. The ring was approximately 150 feet in diameter and several feet deep.

"Tim loves to go there. He says it's around four thousand

years old, like the pyramids in Egypt. He's always digging around, hunting for a spear. Not at the Shell Ring. He knows it's protected. He digs close to streams and ponds. He was really excited when they brought up an old cannon from the harbor."

Annie nodded. These sites were on the north end of the island, where Max and the others had used megaphones to encourage Tim to come home. "I'll take a look around."

Handler Jones shook hands with Billy Cameron. "If you have no objection," he nodded toward Jean, "Ms. Hughes would like for Max to be present for our discussion." Handler's tone was good-humored, his Southern drawl as thick as good grits. "I've often hired Confidential Commissions for investigative work and this will keep Max informed."

The chief's expression was pleasant but wary. "I have no objection. If you'll come this way." He led them down a hallway and opened the third door to the left, standing aside for them to enter. The interrogation room contained a narrow metal table with one chair on one side, two on the other. Billy gestured at a chair against a wall as he closed the door. "You can pull that one to the table, Max."

The room immediately seemed smaller. There were no windows. The overhead light threw the metal table and white walls into stark relief, emphasized the silver streaks in Handler's thick chestnut hair, the dark circles beneath Billy's eyes, the heavy makeup that did not hide the puffiness of Jean's swollen face.

Max placed the third chair a little behind and to the left of Handler's seat.

Billy settled heavily in his chair, flicked on a tape recorder. "Chief Billy Cameron." He glanced at the round, schoolroom-style clock on the wall. "9:06 a.m., Monday,

July 13. Present are Ms. Jean Hughes, her counsel, Handler Jones, and Mr. Jones's investigator, Maxwell Darling. The interrogation concerns the murder of Booth Wagner, Friday, July 10; the shooting of Darren Dubois, Sunday, July 12; and the suspicious death of Hubert 'Click' Silvester, Thursday, July 9. Ms. Hughes has been named a person of interest in this investigation." Billy cleared his throat and recited the Miranda warning, the words clear, distinct, and ominous. "Ms. Hughes, do you clearly understand what I have said to you?"

Her eyes enormous in her pale face, Jean nodded.

"Please answer aloud, Ms. Hughes."

"Yes. I understand."

Handler gave her an encouraging nod. His face reflected easy confidence.

Max wasn't into women's fashions. Women's shapes, yes. But what colors were popular and whether skirts were long or short mattered to him not at all, though short skirts got his attention every time. Yet he sensed, and the understanding made him sad, that Jean had tried hard this morning to look her best, her formal best, in a navy linen dress with a lustrous pink pearl necklace and matching bracelet.

Billy began with questions establishing her identity.

Jean relaxed a little, answering quickly, as if eager to put the inquiry behind her.

"When did you meet Booth Wagner?"

"A year ago last March."

"Describe your friendship."

"He came to the club—"

"What club was that?"

"Boogie's Blues. In Atlanta. On Highland Street. I was a singer. I *am* a singer." She spoke almost defiantly.

Billy's expression didn't change.

"One night he bought me a drink. We started to be friendly."

"Did you know he was married?"

"He said he was separated from his wife."

"You believed him?"

She looked forlorn and vulnerable. She stared at the blank white wall. "I shouldn't have. I did."

"He became your lover?"

Her hands twined together tightly. "Yes." The answer was almost inaudible.

"Please speak loudly enough for the recorder, Ms. Hughes."

Her face flushed a deep red. "Yes." Her voice was loud and harsh, echoing with anger and hurt. "I thought . . . oh, it doesn't matter now what I thought. I was stupid. He didn't care about me." Tears glistened in her eyes. "He was making fun of me, just like he made fun of everyone. I—"

Handler moved forward in his chair, interrupting, his voice mellifluous. "Let's help the chief with his investigation and confine our answers to his questions." His smile was kind, but his gaze commanding.

The questions continued, one after another, inexorable and penetrating. Finally, Billy brought her to this past week. "When did you learn that Wagner wanted you fired from the Haven?"

"Wednesday afternoon."

"How did you find out?"

Jean gripped the huge rounded fake pearls of her bracelet and edged the circlet around and around her wrist. "I was supposed to check with the board members, ask if they had any new business to submit for the agenda. Larry Gilbert acted real strange, like he was uncomfortable. Finally, he asked, like he was puzzled, 'Are you still doing the agenda?' I asked what he meant. He stammered around and said he thought Booth was taking care of everything since I was— Then he stopped and said maybe I ought to call Booth. I told him if he knew anything I should know, he should tell me. He said maybe it was all a mistake, but Booth had told him my contract wouldn't be renewed. I told him I'd call Booth. After Larry left, I called and called and he never answered the phone. I guess he knew it was me. Finally, I got a text from him."

"What was in the text?"

She stared at the wall. "He liked texting. He liked making up abbreviations to see if people would get them."

Billy pulled off a sheet of paper, pushed it across the table with a pen. "Please re-create the message."

She hesitated, then, face puckered, picked up the pen and wrote:

BRD WL VT U O BTR LK NX TM LOL

Billy glanced at the sheet. "Please read the message aloud."

"You can read it." She was defiant.

Billy's voice was uninflected. " 'Board will vote you out. Better luck next time. Laughing out loud.' Was that your understanding?"

She nodded, her lips trembling, her hands tightened into fists.

"Please speak up."

"Yes."

"Did you contact him?"

"I called and called. He never answered that day. I tried again Thursday morning. Finally, he answered."

Billy leaned forward. "You received the text message Wednesday. You called repeatedly without reaching him. You spoke to him Thursday morning?"

"Yes. After I'd stewed a lot." Her voice was bitter. "He told me the joke was over. I was history."

Billy looked quizzical. "Yet you contacted Max Darling Thursday afternoon and asked him for help to keep your job. Why?"

Jean jammed her fingers together in a tight knot. She didn't look at Billy. Her gaze was distant. "Wednesday night Giselle and I were sitting on the porch, listening to the sounds of the marsh at night. I started to cry. She asked me what was wrong. I didn't want to tell her I was going to lose my job. I told her I wished I could take her somewhere and help her get well. She reached out and took my hand and her fingers were so thin and cold. She told me not to be silly, that nothing could be done. And then she said she didn't want to ever be anywhere but here, that the cottage was the nicest place she'd ever lived and that's where she wanted to die and she wanted to be buried on the island and that I should never cry but whenever I saw an egret or a great blue heron or heard an owl, she wanted me to think of her and know how happy I'd made her by bringing her here. That's when I decided to fight him. I didn't think I'd win. But I had to fight. For Giselle."

Billy studied her, his gaze intent and considering.

Max knew she had presented him with a clear and urgent reason to kill.

She took a deep breath. Her hands relaxed, fell loose in her lap. "That's why I decided to ask Max for help."

"On Thursday?"

"Yes."

Billy leaned forward. "I understand you were hunting for Click Silvester Thursday morning."

Jean stared at him in surprise. "That's right. I looked for him in the computer area. I was having trouble with my e-mail. Oh." She seemed to come to a realization. "I guess you talked to Rosalind. She told me he'd just left. I think it was around nine o'clock. I hurried out and caught him near the bike stands. He promised to check everything out in the afternoon."

"Did he say where he was going?"

She looked puzzled. "I didn't ask him."

Max wished she had asked that simple question.

"What was Click's demeanor?"

Her face was suddenly sad. "He was Click, sweet and kind and nice. He had no idea anything awful was going to happen to him."

"Did he mention the program? Or a secret?"

"No. I don't see what kind of secret he could have had that was connected to the program. Everything was set for the show."

Handler said smoothly, "My client is quite willing to provide information about the program and its participants."

Billy wasn't distracted. He ponderously questioned Jean concerning her whereabouts on Thursday. There were four periods when she was not at the Haven: a morning errand to pick up the programs from the printer, her lunch at home with Giselle, a trip in the afternoon to the lumber yard for two-by-fours, and finally to Confidential Commissions in search of Max.

Max saw Billy's satisfied look. That afternoon trip had taken Jean very near the entrance to the nature preserve. Although the time of Click's death couldn't be pinpointed, Jean was now revealed to have been in the vicinity within the general time frame.

Max wondered if she realized that Billy was spinning a web as large and enveloping and strong as any by the island's golden silk spiders, whose webs could span twice the length of a car and were stronger than steel. He shot a worried look at Handler.

The lawyer appeared untroubled, but he made several notes on his legal pad.

Occasionally, Billy glanced at the clock.

Max noted the time. Why was Billy so cognizant of the passing minutes? Certainly, he wasn't concerned about tiring Jean Hughes, though he stopped twice to permit her time to drink water.

The questions continued, one after another, concerning her actions on Friday leading up to the program at the Haven. Billy was painstaking in going over the events of Friday night.

At half past ten, he reached Sunday.

"Where were you at one o'clock Sunday afternoon?"

"At the Haven."

"Can anyone vouch for your presence there?"

"I was alone. I wanted to get everything in order in case . . ." The words trailed away.

"Were you in the woods opposite Fish Haul Pier?"

"No."

The door opened. Lou Pirelli walked toward Billy, a sheet of paper in his hand. He paid no attention to Jean or her lawyer or Max.

Billy looked at him.

Lou answered an unasked question with a quick nod. His expression was one of subdued triumph.

Billy stood. He was always an imposing figure, well over six feet in height, broad-shouldered, muscular. Now his blunt face was stern. "Ms. Hughes, I am placing you under arrest for the shooting of Darren Dubois at three minutes after one o'clock on Sunday, July 12."

❁ *Fifteen* ❁

EMMA CLYDE LED the way down the center aisle of Death on Demand, square face as forbidding as an iceberg, a large legal pad clutched tightly in stubby fingers, pink-and-silver caftan swirling. Her stride checked as she glanced at the display of her newest book. She barked over her shoulder, "It's time to add more copies of *The Clue in the Queen's Tiara*," then resumed her march to the coffee bar.

Laurel Roethke paused at the cash desk. She was, as always, exquisitely beautiful with the loveliness of chiseled features that would never age. Her smile was buoyant. "Dearest Ingrid, how are you this morning?" Her husky voice exuded good cheer and genuine care.

Ingrid poked red-framed glasses higher on her nose. "Tell Her Majesty the book's on order."

"Oooh." Laurel understood the import. Emma never took kindly to less than ten copies of each of her titles available at all times, notwithstanding the grim (to Annie) fact that she had sixty-six books in print. Moreover, Emma expected Death on Demand to stock a minimum of fifty copies of the newest book. Laurel clapped her hands together. "Emma will be pleased to know that the last customer demanded sixteen copies for her relatives." She gave Ingrid a quick wink as she whispered, "Fiction is addictive, isn't it?"

Ingrid's eyes glinted. "The last customer was eighty-seven and her nearest and dearest are all in the cemetery. One for every tombstone?"

"Oooh. I suppose it must have been the next-to-last customer." Laurel's silvery laughter brought a reluctant smile to Ingrid's face.

Henny Brawley patted Ingrid's shoulder. "We'll run interference. Emma's in a snit because she has been, as she sees it, rudely dismissed by our stalwart police. Or as she is now calling them, 'the island's befuddled constabulary.'"

"What a shame." Ingrid's smile was saccharine. And pleased.

Henny walked swiftly down the center aisle to the coffee bar. Emma had already taken over the largest table. Henny stepped behind the coffee bar. "The usual, *mes amis*?"

Emma's primrose-blue eyes narrowed in thought as she flapped a hand in the affirmative.

Laurel hurried to help, choosing the mugs: *Murder Is My Business* by Brett Halliday for Emma, *Murder Is My Dish* by S. Marlowe for Henny, and *Murder in Show* by Marian Babson for herself.

When they were seated—Emma with a double espresso, Laurel with fruit tea topped with whipped cream and cherries, and Henny with Colombian brew streaked with caramel—Emma exploded. "If I had time, I'd arrange a citizens' rally to protest."

Henny spooned out a delectable thread of caramel. "I'm sure Officer Harrison didn't intend to offend you. After all, she thanked you for attempting to aid the authorities."

"Did she pay any attention to my suggestion?" Emma bristled.

Laurel nibbled on a cherry. "They seemed rather busy. You know, with an arrest just made and the press there, trying to get information, and the mayor announcing how the quick solution to this weekend's crimes was a direct result of his emphasis on support for law and order."

Henny was placating. "After all, Billy had already sent an officer to check out the apartments right after the shooting Sunday."

Emma wasn't impressed. "I don't care. They should try again. Someone always sees something. Why, in *The Case of the Kissable Kiwi*, Marigold unearthed the truth by discovering the hidden lair of a panhandler who saw everything."

There was a silence.

It might not have been as respectful as Emma considered her due.

Henny returned to the coffee bar, added more caramel. Before Emma's affronted expression could lead to sharp words, Henny said briskly, "It's up to us. There's no law we can't canvass the apartment house. I agree with your theory, Emma. There are two paths through the woods opposite Fish Haul Pier. The gunman who shot Darren was more likely to take the path to the apartment house instead of the path to the pavilion where there would probably be picnickers on a Sunday afternoon."

Emma made a chuffing sound like an irritated cat. "Inspector Houlihan would see the necessity for such action."

Henny took a sip of coffee to hide her smile. Emma automatically summoned her characters, the sleuth Marigold Rembrandt and the hapless Inspector Houlihan, when addressing any puzzle. "Of course he would," she said soothingly. "However, if the police decline to canvass the apartment house again, we can do it."

Emma's blue eyes gleamed. "I'd already thought of that."

"Had you indeed?" But Henny said it very nicely. Emma always had to be the leader. "That's a very good idea."

There was a hint of suspicion in Emma's quick glance, but Henny's expression was bland.

Laurel beamed; then, slowly, her smile faded. "My dears, why would any of those sweet people in the apartment house talk to us? We can't just go door-to-door and out of the blue ask people if they were home on Sunday afternoon and happened to look out of their windows around one o'clock. They'll want to know why."

Emma thumped a fist on the tabletop. "We can say we are prosecuting inquiries that should have been pursued by the police."

Laurel turned an admiring gaze on Emma. "You are so forceful, so direct, so honorable. But some of the residents might not feel it is their duty to answer one of us."

"And some don't like the dirty coppers." Henny's tone was light. "We might go about it a different way. Everyone loves to win a prize. We can announce we are doing a survey with only a few quick questions and everyone who responds will have a chance to win a prize."

"A prize." Emma looked doubtful, then abruptly, she clapped her hands together. "That's a bully idea."

Henny knew her plan had been accepted.

"The prize is obvious."

Laurel tipped her head and looked inquiring. Henny bent forward to listen.

"An autographed copy of *The Clue in the Queen's Tiara*."

* * *

Annie ducked a bumblebee, flapped her hands at a cloud of gnats. Sweat streamed down her face. Her once-fresh, candy-striped T-shirt clung to her. She had a snag in her new linen slacks and her pink sandals were mud-stained. Next time she went on a safari, she would dress properly. She'd been to the remnants of a schooner that had come aground on the bluffs in a remote area. She'd checked out the ruins of a nineteenth-century plantation. Now she moved uneasily on a shadowy trail deep in the nature preserve. Finally, she reached the remnants of the four-thousand-year-old Shell Ring, whose antiquity had impressed Tim. She tried to move quietly but a crow flapped overhead, squawking. She clambered carefully up and down the grassy sides. The Shell Ring was so deep in the nature preserve she felt like she was on another planet, a tropical planet teeming with insects, wildlife, and steamy heat.

"Tim? I'm a friend of your mother's. Please come home. The police aren't hunting for you. She's very upset." Her voice sounded thin and very lonely.

Annie shook her head. If he was anywhere near, he was a stubborn idiot. She brushed back a damp tangle of hair. Anyway, she'd fulfilled her promise to Neva. Annie turned to leave. Where was the path? She felt an instant of panic until she sighted the boardwalk about twenty yards away. She was climbing the steps when her cell rang. She flipped it open. "Hey, Max, what has two legs and a sweaty hairdo and enough chigger bites—"

"Jean's in jail." Max talked fast. "She'll be arraigned tomorrow. I'm going to take Handler to the ferry after he finishes talking to her. I checked and the friend who's staying with Giselle arrived this morning. Jean doesn't want

Giselle to know she's been arrested, but I don't see how we can keep the truth from her."

Annie pictured Giselle sitting on the porch, wrapped in her quilt, always cold, kept apart from the sister who loved her. "Oh, Max." Being arrested for murder had to be horrible, but for Jean separation from Giselle had to be devastating.

Max was still talking. "The news is grim. The gun found beneath her house is the weapon that shot Darren."

"Someone threw the gun there!"

"Billy doesn't believe there was a prowler."

"Excuse me." Annie was angry. "With the Atlantic Ocean all around, why would she be dumb enough to throw the murder weapon under her own house?"

"Billy's got answers for everything. She was being clever. Throwing the gun there kept her from having to carry the weapon with her to toss in the ocean or a lagoon."

Annie saw Billy's point. If Jean had been stopped and the weapon found, she would have been fatally compromised.

"That's not all." Max sounded bleak. "That was her cell phone under the house. There's a record of a call to Darren Saturday afternoon. Jean couldn't find her phone before lunch Saturday. I was there and saw her hunt for it. So did Marian Kenyon. Billy's not impressed. He thinks Jean had already planned to shoot Darren and pretended the phone was lost so she could claim that if a call was made to him on her phone, it was made by someone else."

Annie shivered despite the heat. Someone had indeed planned ahead after Darren made his pitch for money to keep quiet about what he had seen Friday night.

Annie tried to figure out the timing. "Saturday morning Darren asked for money."

"Maybe he asked someone straight out." Max spoke in a considering tone. "Or maybe he left a note with his cell number. The murderer had to silence Darren."

Annie rushed to speak. "That narrows down the possibilities. Who had access to Jean's office Saturday morning?" Names fluttered through her mind: Neva Wagner, Van Shelton, Tim Talbot, Meredith Wagner, Ellen Wagner. "I guess it could be anybody. She didn't believe in locking up. My guess is that the murderer brought the roll of phosphorescent tape to hide in a filing cabinet, figuring she would be the chief suspect and a search would eventually be made. Her cell was probably lying on the desktop. A quick look around, a grab, and the phone's taken."

"That makes sense, but Billy doesn't agree."

Annie fastened on her suspect list. "Since Booth was killed there the night before, wouldn't it have looked odd for any of his family members to show up at her office on Saturday?"

Max was silent for a moment. His words came slowly as he thought out loud. "Some excuse would have been made if the murderer had been seen, but it isn't far from the woods to the front door of the Haven. Attendance was down so there weren't many kids around. Officer Harrison was on duty, but I imagine she patrolled the grounds, checked in and out of the building. Probably the murderer stood in the woods and waited until no one was about, then moved fast to get inside. Once in the hall, it's only a few steps to Jean's office. The door could have been closed long enough to hide the tape and pick up the phone. When leaving, it would have been the same procedure in reverse."

"Van Shelton? Ellen Wagner? Why would they know anything at all about how Jean ran the Haven?"

"Van's taught beginner's golf at the Haven. As for Ellen Wagner, you can bet Meredith told her all the rumors swirling about her dad trying to get Jean fired. After all," Max was unrelenting, "Ellen Wagner knew enough to bring her little pearl-handled friend to the program Friday night. If she shot Booth, she was sober as a judge."

A grasshopper jumped on Annie's wrist. She wriggled her arm, but the grasshopper clung. Fortunately, she liked grasshoppers. "There's not a shred of evidence against a single one of them."

The harbor breeze riffed the water with white caps. Handler Jones paused at the bottom of the gangplank. "Try to track Click Silvester on Thursday. We know he ended up at the nature preserve. I doubt he was trying to escape notice. Our best bet is to locate him at the nature preserve at a time when Jean has an alibi."

"I'll try." But Jean's responses to Billy's questions had revealed several times Thursday when she couldn't account for her whereabouts.

The ferry whistle sounded.

As Handler started up the gangplank, Max called out, "Do you think we can get Jean out on bail?"

Handler turned and gave a thumbs-up. "I'll do my best. I'll have testimony about her sister's health. I'll contact the doctors when I get back to Savannah."

Max walked swiftly to his Jeep. He sat behind the wheel for a moment, studying an island map. A single road, twisting and unpaved, led to the nature preserve where Click died.

Max drove to Barred Owl Lane. He passed a shack that had tumbled in on itself, the broken roof slats bleached by the sun. Along the way, he visited several houses and had no luck. Either no one was home or the resident hadn't seen Click. A half mile from the preserve he stopped at a neat gray bungalow. Despite the heat, a woman sat in a white wooden rocker on the front porch, shelling green beans in a bowl.

She looked up with a smile. "Can I help you?" Her island accent was as Southern as the faraway bay of hounds.

Max smiled in return. "Yes, ma'am. I hope so. I'm trying to find out more about the teenage boy who died in the nature preserve Thursday. It would be a help to investigators to know what time he arrived at the preserve. Did you happen to see a black teenager who was about my height, but chunkier? He was wearing a Braves T-shirt and cutoff jeans and was riding a bicycle."

Her face reflected quick distress. "I read all about that boy and I saw his picture in the paper. I didn't see him Thursday. Of course," and she hitched the bowl a little closer, "you just happened to catch me when I'm resting a spell. We get up early and by mid-morning I'm starting to tire a little. But I'll only sit 'til I get these beans done, then I'll be back in the kitchen. There's a lot of canning to do this time of year. I don't want my tomatoes to go to waste. I'm mighty sorry I can't help. I sit out here morning and afternoon and the only person I saw on the road was in the afternoon around two o'clock."

Max was ready to turn and go, but he asked without much hope: "Did you know that person?" Perhaps someone she knew had passed by and might have seen Click in the preserve.

She lifted her eyebrows in mock horror. "I should say not. The people I know don't dress like that. 'Course I just caught a glimpse. I was coming out my front door and there went a bicycle. I couldn't tell whether the rider was a man or woman, though I guess it was a woman. Can you believe someone in a witch's robe and cone-shaped hat and straggly gray hair on a day as hot as Thursday? I declare, I don't know why anybody'd be in a getup like that when it's hot enough to fry an egg on top of my car. Some kind of joke I guess."

Annie stopped in the women's locker room to freshen up, but Van Shelton had to be accustomed to talking to sweaty golfers. Maybe he'd think she'd been on the driving range, though she would have worn Bermuda shorts, not linen slacks. She strolled toward the putting green. Van was helping a teenage girl. He was, as always, encouraging and soft-spoken. His hair was sun-bleached, his rounded face ruddy from too many years under a Southern summer sky. Annie waited patiently until the lesson ended.

As he walked off the green, she smiled and called out, "Van, I'm looking for a little help."

His smile was automatic, pleasant, but never too personal. "I'm booked solid this morning."

"I'm helping Neva hunt for Tim. He's still missing."

His reserve fell away. "I could shake that kid. I hope he comes home pretty soon. Neva's real upset. I told her he's okay. That was a dumb stunt to take his twenty-two to the program. No wonder he got scared when the police came to the house."

Annie pretended to share his exasperation. "Kids can do crazy things. Neva and I were talking about Friday night after the lights came back on." Neva had claimed she was with Van when the gun was fired. If that was true, surely

Van wouldn't have left her in the dark. "She didn't see Tim. Did you see him?"

Van shook his head. "I was almost to the parking lot when I heard the shot."

Annie managed not to change expression. Neva had lied. She had been alone when the gun was fired. And so had been the man who was furiously angry because she had elected to stay with her overbearing husband.

Van looked grim. "I knew there was trouble. I turned around and headed back to the field. I waited in the back until the lights came on. Somebody told me Booth had been shot, so I started looking for Neva. I didn't see Tim until I got to the stage." His frown was dark. "He wasn't any help to his mother." His expression softened. "Of course, he's just a kid. I guess he was scared, but he should have stayed with her."

Annie thought of the twenty-two with Tim's initials, found in the magnolia behind the stage. Obviously, Tim had climbed the tree. Had he waited for his stepfather to speak? Had he lifted the rifle? She shook her head in confusion. No matter. It wasn't a twenty-two bullet that killed Booth Wagner.

Max had been hot on Barred Owl Lane. It seemed hotter in Billy Cameron's office. Thunks and thuds in the attic indicated work on the air-conditioning. ". . . Hope you'll send someone out to get her statement."

Billy took a deep gulp of iced tea, wiped sweat from his face. "So a woman sees somebody in an odd costume on the road to the nature preserve. So what? Have you ever counted how many people there are on the island in July in weird clothes? My favorite was the woman in a homemade octopus dress who was protesting aquariums. Weirdest thing I've ever seen. Her hair was divided into a bunch of separate braids dyed red, orange, yellow, black, and brown because octopuses can change color in an instant. Who knew?"

Max wasn't to be diverted. "Click died in the preserve. Here was somebody spotted at ten minutes after two in what could easily be a disguise. Billy, this may be a link to the killer."

Billy's good humor at the memory of the octopus protester evaporated. He looked obdurate. "I got my link, Max. The forty-five that shot Darren Dubois and very likely killed Booth Wagner."

Outside the police station, Max made a sudden decision. It would be good to figure out what time Click arrived at the preserve, but Max thought he had the timing of the murder. Billy could dismiss the bike rider dressed as a witch, but Max remembered the highwayman costume wadded up and thrown in the lake at the Haven. Max was convinced the murderer wore the witch costume Thursday afternoon and dressed as a highwayman Friday evening.

He started down the steps, paused, figuring days and times. The broken hasp of the costume shed had been noticed Friday morning. The oddly dressed rider was seen on Barred Owl Lane Thursday afternoon. Either the witch costume didn't come from the shed or the murderer had access to the shed before the break-in. However, more than likely, the shed wasn't locked during the hours the Haven was open. He almost turned to go back inside, then shook his head. Billy would see the discrepancy as another indication of Jean's guilt. She had access to the shed, locked or unlocked, at any time. In Billy's mind, the broken hasp had been another ploy, like the gun and cell phone thrown under the cottage.

The important thing was to find out where the suspects

were at shortly after two o'clock Thursday afternoon. There was another matter Max was determined to explore. Larry Gilbert had insisted all was well between him and Booth and that Booth had repaid Larry the five hundred thousand for the fake stamp. They only had Larry's word that the exchange had occurred.

Max wanted proof.

Annie carried a pink limeade from the golf course grill and sipped thirstily as she walked to her car. Should she confront Neva? Maybe the better choice would be to report to Billy.

She'd left the car windows down, but the interior was oven-hot. Using the edge of her T-shirt, she opened the driver's door. Reaching over the seat, she snagged a beach towel and draped it to cover the leather. Once behind the wheel, she plucked Kleenex to shield her hands from the hot plastic wheel. She put the air-conditioning on full blast.

As she drove toward town, she realized Billy wouldn't be interested. He had his murderer. Lies by Neva didn't matter now.

Ellen Wagner had no reason to protect Booth's second wife. Ellen appeared to be drunk Friday night and claimed she lost the gun from her purse. The gun was found in the lake behind the stage.

Annie felt a flicker of hope. The gun had been dredged from the bottom of the lake. It had to have been thrown there. If Ellen threw the thirty-two, she had been sober enough to decide to get rid of the gun and to toss it. Maybe she saw something that would help vindicate Jean. And maybe Meredith would have some idea of places where Tim might be hidden.

With a decisive nod, Annie headed for Sea Side Inn.

* * *

Larry Gilbert was straightforward. "Look, you know I want to help." He glanced at his watch. "But I'm scheduled to take some papers over to Mrs. Willoughby's to sign."

It was a reminder to Max that everyday life with all of its demands and commitments claimed the attention of most island residents, despite three murders or, as Billy emphasized, two murders and a suspicious death. "Right. I'll be quick."

Larry gestured toward a comfortable chair in his spacious office. He looked stressed, his bony features taut, though his surroundings spoke of languorous ease: wallpaper with palms against a cream background, a banana tree plant that glistened in the sunlight through unshuttered windows, and a rattan floor mat. Bright cushions in several wicker chairs completed the tropical motif. As Max dropped into a comfortable chair, he thought all he lacked was a rum and coke with a swizzle stick and "Sweet Leilani" playing in the background.

Larry's face tightened in aggravation. "If Sybil weren't such a good client, I'd insist on seeing her tomorrow. But Sybil never met a tomorrow she wasn't determined to have now. She's changed her mind a half-dozen times, but she's finally set on an annuity, and I want her signature on the dotted line before she waffles again. Sorry. You aren't interested in my problems. What can I do for you?"

"I'm trying to get a better handle on times Friday. It may turn out to be very important when you saw Meredith Wagner with the money from her dad's desk." Max hoped Larry Gilbert was too distracted by his upcoming appointment with Sybil Willoughby to question Max's logic.

In fact, Larry scarcely seemed interested in Max's confident assertion. His focus was clearly elsewhere. "Friday morning." He spoke as if the time were far in the past. "Oh, I don't know exactly. Maybe ten o'clock. Maybe a quarter past."

Max looked chagrined. "Isn't there some way we can narrow it down?" He stopped, blinked, hoped he wasn't overdoing the posture of a man suddenly struck out of nowhere with a thought. "You said Booth arranged for a transfer of funds, taking care of the money you'd paid him for that fake stamp. How about you check your accounts, see what time the transfer was made, then we can work back ten minutes and we'll know when Meredith was there." It had been a few years since he'd had a Cary Grant role at the Little Theater. Had he played his part convincingly?

Larry swiveled his desk chair to his computer. "Yeah." He sounded interested. "We can do that."

Trying to appear eager to learn the time, Max got up and leaned on the desk, the better to see.

In a few clicks, Larry had the bank statement on his screen. He moved the mouse, and the cursor touched the time of deposit, but Max was looking at the amount. The entry confirmed Larry's story of what had unfolded in his meeting with Booth Wagner. Deposited in his account at 10:09 a.m. Friday was the sum of five hundred thousand dollars. Though there was no proof the deposit came from Wagner, it was for the precise amount Larry had paid for the counterfeit Inverted Jenny. It was reasonable to assume Larry had told the truth about his rapprochement with Booth and Booth had reimbursed him in exchange for Larry's vote on the board to terminate Jean.

Max made a show of working out when Larry saw Meredith.

Larry nodded. "I'd think it was right around ten. I got there a few minutes early and Booth came about five minutes after ten. As always, he was running behind. Typical Booth."

Max was enthusiastic. "Larry, that's a great help." He felt a sharp disappointment. Jean was in jail and there she would stay unless they came up with a solid suspect, backed by evidence.

He frowned as he clattered down the steps of the small brick building on Main Street that housed Larry Gilbert's insurance agency. Max moved fast but he had nowhere to go, no more ideas.

He was on the sidewalk when his cell phone rang. He glanced at Caller ID. "Hey, Ma."

"Sweetie, you are discouraged." Her husky voice resonated with care.

Max grinned. How did mothers always know? Of course, he never underestimated his mother's intuitive insight. He and his four sisters knew that Bergdorf Goodman would sell plastic ukuleles before he and his sisters would put one over on their mother. "Hot, tired, disgruntled, and discouraged. Make it better, Ma."

"Oh my dear, of course I will." The sweet, throaty response took him back to the years when a kiss on a scraped knee instantly took away the sting, a butterfly-light touch on his cheek said I love you, and flashing blue eyes presaged a tigress mother springing to his defense. If only miracles still . . .

". . . And we went door-to-door. I met some of the loveliest people. One woman stays home to care for her husband with Alzheimer's, and she raises hamsters. Don't you think Annie would like a dear little calico hamster? I told her I'd be back to pick one up. The third time is the charm—you know, the third door, the third floor—Henny and Emma are so proud of me." A pause. "At least Henny is pleased, though Emma does like to be the one who strikes gold. The lady's name is Gold, Herwanna Gold in 310. She immediately noticed someone dressed like a witch on a sweltering July day."

Max felt a surge of triumph. Laurel had gotten the goods. Billy would be forced to pay attention now. A witch had been seen en route to the nature preserve on Thursday and now a witch had been seen near the apartment house on the other side of the woods from Fish Haul Pier shortly after Darren had been shot on Sunday.

Emma's imperious voice sounded in the background. "I'm not waiting. Come along if you wish."

Laurel spoke hurriedly. "Emma does take charge." A trill of laughter. "I'd better go help. We think the costume was probably hidden almost immediately. And I'm feeling lucky today!"

Max was quick. "Don't do anything until I get there. I'm—"

The connection ended.

∴ Sixteen ∾

ANNIE KNOCKED. SHE waited a moment, knocked again.

Slowly, the door opened. Ellen Wagner looked small and shaky and sick. She held to the edge of the door for support. "I don't think I want to talk to you."

Annie spoke gently. "I was hoping to catch Meredith. Her stepbrother ran away last night and he's still missing."

"Actually, Meredith's gone to help hunt for him. Neva called and of course I wanted Meredith to help." She started to shut the door.

"Mrs. Wagner, you've had tough times. I think you are very kind. Will you let me tell you about Jean Hughes?"

"The director of the Haven?"

"Yes."

"Meredith likes her very much even though her dad . . ." She trailed off.

"I won't stay long, but please let me tell you what's happened."

Without a word, stumbling a little, Ellen turned and Annie followed. They sat at the small circular table. The blinds were drawn. The room still smelled of whiskey, but today Ellen Wagner, her face pale, her hands clasped tightly together, was sober, painfully, miserably, shakily sober.

She sat quite still for a moment after Annie finished speaking. Ellen sighed. "Life is funny. When you're a little kid, at least I guess if you're a lucky little kid, most days are happy and you never think bad things will happen to you. When you grow up, there are bad things everywhere you look." She took a deep breath. "Meredith says Jean Hughes is really nice. I'm sorry about her sister." Her gaze was troubled. "I don't know who killed Booth. I want justice. For Meredith. For Booth. Maybe," she looked a little surprised, "maybe even for me. I loved him once. He was the sweetest daddy when Meredith was little. I've loved him. And hated him. But I didn't want him to die like that. If she shot him, she should be in jail."

Annie marshaled the same arguments they'd made, to no avail, to Billy. ". . . And most of all, she wouldn't have done anything that would take her away from Giselle. Please help us if you can." Annie looked at her steadily, not in accusation but with quiet confidence. "You were at the Haven Friday night. Were you sober?"

Ellen picked up a Coke can, drank thirstily. Her hand shook. Her brown eyes looked haunted. "Kind of sober. Kind of not. Today's the first day I've been really sober in a long time." Her voice was weary. "I had to talk to Booth. I wouldn't have shot him. I really wouldn't have. I don't know what got into me. I bought the gun in a pawnshop. They've probably traced it by now. But that's all right. Sometimes at night, I'd get the gun out and hold it in my lap and I'd think that all I had to do was lift it up and I wouldn't be unhappy anymore. I'd be finished. Because I was finished. I lost everything that mattered to me. Do you know how much I missed Meredith?" Her voice was anguished. "Seeing her in the morning, kissing her good night. Instead there was just me and a dirty apartment and not enough food sometimes. I'd get a job, then I'd lose it. Finally I decided to come here. I couldn't stand being away from her."

She raised a trembling hand to press against her temple. "I feel awful. My head hurts. My stomach hurts. I haven't had a drink since last night. I didn't have much to drink Friday. I had to be able to talk to Booth." A sudden look of cunning made her pale face sharp. "I knew things that could get him in trouble with his taxes. I was going to tell him I'd keep quiet if he'd let me have Meredith back."

"Why did you take the gun with you Friday night?"

Her brown eyes flickered. "I don't know." Suddenly she gripped the chair arms. "Oh, I'm tired of lying. Maybe I was going to shoot him. I don't know. I took the gun with me. Just in case. I tried to keep in the shadows. I didn't want Meredith to see me and make me go back to the inn. When I saw him walk toward the stage, I edged toward the back, that area between the stage and the lake. I stood and watched him. When the lights went out, I thought something was just broken. Then there was the sound of a shot. Even though it was dark, I heard Booth cry out. I knew it was him even before a man came with a flashlight. My hand was in my purse, and I was gripping the gun. I was terrified. I didn't know what to do. I pulled out the gun and threw it into the lake. When the lights came on, I saw Meredith coming toward the stage. I started to go to her and then I realized I didn't dare. I turned and ran back toward the inn. Somehow I got off the path and I heard people coming, so I hid behind a bush. When I got back to the path, I was turned around. By the time I got to the inn and upstairs, you and Meredith were there. I pretended to be really drunk. I thought I'd better act like I'd lost the gun. Maybe that was dumb."

Annie wanted to know more about that last instant before the lights went out. The murderer pulled the cord from the battery pack. "You were standing near the back of the stage. You must have looked around." If Ellen stood with her hand in her purse gripping the gun, surely she would have wanted to know if anyone observed her. "Before the lights went out, what did you see?"

Ellen massaged one temple. "It was dark behind the lights. Really dark. I could see figures, but no one was distinct." Her eyes narrowed. "There was a group of kids in shiny costumes. The last thing I saw before it got dark was somebody bending forward in a hat with a big feather."

Annie gazed steadily at Ellen. Either she was innocent and she had seen, oh so briefly and indistinctly, the murderer in a highwayman costume bend down to pull out the plug or she was clever enough to describe her own actions. "Was that just before the lights went out?"

"Just before." Ellen leaned back in her chair. "If you don't mind, I'd like to rest. I'm very tired."

"I'll go now." At the door, Annie looked back. "Do you know when Meredith will be back?" Annie glanced at the bedside clock, was surprised to realize it was almost one o'clock. No wonder she felt hungry. "Is she coming back for lunch? I'd like to talk to her."

Quick alarm flared in Ellen's eyes. "She can't help. She wasn't close to the stage. She ran to the stage from the center aisle."

Neva had lied. Now it was Ellen's turn. Annie distinctly

recalled Meredith coming from the direction of the woods as she ran toward the stage and her fallen father.

Max slammed out of the Jeep. The large parking lot behind the stucco apartment house was almost empty. Many residents were likely at work. Retirees might be out fishing or they might be enjoying a quiet rest after lunch. In a little while he'd call Annie. If she hadn't already eaten, they could meet at Parotti's. Right now, he wanted to find his mother and her cohorts.

He gazed at the woods that separated the apartment house from the boardwalk and Fish Haul Pier. He took a step toward the path, then shook his head. He'd better get an idea where they were. He turned and hurried to the corner stairs. He found 310 at the near end of the third floor. He knocked.

A tiny woman with curly red hair held in place by a bandana opened the door. She looked up at Max with bright, dark eyes, prominent in an age-wrinkled face. She was trim in a white blouse and crisp blue slacks.

Max introduced himself.

The small woman was instantly friendly. "I'm Herwanna Gold. Your mother is a delight." She spoke softly. Her head nodded toward a closed door. "Raymond's asleep, so, if you don't mind, I'll step out on the balcony with you."

Max glimpsed a living room with three rows of cages, a brown plaid sofa, and a black leather recliner. The mingled scent of wood shavings and disinfectant tickled his nose.

She left the front door ajar and stepped to the railing. "I'd just finished feeding the hamsters. I keep to a schedule. When I finish, I take a few minutes and stand on the balcony and look at the woods. We used to love to walk in the woods when Raymond was still able. I was on the balcony a few minutes after one yesterday."

The dark asphalt parking lot reflected the heat. A sea breeze would be rippling the surface of the harbor, but the intervening woods blocked the cooling effect.

She pointed. "Someone in a witch's costume came out of the woods. I wondered if there was a children's party and the entertainment was running late. The witch ran across the parking lot and around the far corner of the apartment house."

"A man?"

Her brown eyes were thoughtful. "It might have been a man. It could have been a woman. Looking down from this floor may have made the figure seem smaller. I'm sorry I can't be of more help. But I'm sure about the conical hat and the black robe and stringy gray hair."

Stringy gray hair. Max felt a twist of anger. A wig could disguise either a man or woman.

"What's on that side of the building?"

She smiled. "More woods."

Max hurried around the far end of the apartment house. A pedestrian had two choices: to continue straight and reach the paved road that ultimately connected to Main Street or take another path into this section of the woods, which ended at a small fishing lake.

As Max debated which way to go, a police car jolted to a stop near him. Officer Harrison gave him a brief nod and walked swiftly toward the woods.

Max followed. He stepped into the dimness beneath the overreaching branches of live oaks. As he came around a curve, he saw Officer Harrison stepping stealthily, hand on her holstered gun.

Voices rose not far away.

"Leave everything in situ." Emma was didactic. "The doltish constabulary must be consulted."

"I'll call." Henny sounded pleasant. "I'll say we've discovered material linked to the murder on the pier."

"I've never liked witches. Those long pointed noses and bony hands." Laurel's voice was shuddery.

Officer Harrison's hand fell from her gun. She straightened and walked forward.

Max continued forward, then stopped to watch, screened by a royal fern growing in a brackish low spot.

"Ladies." Officer Harrison gazed at them with a suspiciously wooden face.

Laurel's blue eyes glowed with amazement. "How serendipitous for you to be here."

The policewoman sounded phlegmatic. "We had a call." Her thin lips gave a twitch of amusement. "Women behaving suspiciously in the woods."

Henny laughed aloud, then was abruptly serious. "It's too bad your informers weren't in the woods yesterday. We think we've found what the murderer wore on Sunday. There's a witch's outfit bundled into that hollow tree trunk."

"We have testimony, officer." Laurel gestured gracefully. "Mrs. Gold on the third floor. She saw someone dressed in a witch's costume exit the harbor woods shortly after one o'clock. Obviously, the murderer was escaping an area sure to be quickly searched. However, it was necessary to jettison the costume, so we believe the murderer ran to the woods on the south side of the apartment house."

Emma nodded. "Clearly the killer ran from the harbor woods, came around the side of the apartment house, darted into this patch of woods, and pulled off the costume."

Officer Harrison pushed aside a feathery fern to inspect the cache.

Max strode forward. "Those clothes match the description of a person observed near the forest preserve shortly after two o'clock on Thursday. I've given that information to Chief Cameron."

Officer Harrison reached for her cell phone.

Emma gestured to Laurel and Henny, a wave beckoning them to follow her. The author's expression was one of supercilious disdain. "Now that the dol—"

Henny interrupted swiftly: "We're glad our efforts have been helpful. Perhaps we are rather in the way for a crime scene investigation." She took Emma's elbow. A quick glance brought Laurel to Emma's other side, and they nudged her toward the path. Henny's farewell was courteous: "Officer, if we are needed we'll be at the bookstore."

In the parking lot behind Sea Side Inn, heat pressed against Annie like a hot, wet sponge. She walked slowly toward her car. She was sweaty, thirsty, and hungry. Tim Talbot was probably sweaty and scared.

Where was Tim? She'd hoped Meredith might suggest places to check, but maybe some of the kids at the Haven could help. It was quicker to walk through the woods than to drive. Annie popped her trunk and tossed in her purse.

Once again she plunged into hot gloom. Somebody needed to prune back the ferns and vines. Maybe she could suggest a cleanup of the path as a project for the Haven. Maybe Max had found new information and Jean would soon be free and her biggest work decision would be a new net for the tennis court.

As always in semitropical growth running wild, Annie

stepped carefully. She drew in a quick breath when an eastern king snake slithered beneath a shrub. No matter how many times Max extolled the virtues of eastern kings, who loved to dine on poisonous snakes, Annie declined to join their fan club. "Go eat a diamondback." A bush rustled. She slid a nervous glance to her right. The sudden *tock-tock-tock* of a woodpecker startled her. Horseflies dipped near. She moved through the hazy tunnel of heat, sweat running in rivulets down her back and legs.

When she reached the clearing, she realized how near the path came to the Haven's outdoor stage. She stopped and gazed at the dock that jutted into the lake and was surprised not to see anyone fishing.

It was very quiet. Too quiet. Where were the kids? The sand volleyball court was empty, as was the soccer field. She shaded her eyes and looked across the grassy expanse at the main building. She couldn't tell if the lights were on, but there was something odd. The windows were closed. It would be stifling inside the old building, which had ceiling fans but no air-conditioning.

Disappointed, she turned to retrace her steps, then her gaze stopped on the stage. She tried to re-create in her mind the location of the lamp stands and where Ellen Wagner might have stood. Annie found a likely spot near the willowy fronds of a weeping willow, nearer the lake than the woods. Ellen would have been almost hidden from the audience, yet with a clear view of the stage.

The stage glittered a dazzling white in the midday sun. She squinted against the glare and looked at the dark line of trees. Everyone said the shot came from the woods, not from the side of the stage where Ellen had stood.

Annie crossed behind the stage. She walked into the woods and continued a few feet. A huge magnolia towered above her. Depressions and scuffed spots at the base indicated recent activity. She pictured Emma standing with folded arms and a circle of onlookers as an agile kid climbed the tree.

Annie looked up, wondering which branch might have held Tim. Her sandals wouldn't be much help in climbing a tree, but she could manage. She reached up and pulled herself into the tree and began to climb. It would have been fun if she hadn't carried with her a memory of a dead man with a bloodied shirt.

She was about twenty feet above the ground when she spied a branch that would have been a perfect platform for Tim and his rifle. Cautiously, she eased out on the branch. Two big limbs forked, a perfect spot to rest a rifle. When his stepfather was shot, Tim would have been looking down.

Annie looked down. She imagined a figure in the highwayman hat and cape bending to unplug the lights. Once it was dark, the killer must have been quick to stand and fire before Booth turned.

Very quick.

The gunman had probably taken about three strides to reach a point in line with Tim's view and directly behind Booth. There was nothing behind the stage to impede that movement. The gun was raised and fired, the target made clear by the patch of phosphorescent tape.

All the while, the killer's heart must have thudded, fearing light. As soon as Booth fell, the murderer removed the cape and feathered hat, wadded them into a ball, tossed the bundle into the lake, and ran into the woods to reach the path that led back to the field.

It was as if Annie were struck sharply in the chest.

The murderer's escape had depended upon speed and precision that could not have been achieved in darkness. There were two possibilities. The murderer had night-vision glasses or the murderer used a light. Night-vision glasses would surely have been discarded when the murderer regained the field. They would likely have been found. Billy's officers were thorough. Every trash can would have been emptied and the contents checked. However, night-vision glasses hadn't been necessary to shoot Booth. He had been marked by phosphorescent tape. It was much more likely the murderer used a tiny key-ring flashlight to find the way to the path.

From his vantage point, Tim could not have missed seeing a flash of light. Tim came down from the tree shaken and terrified. What had he seen?

Annie scrambled down the magnolia. What fools they'd been. Everyone on the island probably knew by now that Tim Talbot had run away and was hiding because the police had come to ask him about the rifle he'd carried up to the tree behind the stage the night his stepfather died.

Scarcely anyone was now seeking Tim, comfortable in the thought that he'd come home when he realized the police didn't want him.

Scarcely anyone was now seeking Tim, except for a desperate murderer who had to fear that Tim Talbot had seen too much from his perch in the magnolia.

Officer Harrison held back the feathery fronds of a royal fern. Billy Cameron stood with folded arms, watching as Mavis photographed the crumpled witch's robe and smashed conical hat. A flash blinked sharp white.

Billy was matter-of-fact. "When you get to the crime van, check the hat and jacket for fingerprints." He turned toward Max. "It looks like you had the right idea. The murderer wore that stuff Sunday just in case anyone was around. The costume served as a disguise until the murderer was out of the harbor woods and across the apartment house parking lot. Once around the corner, it was time to get rid of this stuff."

Max didn't say I told you so. He was feeling anything but triumphant. "Looks like the stuff was put where it would be easy to find."

Billy's stare challenged Max. "You want my take on it? Jean Hughes wore the outfit to the nature preserve and pushed Click off the platform Thursday afternoon. I'd guess she shoved him from behind. She probably put the costume back where it belonged. The stuff would have stayed there, but Darren Dubois thought he was a junior G-man. He tried to get evidence against her with a fake blackmail scheme. My guess is he didn't think anyone would believe him if he said he'd seen her in the highwayman costume. She promised she'd have a payoff taped under Fish Haul Pier by one o'clock Sunday. When he shows up on the pier, she's standing in the woods in the witch costume. She pulls a gun out of one of the deep pockets and blows him away. She ducks behind a bush and waits to see if there's anyone coming on the path. When the coast is clear she runs out of the woods into the parking lot of the apartment house. Once around the corner, she darts in here and hides the costume. It's too hot to handle now. She doesn't want to be found with it."

Max felt backed against a wall. "Both women who saw the murderer said the figure could have been a man."

Billy wasn't impressed. "Or a woman. We'll get statements. What matters is where the costume came from and whether we find her fingerprints on it."

Max very much feared he knew the origin of the costume: the trunk in the prop shed at the Haven. If he was right, Jean Hughes's fingerprints would be all over it.

"In fact," Billy started to move, "I'm going to the Haven right now. Jean Hughes's assistant called and said someone broke into the kitchen. I'll see about that and check the costumes, too. You're welcome to come and see if I'm right."

Annie hurried out of the woods. The Haven was much nearer than her car with her purse in the trunk. She wanted to call the police as soon as possible. She walked swiftly across the field. Even if the kids had been sent home, Rosalind Parker was on duty. The sooner the police started looking for Tim the better, but he'd done such a good job of hiding, he should be safe from the murderer.

Rosalind Parker bolted out on the porch, clutching a sheet of paper and a roll of tape. She slammed shut the front door to the Haven.

Annie ran to the steps. "I need to use the phone."

Rosalind shook her head. "Everything's locked up. I'm not staying another minute. That policewoman didn't come back this morning, so there's no one to look after us." She turned and held the sheet on the front door, taped it with a shaking hand. "I've closed everything down. Too much has happened here. A man killed and two kids dead. This morning there was a muddy footprint in the kitchen sink. Maisie quit, saying she wasn't going to stay someplace where people got killed and somebody had broken into her kitchen and maybe they would be coming for her with an ax and she ran out the door. I couldn't have lunch ready for the kids, and then I got scared too. I called the police. They wanted to know if anything was missing. I said I didn't know, but the cabinets aren't locked in the kitchen. The woman said I could come by the station and fill out a report. What good would that do? So I sent the kids home." Rosalind slapped another piece of tape on the sheet and stepped back to look at it. "There. That tells everyone." She started down the steps. "I called the directors and told them I wasn't going to stay someplace where people broke in. I told them I sent the kids home. I don't care what they say, but I'm not coming back here until they let Jean go. She'd never in a million years hurt any of the kids. It's all a lie. No matter what happens they blame Jean. But something's wrong when somebody breaks into a place. It's dangerous. Somebody's out there," she waved her hand toward the woods, "and I don't know who they might hurt next. If you've got any sense, you'll get out of here, too." She brushed past Annie, hurrying down the steps.

"Rosalind, please," Annie called after her, "I need to call the police. Let me use your cell."

But Rosalind was running toward the line of pines that screened the Haven parking lot.

Annie looked after her, hot, irritated, and thwarted. She started down the steps. Now she'd have to walk back to her car to call. So someone had broken into the kitchen. Big deal.

Annie stopped on the third step. A muddy footprint in the kitchen sink. Why did anyone break into a kitchen?

For food.

Tim Talbot ran away Sunday afternoon. By nightfall, he would have been hungry. Annie looked toward the woods that stretched into the distance behind the stage and curved around the far side of the lake. There were no roads into that patch of woods. Max and the others had driven around the north end of the island, shouting out to Tim, telling him it was all right to come home.

No cars or trucks had traveled into those dark, thick, heavily overgrown woods. There were only a few paths. Annie remembered Rachel describing a walk there sponsored by the Haven with a local historian. "Clouds of mosquitoes surrounded us. That's why they abandoned the fort. They died with yellow fever. There's not much left now. Three big grassy hills with wooden timbers poking out. Down beneath some of the broken timbers, there's a cellar that was used as a storeroom. I'll bet it's got snakes and spiders in it."

Tim Talbot loved old places on the island. She'd not thought of the remnants of this ruin because it wasn't a tourist attraction. There wasn't enough left, a few humpy hills and part of an emplacement. The other historic sites were maintained, accessible. She didn't remember the name of this fort. Tim would have known. She remembered the lines of metal soldiers in his room, Confederate gray and Yankee blue.

Annie hesitated. She could go to her car, phone Billy.

Could she convince Billy that Tim might have seen the murderer, a quick, bright, brief glimpse of a face when a tiny flashlight was used to gain the path in the woods?

She felt confident she knew what had happened. But what could she actually offer Billy? She'd climbed a tree and looked down on the stage and decided that the murderer could not have reached the path in the woods without using a light.

Billy had arrested Jean. Jean had no need to dart into the woods. Jean could have taken a few steps and returned to her place near the darkened lamp stands.

Why would Billy pay any attention to Annie's idea?

She could tell him about an intruder in the Haven kitchen and her certainty that Tim was nearby.

Nothing she could offer had much substance, a climb into a tree and a footprint in a sink and Tim's preoccupation with historic sites. Annie shook her head. It would be better by far to find Tim, persuade him to come with her, explain that he might hold the key to the murders of Booth and Click and Darren.

She struck off across the open field. She hoped Tim had filched some water bottles from the kitchen. Maybe he'd share one with her. She was miserably hot and thirsty, but in only a little while Tim would be safe, Jean would be freed, and Annie would drink a big, tall glass of achingly cold iced tea at Parotti's.

She shaded her eyes, searched for a break in the trees. What was it Rachel had said? ". . . Way cool. I mean, actually really, really hot. The path is kind of jungly. You go past the dock and about halfway around the lake there's an old bateau . . ."

Annie found the rotting hulk of the shallow draft boat. Almost directly opposite was a barely discernible gap in the woods.

Max looked around the empty parking lot of the Haven. "This doesn't make sense. Nobody's here." He turned his head, listened. "I don't hear the kids. Some of them play volleyball no matter how hot it is. Come on, Billy, let's see what's going on."

They came through the pine trees. The dusty field was quiet and empty, the tether ball hanging limply at its pole, the volleyball court deserted.

Max pointed toward the front door of the building at the sheet taped on the door. He and Billy strode quickly across the ground. Max hurried up the steps and read the uneven printing out loud.

CLOSED UNTIL FURTHER NOTICE.
DIRECTORS NOTIFIED.
ROSALIND PARKER

Max frowned. "I suppose the break-in scared her."

Billy shrugged. "I can't follow up on her complaint, but we're here. We might as well check out the shed." He glanced across the field at the metal shed near the stage.

They walked in silence. Beyond the field, the lake shimmered beneath the overhead sun. Billy used a handkerchief to mop his face. "I'm sorry you were wrong about Jean Hughes." His voice was heavy. "Kevin thought she was great."

"Remember that someone broke into the shed. She had keys."

Billy gave him a sardonic glance. "The same bogeyman who threw the gun and cell phone under her cottage?"

At the shed, the broken hasp still dangled, the lock useless.

Billy nodded at Max. "I don't have a search warrant. As a Haven volunteer, you can open the door."

Annie edged into a dim tunnel that was much worse than the path between the Haven and the inn. Ferns and vines had almost obliterated the faint trail, but the overgrown plants clearly showed that someone had recently passed this way, ferns broken off, vines trampled, depressions in mucky spots that hadn't drained from a recent rain.

The trail curved, once almost turning back on itself. Sweat drenched her. Flies hovered. Every step took courage. Any pile of leaves might harbor a diamondback or a copperhead. She felt caught up in a verdant nightmare. Her breathing was shallow and strained by the time the tunnel lightened. She reached the end of the path and looked gratefully at a broad sweep of marsh. About thirty yards away, the remnants of embanked earth formed grassy hillocks. The wooden support for the cannons would have been on the side facing the marsh.

Annie drew in a deep, calming breath. The marsh was beautiful, a breeze rippling the spartina grass. She loved the rank scent. The tide was going out and fiddler crabs swarmed on the mudflats. The blistering sunlight felt good after the sweltering dimness of the forest. She felt buoyant. Tim was here. She was sure of it. The broken foliage on the overgrown trail was all the proof she needed. He was here and if she was right, he could reveal the identity of a three-time killer.

"Tim? Hey, buddy, come on out." The call was robust.

But the voice wasn't hers.

"Hey, fellow, it's hot and your mom wants you to come home. Come on, now. I know you're here. You broke into the Haven, probably to get some food. Come on out and you can have all you want to eat."

Max felt dour as he pulled the door wide, flicked on the light. He had spent the day trying to find evidence in support of Jean. Instead, he was contributing another strand to the web that enmeshed her. He went directly to the costume trunk and lifted the lid.

Billy knelt and focused a small camera he'd taken from his pocket. "Got a nice feature. The time and date of the photo is recorded." He pressed and the flash flickered.

The costumes were listed in order on a sheet of paper pasted on the interior of the trunk lid. Number 12 read: *Witch's robe and hat.*

Billy looked at the picture, nodded in satisfaction. "I'll take a couple more. Just in case." He finished, then nodded at the chest. "As a volunteer, do you feel comfortable checking the trunk to see if the costume is there?"

Max nodded. He carefully sifted through the stacked costumes. He reached the bottom of the trunk. There was no witch costume in the trunk.

Billy made no comment. He turned and walked outside.

Max followed. He closed the door, his face drawn in a tight frown.

Annie didn't take time to think. Evil called in a reassuring voice on the other side of the hill. "Don't come out, Tim," she yelled with all her might. She wanted to run, seek sanctuary, hurl herself on the path to safety.

She couldn't leave a thin, scared kid alone to face death.

Larry Gilbert came around the side of the hill. He held a knife in his hand. His deep-set brown eyes looked opaque, inhuman. His bony face twisted in fury.

Annie screamed: "Don't come out, Tim. Don't!"

The scream was distant, yet near.

Max jerked around, stared across the lake. "That's Annie." The water glittered in the hot sun. There was no one to be seen anywhere. He opened his mouth to yell, and a heavy hand clapped across his face.

"Don't give warning. There's only one place where the sound carries across the lake like that. Follow me." Billy broke into a run. He was a big man, but he could move fast.

Max was right behind him. The forest looked impenetrable, but Billy knew where to go. Billy was an island boy. If anyone could reach Annie in time, it was Billy. Abruptly, Billy swerved to his right, plunging into a dim tunnel in the woods. Despite the vines and creepers and broken branches, Billy didn't slow, nor did Max. They thrashed along the path, bulling through obstructions, their breathing increasingly labored.

Annie, I'm coming, Annie, I'm coming . . .

* * *

Gone was the cool, wry, self-contained Larry Gilbert popular with island hostesses. How many times had she danced with him at the country club, felt the light pressure of his hand on her back, looked up into his smiling face? Now his features were ugly with hate, his dark eyes wild and unreasoning.

Annie backed away. "Stop, Larry." She yelled with all her might. Yet she despaired of being heard. If no one came, she and Tim were alone against a man with a knife, a man who could not let them live. There was no one to help her, no one to help Tim. The Haven was closed. The woods were thick and wild and the only ears belonged to birds and beasts.

"Shut up." Larry's voice was a rasp. Sweat beaded his face. He moved toward her, one step at a time, death gleaming in his eyes.

Behind him, a dark head eased up to look over the top of the mound.

Annie's throat was parched. It was an effort to speak. "You can't get both of us, Larry. Tim will stay hidden." She raised her voice, hoping Tim would understand, heed her warning, slip back down the other side of the hill. "Tim isn't going to come out. He's going to run into the woods. If you come after me, he'll run and escape and then you're finished."

Instead, Tim came to his feet on top of the hill. He was dirty and shaking, his clothes thick with dust, his hands grimy. His face was slack with fatigue and despair. "She didn't have anything to do with killing him." His voice was ragged. "Let her go. I'll come."

The words made no sense.

Tim began to cry, sobs shaking his shoulders. "I didn't mean to shoot him."

Larry swung toward the hill. "What are you talking about?"

At that instant, Larry wasn't looking toward Annie. He might sense peripheral movement, but that was a chance she had to take. She eased to her left, flicking her glance between Larry Gilbert and a mound of rubble behind a weathered spar uncovered by erosion.

"Booth." There was despair in Tim's thin voice. "I was lying there and I sighted him. I was holding my rifle and counting down and the lights went out. I heard the shot. I don't remember pulling the trigger."

Larry's ravaged face was incredulous.

Annie leaned down and grabbed a piece of brick. She straightened, the sharp-edged fragment in her right hand. It wasn't much of a weapon against a knife. The rough lump was all she had or was likely to have.

Larry took a step toward the hill. "I thought you saw me." His voice cracked.

Tim looked puzzled. "You came toward the path. I saw your face in the little light. I thought you were scared because of the shot and then I looked back at the stage and they had some light and Booth was bleeding."

"Let him go, Larry. He didn't connect you to the shot." Annie felt a wave of terrible sadness. Tim had disappeared because he thought he'd killed a man. He'd carried anger and a rifle to the Haven Friday night and lain on the thick tree branch and looked down at the man he blamed for his injuries. Was it any wonder that when the lights went out and a shot sounded, he believed he'd pulled the trigger? All he knew was what he had intended, and his stepfather lying dead. When the police came to his house Sunday, he'd run away, terrified. He hid because he thought he was guilty of murder. He didn't know Click and Darren had been murdered. He didn't realize he'd looked down from the tree and seen a murderer pass.

Larry's head jerked toward Annie. He was breathing fast, like a man at the end of a long run. His face was gaunt, despairing, driven. Merciless.

Annie saw her death and Tim's in his eyes.

"You know." His voice was toneless.

"Let us go, Larry. It's too late now. Max is on his way here." If only that were true. "There's no point in killing us. They're going to catch you." She forced herself to keep her eyes on Larry, hold his attention.

"Maybe we can work something out." Larry's voice was hideously ingenuous. His face was cunning and feral with a travesty of a smile. "Tim can come down and we'll talk about—"

"Don't come down, Tim." Annie's voice rose in desperation. "He's going to kill us. He shot Booth."

"Damn you." Larry sprang toward her.

Tim disappeared behind the mound.

Larry grabbed Annie's left wrist. He lifted the knife, then gave a yell of pain.

The knife fell to the ground.

Struggling, Annie wrenched free, kicking him hard.

On top of the mound, Tim wound up and threw again with force and accuracy.

A dirt-encrusted ball struck Larry in the back of the head. He dropped to the ground.

"Police. Hands up. Police." Billy's shout was breathless. He thundered toward them.

Larry rolled to his feet, hunting for the knife. As he bent to grab the handle, Max tackled him and Larry slammed into the ground.

∴ *Seventeen* ∾

ANNIE SAT IN the backseat of Max's Jeep, one arm around Tim's thin shoulders. He cried in jerky, gulping sobs.

"It's all right, honey." Annie's voice was soft. "We're taking you home to your mom. Everything's all right now."

Max glanced over his shoulder. "You were brave, Tim. You've had a tough time, thinking you'd shot a man. Now you know you didn't. If you hadn't been quick and smart, Annie could have been killed. Where'd you learn to throw like that?"

Tim sat a little straighter. His breathing began to ease. "I'm a pitcher. At least," now his voice drooped, "I used to be. But," he sounded eager, "I'm going to have another operation and they think a rod will work and I'll be able to walk right again and maybe even run. If I do, I'll go out for baseball. I can throw." He spoke with quiet pride.

"Yes, you can." Max's admiration was obvious. "Thank God."

Tim swiped at his splotchy face. "It all happened pretty fast. I wasn't thinking about being brave. But," and he slid a shy sideways glance at Annie, "you tried to help me. I couldn't let him hurt you. I had a bunch of grapeshot I'd dug out of the hill. I was half-nuts wondering what I was going to do, so I started digging. I used a piece of old brick. I found almost a dozen." He twisted against the seat belt and shoved his hand in his pocket and brought out a couple of dirt-encrusted iron balls. "See? They're real dirty, but they're solid iron."

The Jeep turned into the big circular drive. Sunlight sparkled on the red tile roof. Neva Wagner flew down the shallow front steps and ran toward the car.

Max stopped the Jeep.

Tim flung open the door and tumbled into his mother's arms.

She held to him, sobbing. "Timmy, Timmy, Timmy. I'm so sorry."

He pulled back, looked up at her, his face earnest. "Mom, listen, I wasn't going to really hurt Booth. I was aiming at his leg. 'Cause of my leg. And now I'm sorry. Oh Mom, I'm sorry."

Violet, mauve, rose, and gold streaked the sky above the darkening marsh as the sun set. Brilliantly green spartina grass swayed in a gentle breeze, rustling like softly snapped cards. An unseen clapper rail cackled.

Giselle, her wasted face illuminated by joy, pointed at a great blue heron stalking in shallow water.

Jean watched her sister. "He's a big guy." She'd never been much to notice birds until they'd moved to the island. Now she knew so much about so many of them, thanks to Giselle. Jean doubted her sister could see the four-foot-tall, slate-colored bird with great clarity, but she still took pleasure in whatever fuzzy image she perceived.

They sat, as they did every evening, on the deck overlooking the marsh. Jean reached over to tuck the quilt more snugly around Giselle's waist.

Giselle turned. "I'm so happy." The glow of the sunset made her face lovely despite its thinness.

Jean took her sister's hand and smiled through her tears. Whatever days remained, she and Giselle could spend them together in this peaceful place on this beautiful island, thanks to good people. She knew suddenly that when Giselle was gone, she would stay on the island, do her best for all the kids.

Whenever she saw the marsh, she would remember Giselle.

Meredith's heart-shaped face was eager. "I'll come and see you, Mom. You'll do great. When you get out, we can go home to Atlanta."

Ellen trembled. She wanted a drink so badly. Just one drink. That would make her feel steady, give her strength.

A car pulled up in front of the inn.

She felt Meredith's hand, warm on her elbow. "They're here."

The car from the rehab clinic stopped and a middle-aged woman stepped out and came briskly toward them.

Ellen pulled Meredith into her arms. "I'll do my best, baby. I'll do my best."

"Mom?"

At the soft cry, Darren Dubois's mother came out of the chair next to the hospital bed. She leaned down and took her son's hand. "Darren." Tears spilled down her face.

He blinked, looking puzzled. "My shoulder hurts." He gazed around the small narrow room at the white walls and the television mounted high on the wall opposite the end of the bed. "Where am I? What happened to me?"

"Oh, Darren." She told him in a rush, the shooting, the helicopter ride to Savannah, the long days and nights as the swelling decreased in his brain. "You were hurt so bad. Not so much from the shot but when you hit your head."

His eyes widened in terror. He struggled to sit up. "Click told me . . . a joke with Mr. Gilbert . . . that night I followed Mr. Gilbert . . . he was in a highwayman costume with a mask. I saw him go into the woods . . . the next day when they found the costume in the lake I thought he had to be the one who shot Mr. Wagner. I didn't think anyone would believe me. I set a trap . . ."

"He's in jail, honey. But when no one was sure who shot you, the police chief put out the word you'd died and he sent an officer to sit outside the door," she nodded her head, "to protect you. He kept you safe. And when you get well," her voice was stern, "you are going down to that police station and thank everyone there and you are going to do cleanup and whatever work you can do to help."

"The police chief sent somebody to see over me?"

"He did. He's a fine man, Chief Cameron. I told him you'd be coming."

"Maybe," there was an eager gleam in Darren's eyes, "he'll let me watch them work. I'd like to be a policeman. I can figure things out."

Emma Clyde exuded self-satisfaction. "The solution came from the Rectangle of Interest. As I told everyone." Her supercilious gaze swept around the coffee area at Death on Demand. It was after hours.

Annie loved her bookstore when the aisles teemed with

readers. She also loved the store when the front shutters were closed and old and dear friends gathered.

Emma was a picture of summer comfort in a seersucker caftan that improbably featured bat-size red butterflies against a white background. Laurel's lime-green linen dress and matching headband emphasized the camellia perfection of her skin and the silver gold of her hair. Henny was bright in a raspberry T-shirt and slacks.

Emma, as always, assumed that she was the central figure. She nodded emphatically. "Tim Talbot's knowledge meant the murderer's apprehension was assured."

"Not quite." Annie intended to sound crisp. Instead, her voice was wobbly. "Tim saved our lives. If he hadn't dug around in that old site and found grapeshot, Larry would have killed us."

Max's tone was admiring. "He found a perfect weapon. They're made of iron and about the size of a golf ball. He zinged Larry's arm, knocking the knife out of his hand, then got him in the back of the head." Max's grin was huge. "It turns out Tim was a super Little League pitcher."

Henny commented mildly, "Sometimes it seems so much a matter of one card falling and then another. Once Larry realized Tim must have seen him when he darted into the woods, Larry had to try and find him. When Rosalind Parker called the directors to say someone had broken into the Haven kitchen, Larry started searching in the vicinity of the Haven. Larry considered himself something of an authority on island history. He knew all about a fort there."

Laurel spoke proudly, "If Max hadn't kept trying to help Jean, he and Billy wouldn't have been there to hear Annie's shout."

Max was grim. "I had all the pieces and I didn't fit them

together. Larry said he tried to sell a rare stamp he'd bought at a discount from Booth, and the stamp was a fake. Larry figured if he could get access to Booth's computer he could switch funds to his account and later claim that Booth had agreed to give him the money in exchange for his vote against Jean. Everything depended upon Click. Larry spun Click some kind of tale about putting a joke program into Booth's computer. What Larry needed were passwords. Click thought he was part of a joke that would be explained at the program Friday night. Instead, Larry got the information he needed, met Click at the nature preserve, and killed him. Larry pulled out Click's pockets to get back the money he'd paid. When Booth was playing golf Friday morning, Larry slipped into his study. He switched the funds. That's why Booth had to die that night. When he ran into Booth at the Haven that night, Larry clapped him on the back and placed the tape on the back of his shirt. He would have gotten away with everything if it weren't," and his voice was proud, "for Annie."

Emma looked dour.

Annie felt a moment's compunction. Fair was fair. "If I hadn't gone to look at Emma's Rectangle of Interest, I wouldn't have realized what Tim probably saw. As Emma said, Tim made all the difference."

"A celebration is in order." Henny opened a special cabinet. She worked swiftly, bourbon and Coke for Emma, sherry for Laurel, gin and tonics for herself and Annie, a Dos Equis for Max.

Henny served the drinks to murmured thank-yous. She lifted her glass. "A toast to our dear brave Annie, to persevering Max, to prescient Emma—"

Emma's nod was regal.

"—to perceptive Laurel and to *moi*—"

As they raised their glasses, Henny cleared her throat and nodded toward the watercolors: "—The island's champion mystery reader." Her glance at Emma was triumphant. She pointed at the paintings in order. "*Her Royal Spyness* by Rhys Bowen, *Southern Fried* by Cathy Pickens, *The Witch Doctor's Wife* by Tamar Myers, *A Vicky Hill Exclusive!* by Hannah Dennison, and *All the Wrong Moves* by Merline Lovelace."

*Turn the page for a sneak peek at Carolyn Hart's next
exciting Death on Demand mystery*

DEAD BY MIDNIGHT

*Available in hardcover in April 2011 from
William Morrow*

∻ *One* ∻

GLEN JAMISON LOOKED every one of his fifty-two years, his fair hair flecked with silver, his aristocratic face mournful, his six-foot-two frame too thin. He hunched at the desk in his study and felt a sense of panic, like the beginnings of a fire flickering at his feet then billowing to an inferno. How much longer could the firm go on?

There wasn't enough money coming in. The appointment book had too many empty spots. Maybe they shouldn't dump Kirk even though cutting him should save at least a hundred thousand a year. He hated looking into Kirk's blue eyes that held the hurt puzzlement of a kicked dog. Of course, Kirk was young. Not yet thirty. He was a brilliant lawyer. He'd find a job. But he wouldn't find a job on the island. There were only two other firms and neither intended to expand. Not in times like these. Kirk needed to stay on Broward's Rock. Glen tried not to think how desperately Kirk needed to be here.

Glen wondered if it would do any good to talk to Cleo again. If Kirk stayed, Laura wouldn't be so angry with him, either. It was a misery to go to the office and see Kirk, tight-lipped and grim. Then he shook his head. He knew in his heart that Cleo wouldn't agree to keep Kirk. Maybe it had been another mistake to give Kirk a couple of months to wind down his cases. But that had seemed the decent thing to do and Cleo had agreed.

Glen had been a little surprised at her acquiescence, but grateful he didn't have to face her disapproval. He was getting enough disapproval around town. A couple of times at the Men's Grill, he was sure he'd been avoided by clients. In fact, Ted Toomey had canceled an appointment a few days after word got around that the firm was letting Kirk go. Ted had said evasively that he was still giving the matter that they had intended to discuss some thought. One more empty slot in the appointment book. The money wasn't coming in and Cleo wanted . . . Cleo wanted many things. He'd given in over the trip to Paris for Christmas.

When the kids were little, he and Maddy and the kids came home from the midnight service and put the baby Jesus in the crèche. Now the crèche was in the attic with the other Christmas decorations that had been in his family for generations. The decorations Maddy and the kids had made together were boxed up, too.

Cleo had wanted all new decorations for their first Christmas together. He'd hated the tree. Shiny white with all blue balls, the tree reminded him of a department store. The kids hated the tree, too. They hated everything Cleo did. This year she had waved away the idea of decorating. After all, they'd be in Paris . . .

The kids had been unhappy ever since he married Cleo. He used to be excited to have his children home. Not anymore. Maddy had been gone so long now. He still felt the clutch of emptiness in his gut when he thought of her and the night the police came to the door to tell him about the accident. The first few years he'd been in a daze, working, trying not to think, hurting. He owed everything to Elaine. She'd given up her job in Atlanta and come to help and be there for the kids. The kids loved their aunt.

He felt guilty every time he passed the first bedroom on the second floor that had been Elaine's room. Now she lived in the cottage not far from the gazebo. She'd acted as if the new quarters were fine. Maybe she liked the cottage, but she didn't like Cleo any more than the kids did. Cleo had insisted Elaine needed a life of her own. After all, she'd done a good job with the kids. Maybe she'd like to go back to Atlanta. But Elaine had been on the island for so many years now. She had her friends, a life she'd built, and of course Tommy was still in high school. That was another problem. Well, Tommy had acted up. He had to find out who was boss. The matter was settled.

Anger was everywhere around him. Pat Merridew had worked for the firm for so many years, but Cleo had insisted Pat was frumpy and they needed a young and charming receptionist. Firing Pat hadn't saved money. Cleo was paying the new girl even more. Glen hated to remember the ugly look on Pat's face when he saw her yesterday on the street. And then there was Kirk . . .

Glen shied away from thinking about Kirk. It would be a relief not to have to face him every day. They'd given him two months to close down his cases. Three more weeks and he'd be gone.

Cleo told him to buck up. Everything would get better.

The money flow would have to get better soon.

* * *

Richard Jamison parked his rust-streaked 2004 Pontiac in the shade of a live oak. He left the windows down and pulled a stained duffel from the trunk. The house looked just as he remembered it, a gracious Lowcountry antebellum home, tabby exterior moss green in the June sunshine. Wicker furniture on the shaded verandah looked inviting. He'd like to settle in a rocker with a rum collins. He and Glen could talk over old times. He'd have to go cautiously with Glen. It would never do for Glen to realize that Richard had come to the island to seek financial backing. If he presented everything just right, he could persuade Glen that he was giving him a good investment opportunity.

Richard hefted the duffel. He was curious to meet his hostess. He'd been in Singapore when Glen remarried. Maddy had been dead for six years now, maybe seven. He wondered how the kids felt about a stepmother. Especially a stepmother who was only a few years older than Laura. And how did Glen's sister, who had since then served as chatelaine of the antebellum home, feel about the new Mrs. Jamison?

Kids . . . As he climbed the front steps, he gave a slight shake of his head. Not kids anymore. Laura must be about twenty-four. Kit was in graduate school. Tommy was in high school.

An old friend had written him about Glen's second wife. "Cleo's hot, a tall brunette, sultry brown eyes, leggy but stacked. Cleo's one lucky lady. Whatever she does succeeds. High school beauty queen. Top grades in law school. Bowls over guys with one glance. Her favorite game's roulette. The ball always seems to fall in her pocket. Don't know what she saw in Glen except he's top drawer when it comes to an old Southern family and her roots are middle class. She grew up in Hardeeville, mom a teacher, dad a fireman. They lived in a modest frame house on an unpaved road. Plus, Glen used to have a lot more cash till the meltdown in '08. Cleo came to work at the firm, made partner in a year, married Glen the next year."

Richard shifted the duffel, punched the doorbell. He'd selected his wardrobe with care, a boring blue oxford-cloth shirt, poplin slacks, and cordovan loafers, a far cry from his usual frayed tee, baggy shorts, and flip-flops. He'd shaved the stubble that he preferred, even sported a short haircut. He hoped the preppy look would reassure Glen that his wild cousin Richard could, with the proper financial backing, become a pillar of the community.

When the white door opened, Cleo Jamison pushed the screen, held it wide for him. Dark brown hair cupped a long face with deep-set brown eyes, a straight nose, and full lips. A summery blouse emphasized the curve of her breasts. Sleek jade slacks molded to her legs. She smiled. "You must be Richard." Her throaty voice made him think of cast-aside pillows and rumpled sheets. She reached out a perfectly manicured hand, the fingers long, slim, and warm, to take his hand.

Richard felt a flood of desire. His response was immediate and instinctual. For an instant, a hot current sizzled between them.

Cleo relinquished his hand. Her gaze was abruptly remote. Her lips curved in a conventional, polite smile.

He stepped inside, once again under control. But she'd responded for a flicker of an instant. Hadn't she?

A door opened toward the end of the hall. A tall man walked wearily toward Richard and Cleo.

Richard felt an instant of shock. Glen's fair hair was silvered, his face drawn and tired, his clothes hung too loosely on his body. "Hey, Glen." Richard forced a robust shout.

Glen's slightly reedy voice was raised in welcome. "Hey, little buddy, welcome home."

Cleo was well aware that Kit Jamison had been in her father's study for almost fifteen minutes. She felt a surge of triumph. It had taken all her cleverness to delicately maneuver Glen into a state of acute dissatisfaction with his daughter. He'd almost proved intractable, but Cleo's will had prevailed. Funny that he should be so devoted to unstylish, awkward, socially graceless Kit. Of course, she looked like her father, fair-haired, fair-skinned, slender, but her pale blue eyes were humorless, her thin face ascetic. Sure, Kit was academically brilliant, but she didn't have the smarts to go after a well-paying career. Kit's plan to go to the Serengeti to help catalog declining lion populations as a volunteer biologist might be admirable, but let her manage on somebody else's dollar. Asking Glen to support her intellectual and nonpaying lifestyle would have been all right a few years ago, but Glen not only lost half of his savings in the crash, he'd been panicked enough to sell when the Dow was plunging down toward seven thousand. Cleo's lips thinned. He should have asked her. But he hadn't.

Despite the thickness of the walls between Glen's study and hers, the sounds of acrimony penetrated.

Cleo rose from her chair. She paused in the sunlight that poured through the large, wide window to admire the glitter of the emerald bracelet on her wrist, a gift from Glen, then strolled toward the hallway. She knocked briskly on Glen's study door, swung it wide.

Kit jerked to face the door, her narrow face folded in a

furious frown. Without makeup, her fair skin was pallid, though marred now by red patches of anger.

Cleo's voice was pleasant. "Kit, won't you stay for lunch?"

Kit flung out one hand. Her hands were graceful and elegant despite chipped nails. "I'd rather eat with hyenas." Head down, she rushed toward the door.

Glen pushed up from his chair. "Kit, come back here. Apologize to Cleo."

The only answer was the clatter of steps in the hallway and the slam of the front door.

Darwyn Jack straightened the collar of the green polo. His fingers luxuriated in the crinkly feel of the cotton mesh. His thick, sensuous lips curled in the half smile that made women his for the taking. Women couldn't resist his tangle of thick chestnut curls and sloe-brown eyes that held a reckless glint. He felt on top of the world, invincible.

He looked around the dim, small room, seeing only its cramped lack of space and shabby furnishings, blind to its scrubbed cleanliness and the lovingly hand-pieced quilt on the bed.

He gave a final approving glance at the mirror and moved into the hall. He was tall, muscular, and well built, but he walked with a slight limp. He'd been the best running back in the state when he was a junior and there was already talk of how he'd have his pick of colleges when he graduated. An accident while mowing a hayfield ended his football dreams and his college hopes. He'd never bothered much about grades. Who needed them if you could run like the wind?

In the kitchen, he walked to the old oak table, pulled out a chair. This room, too, was clean and bright with daffodil-yellow curtains at the windows.

Bella Mae Jack's cotton housedress was crisp and starched. A big woman, she moved slowly now that she'd reached her seventies. She no longer cleaned homes for a living but she baked and cooked for the weekly farmers' market that was held every Saturday in the park near the harbor. She was careful with her money, always frugal, unfailingly honest. She turned, a plate in her hand. "Sausage patties and dilly bread." She stopped, peered nearsightedly, her pale worn face folding into a frown. "You march back to your room and take that nice shirt off. You have work clothes. Wear them." Her voice was stern.

Darwyn hesitated for only a fraction, then, with a shrug, he came to his feet. When he'd played football, he liked to hurt opposing players. Darwyn had a cold, dark core, the product of abusive years before his drug-ridden parents died and he came, a withdrawn and wary seven-year-old, to live with his grandmother. Only for Bella Mae would he ever be meek.

In his room, he shrugged and carefully pulled off the polo. Soon he would wear fine clothes whenever he liked.

Pat Merridew walked back and forth across her small living room, too angry to sit and try to relax. Finally she stopped at the closet, reached for her light jacket. Even though it was summer, the nights were cool in the woods. She slid a small flashlight into her pocket and retrieved her BlackBerry from her purse. She didn't need a BlackBerry now, not since she'd lost her job. But she always carried a phone in the woods in case of an accident.

She edged out of the back door, careful to keep Gertrude from following. "Not safe for you, sweetie." Gertrude was only permitted outside on a leash and their walks avoided the lagoon with its leathery black king, a nine-foot alligator who would see Gertrude as an hors d'oeuvre. "You stay inside." The door shut, muffling the disappointed whine of the elderly dachshund. Pat walked swiftly, the way familiar now. She'd begun her late-night forays when she found it hard to sleep after she was fired.

Pushed by hatred, she walked the half mile to the Jamison property and stood in the shadows of an old live oak, glaring at the dark windows. Long ago, the land had been home to one of the island plantations. There were stories of a ghostly little girl wandering on summer nights, looking for her father, who had been killed in the Battle of Honey Hill. What if a ghost began to haunt the house? Or maybe a poltergeist might make its presence known by little destructive acts.

She stood in the shadows and hugged ideas of revenge.

Oyster shells crackled. She was alert, wary. It was past midnight. Pat watched a dimly seen figure slip through the moonlit garden to the gazebo. Footsteps sounded on the gazebo steps. A flashlight flared, illuminating the interior. The beam settled on a wooden bench. The shadow behind the light knelt for a few minutes, then rose. The light was turned off. Footsteps again thudded softly on the wooden steps. Pat watched the swift, confident return toward the house until the visitor to the gazebo was out of sight behind shrubbery.

Pat waited a few minutes. No one stirred in the garden. She walked swiftly to the gazebo and edged up the steps. She bent and used her pencil flash for a quick flicker. A rolled-up brown towel was taped beneath the bench. She knelt and touched the towel. Oh. She took a quick breath. She didn't need to remove and unroll the lumpy towel to know what it covered. She thought for a moment, then smiled grimly as she reached in her other pocket.

A moment later she moved swiftly along the path in the woods, using the pocket flash to light her way. A thought darted swiftly as a minnow: knowledge was power.

Henny Brawley sat on her verandah overlooking the marsh. The spartina grass glimmered gold in the morning sun, rippling in a light breeze. Fiddler crabs skittered on the mudflats as the tide ebbed. She took a sip of rich, black Sumatra coffee and breathed deeply of the distinctive marsh scent. All would be well in her sea island world except, of course, for the challenge of personalities. But Henny wasn't irritated. Detecting motives, choosing the right word at the right time to achieve a desired effect, provided a never-ending challenge in her role as a volunteer, and was almost as much fun as reading clever, multilayered mysteries.

Henny laughed aloud. As soon as she identified one more of the paintings hanging this month in the Death on Demand mystery bookstore, she would break a current tie with Emma Clyde. Emma, the island's famed mystery author, was also— Henny was willing to give credit where credit was due—an omnivorous mystery reader and a worthy opponent in the contest. Each painting represented a particular mystery novel. The first viewer to identify titles and authors would win free coffee for a month and a new book. She would choose the latest by either Jasper Fforde or Rosemary Harris.

Henny almost could recall the book depicted in the third painting, but not quite. Browsing the store's shelves this afternoon, she was certain something would nudge her memory. However, first she needed to help her old friend Pat Merridew, who had applied for the paid manager's job at the Helping Hands Center, a private charity that threw out lifelines to the sick, the old, the troubled.

There was a fly in the ointment. One of the board members was a stickler for checking references, which seemed a trifle absurd on an island the size of Broward's Rock. All of them knew Pat Merridew, admittedly a bit quirky and sometimes fractious, but whatever her shortcomings, Pat exuded energy and she knew everyone in town.

Of course, there had to be a reason why Pat had lost her job at the law firm. That was the point made by Rachel Thompson in her brusque way. "Depend on it, Henny, there's a story there. We can't hire Pat until we know what's what."

Henny had made no headway when she'd suggested that Pat was simply another casualty of Cleo Jamison's remake of her husband's life and office. Rachel had insisted, "We must know the truth of the matter."

Henny flipped open her cell, punched a number.

"Jamison, Jamison, and Brewster." The unfamiliar feminine voice was obviously young. The new receptionist, no doubt.

Henny raised an eyebrow. Kirk Brewster's name was still included in the firm name. But not for long. Glen should be ashamed. Of course, everyone had been struggling with hard times. "This is Henny Brawley calling for Mr. Jamison." She and Glen had worked together on fundraising for the island youth center.

"May I ask the subject of your call?" The voice was chirpy.

Henny felt as if a door had slammed in her face. If Pat had answered, the call would have been put through without question if Glen was in the office and available. It would take the new receptionist time to learn the ropes. "I'm calling in regard to a recommendation for Pat Merridew."

"How is that spelled, please?"

Henny responded politely, though she was annoyed. Pat had worked at the firm for more than twenty years. Was she already completely forgotten?

"Thank you. One moment, please."

Henny understood that Kirk had started looking for a job on the mainland, but law firms had cut back on hiring in the face of the economic downturn. Kirk's record was amazing. He'd been number one in his law class and made junior partner in a mainline Atlanta firm in four years, instead of the usual seven. He would likely still be on the fast track to an equity partnership except for his sister's serious illness. Both parents were dead and he was the only family she had. Henny felt sure Kirk would eventually receive an offer, but that didn't change the fact that his single-mom sister had leukemia and depended upon Kirk to help with her two little boys. The grim news had come only a few months after he made partner at the Atlanta law firm, but he'd immediately resigned and returned to the island. If he had to leave Broward's Rock, his nephews would suffer.

The chirrupy voice returned. "Mr. Jamison is in conference, but Mrs. Jamison is available."

Henny hesitated. She could call Glen at home tonight. But she'd promised Rachel she'd check this morning. Before she could answer, Cleo came on the line. "Cleo Jamison."

Henny raised a disdainful eyebrow. Cleo dismissed niceties such as hello. Implicit in her tone was the conviction that she, Cleo, was due homage. Cleo had succeeded in conveying her sense of self-worth to the community of Broward's Rock. Since her arrival on the island a few years ago, she'd excelled as a rising young lawyer, married the widowed senior partner, and now she dominated the island's social scene, young, beautiful, and joyously self-confident.

Henny spoke pleasantly. "Hi, Cleo. Henny Brawley. I need a rec for Pat. She's applied to work at Helping Hands. Of course, the job isn't on a level with her work at the firm. She'll be overqualified but we'll be glad to have someone to sort and arrange the clothes and household goods." *And you screwed her royally, so now's the time to pony up some help, lady.*

"Pat?" A sigh of regret. "I wish I could be helpful, but as I told Rachel this morning—"

Henny's eyes narrowed. Rachel was humorless, didactic, pompous, and perhaps the wealthiest member of the Helping Hands board. Rachel was pleased to provide support, but only if people and proposals met with her approval. Had she called Cleo?

"—I'm afraid Pat's become a bit unbalanced. She wasn't the right face for the firm now. The firm wants to project an up-to-the-minute image, youthful, forward-looking. Glen explained it to her as kindly as possible—"

"Pat doesn't need a youthful image at Helping Hands." Henny's tone was sharp, but she knew it was a stiletto flick at an opponent who wore emotional chain mail.

"Of course not." Cleo sounded amused. "But Rachel agreed that it wouldn't do to hire someone who is emotionally unstable." Now Cleo's voice was metallic. "Last weekend she slipped into the house and accused Glen of ruining her life. There was a dreadful scene. She refused to leave until I threatened to call the police. Of course, she's old—"

Henny was icy. "Not quite fifty." Cleo knew full well that Henny was a septuagenarian. Cleo was arrogantly on the sunny side of thirty.

"Oh, perhaps it's hot flashes." Cleo was dismissive. "In any event, you'd better check with Rachel. I gave her a ring when I heard Pat had applied to Helping Hands. I thought she should know the truth. But I suggested a charming young woman who's working on her certification for home health. Ciao."

Henny listened to the buzzing line, clicked off the handset. Was Cleo's tale of Pat's behavior true? Whether it was or not, Pat wouldn't get the job. It was too late to try to talk to Glen.

Henny sipped coffee. She watched a majestic blue heron poised to capture a fish. The heron's beak darted into the murky green water, lofted its prey. The great bird swallowed and the fish was gone, plucked from its summer moment in the warm water just as Pat had been ousted from her once secure job.

Get cozy with
CAROLYN HART's
award-winning
DEATH ON DEMAND mysteries

laughed 'til he died
978-0-06-145308-3

Mystery bookstore owner Annie Darling and her husband, Max, plunge into a startling web of danger when a trio of deaths is linked to their island's youth recreation center.

dare to die
978-0-06-145305-2

Annie and Max Darling are caught in the middle of a devastating storm of rage, secrets, and murder when they invite the sad and beautiful Iris Tilford to their party at the pavilion.

death walked in
978-0-06-072414-6

A mysterious woman caller leaves word that she's hidden something in the antebellum house Annie and Max are restoring. When Annie finds out, she hurries to the woman's house, only to discover she's been murdered.

Get cozy with

CAROLYN HART's

award-winning

DEATH ON DEMAND mysteries

dead days of summer

978-0-06-072404-7
Annie Darling is understandably upset when her p.i. husband Max
disappears and his car is found with a brutally slain woman nearby.

death of the party

978-0-06-000477-4
Annie and Max Darling are left stranded on an island
with a handful of invited guests—including a murderer.

murder walks the plank

978-0-06-000475-0
Annie Darling's murder mystery cruise is going swimmingly—
until one of the revelers plunges overboard and
faux murder turns all too quickly into real-life death.

engaged to die

978-0-06-000470-5
When wealthy Virginia Neville officially announces
her engagement to Jake O'Neill, her handsome, charming, and *much*
younger fiancé, not everyone is pleased. And before the last
champagne bubble pops, murder disrupts the grand celebration.

CHD2 0111